CW00552921

FIERCE OBSESSION

LA RUTHLESS: BOOK 4

SADIE KINCAID

RED HOUSE PRESS LTD

To anyone who has ever been told that they're not good enough and they will never make it, whether in word or deed, this is for you. You are and you will.

Love, Sadie xxx

LA RUTHLESS

Fierce Obsession is a Dark Mafia, age gap/ dad's best friend romance that deals with mature themes which may be triggering for some, including scenes of extreme violence and graphic sexual content.

It is Book 4 in the LA Ruthless Series, featuring Lucia Montoya and Jackson Decker. It follows on directly from Book 3, Fierce Betrayal which should be read first.

Or of you would prefer to start where it all began and read the first duet in the series, they are also available on Amazon
   Fierce King
   Fierce Queen

PROLOGUE
JAX

My fingers fumble with the black silk as I stand in front of the mirror trying to fix my bow tie.

"Here, let me get that for you," a deep laugh rumbles in my ear.

His eyes catch mine in the reflection. Damn, am I glad to see him. Turning around, I come face to face with my oldest and closest friend, and the man who's about to become my father-in-law in less than twenty minutes time.

"I've never seen you looking so goddamn nervous, amigo," Alejandro chuckles.

"Well, I've never been married before," I remind him, twisting my neck as he fastens my tie.

"Keep still," he orders.

"I'm too fucking hot," I complain. "Have you purposely turned the AC off in here to make me sweat?"

He laughs again. I'm glad he finds the whole thing so funny, particularly as he almost killed me when he found out I was dating his daughter. I suppose hooking up with the only daughter of the head of the Spanish Mafia wasn't the smartest move I ever made, although it's damn sure been the best one. I figure he's earned his amusement at my expense.

"No," he shakes his head. "Why would I want my beautiful daughter to have to kiss you like this? You need to chill."

I nod at him. "I know. Is she okay?"

"She's fucking perfect," he says with a wink.

"She's still going to walk down that aisle and marry me then?"

He narrows his eyes at me. "Is that what you're worried about? That she's gonna ditch you at the altar?"

Yes. "No!"

He turns and looks at the only other person in the room, his five year old grandson, Matthias. "You know this is all kind of the best man's job?" he says with a grin.

"I can't fix bow ties, Papa," Matthias replies with a frown that makes his face look so cute that it almost makes me forget about my nerves.

"You leave my best man alone," I say, scowling and making Matthias laugh.

Alejandro finishes my tie and pats me on the back. "I'd better go check on Lucia," he says, "and make sure she isn't about to run away with that new concierge."

He winks at me but I don't find his joke the slightest bit funny. We're getting married at his hotel, and his newest hire is a definite hit with the ladies.

It makes him laugh though and he wraps his arms around me. "Relax amigo, she fucking adores you."

"Yeah," I breathe as I hug him back.

He pulls back from me and turns around to Matthias. "You make sure this guy makes it to the altar and doesn't get drunk on the way, okay?" He holds out his hand for a fist bump.

"Okay, Papa." Matthias grins at him, showing his one

missing front tooth as he connects his little fist on Alejandro's. God, the kid is fucking adorable.

"I'll see you on the other side," Alejandro says with a wink before he walks out of the door, leaving Matthias and me alone.

"What does nervous mean?" he asks, looking up at me with his huge brown eyes. "Papa said you're nervous."

I take a seat on the sofa beside him, picking him up so he can sit on my lap. "It means that I love your mom so much, and I'm so excited to marry her, that I feel a little bit scared."

His eyes widen. "Scared? You? Why?"

"Sometimes when we want something so bad and we're so close to getting it, it can make you feel a little bit scared in case you mess up."

He blinks at me.

"Like when you were chosen to paint the poster in kindergarten for Memorial Day, remember? You wanted it to be perfect and you were worried when your paint got a little smudged that your teacher wouldn't want to use it?"

"Yeah," he says with a nod.

"That's nervous, buddy."

He stares at me, his face so full of innocence and happiness that he calms my nerves completely. He is the finest best man I could have ever asked for.

And as if I wasn't already enough of a trembling mess today, he wraps his little arms around my neck, presses his lips to my ear and whispers. "Don't worry, Dad. I got you."

CHAPTER 1
LUCIA

Taking Jax's hand, I climb out of the car and step onto the runway. Glancing up at the private jet, I see it's not my father's, or my grandfather's either. Technically they belong to Montoya Inc, but my Papa and Grandpa are the company. The rest of the family can use them whenever we want though, and even before he married me, Jax was considered one of the family.

I arch an eyebrow at my new husband. "Don't tell me you've bought a plane now too?"

He shakes his head, a twinkle in his eye as he laughs softly. "No. I borrowed this one, because I'm not taking my wife on honeymoon in her father's plane."

"Why not?" I whisper, even though I know the answer. At least I hope I do.

One of my father's men is unloading our bags beside us, so Jax bends his head close to mine. His lips brush over my ear, making goosebumps break out all over my body. "Because I'm going to fuck his daughter in it. In fact, I'm gonna make her come so hard..."

"Is there anything else you need me for, Mr. Decker?" Raoul our driver asks, interrupting the moment.

Jax's hand coasts down my back until he slides it around my waist, pulling me against him as he straightens up. "No thanks. I've got everything I need right here," he replies before giving me a cheeky wink and I swear my ovaries just exploded.

"Have a good trip," Raoul says with a polite nod of his head. He is a man of few words.

"Thanks, Raoul," I reply with a smile.

"Let's get you on that plane then," Jax says before slapping my ass and making me squeal like an excitable teenager.

WHEN WE BOARD THE PLANE, the first thing I see is the bottle of champagne in a bucket of ice, white rose petals scattered all over the seats, and a huge gold foil sign that says 'Congratulations Mr. and Mrs. Decker'.

"Oh wow! I love it so much." I clasp my hands together and suppress a squeak of excitement. I swear I'm going to need some of that champagne to calm my nerves. We got married ten hours ago in the most perfect wedding in the history of weddings, and I don't think I've eaten or stopped smiling since. The whole day has been perfect from start to finish.

"I think your mom and Jessie planned it," Jax says as he smiles too.

"Aw. That is so sweet," I feel warmth coiling up my spine. I have never felt so loved in my whole life as I have today. I only met Jessie Ryan yesterday. She's a computer genius just like Jax, but she has a wicked sense of humor too. I love her and have already decided she's going to be my friend forever, and the fact that her and my mom arranged this is making me feel all choked up.

I place my hands on his face and pull him to me for a kiss.

He palms my ass, squeezing possessively and his stubble tickles my lip, both of which make me giggle. He was clean-shaven for our wedding, but this man can grow a beard in a day, and I much prefer him with a bit of scruff on his face.

"We'll be taking off in ten minutes," a soft voice says behind us and I blush as I realize the stewardess is standing right behind us.

Less than five minutes later, I'm sitting down with a glass of ice cold champagne in my hand and looking up at my incredibly handsome husband as he buckles my seatbelt for me. His warm hand glides over my abdomen making my insides turn to jelly. My breath hitches in my throat and he must hear it because he gives me a wicked grin.

"Thank you," I whisper. "you always take such good care of me."

"And I always will, baby," he replies, the deep timbre of his voice penetrating my bones and making me shiver. Then he kisses my forehead softly. "I'll take real good care of you once we're in the air. Okay?"

"Hmm," I murmur, taking a sip of my champagne as I notice the stewardess watching us again.

As soon as we are in the air and the plane has leveled out, Jax unclips his seatbelt and jumps up from his seat. He reaches down and unfastens mine too. "Come with me, Mrs. Decker," he says with a wicked grin.

"Where are we going?" I say, biting on my lip as anticipation, nerves and excitement flutter in my stomach, all vying for space.

He pulls me into his arms and then scoops me up. "Oh, you

know, baby," he says pressing his lips against my ear. "I have been waiting for this all damn day."

My breath catches in my throat and warmth pools between my thighs, because I know exactly how he feels.

"I almost tossed Raoul and Jacob out of the car so I could fuck you on the way here, but we'd have missed our take off slot," he chuckles darkly as he runs his nose over my neck and inhales deeply. "You smell so fucking good."

He walks to the back of the plane and kicks open the door that leads to a bedroom. It closes behind us as soon as we're inside and he sets me down on my feet.

"I've been waiting for this all day too," I whisper.

"Yeah?" he growls, his breath dusting over my cheek.

"Yeah," I whimper as my knees wobble.

He arches one eyebrow at me. "You think we'd best get naked then?"

"Uh-huh," I mumble.

My fingers tremble as I start to unfasten the buttons of his crisp white shirt. He runs the back of his knuckles softly over my cheek and down over my neck until he reaches my collarbone.

"Are you nervous, angel?"

Nervous would be an understatement. My heart races wildly in my chest and my stomach feels like it's twisted into a huge knot. "Kind of, yeah."

"Why?" His hand slides to the back of my neck and he holds me there. Dominating and possessive.

"I don't know. This feels different." I chew on my lip, trying to think of the right words. I look up into his dark brown eyes. "Special?"

"Every single time with you is special," he whispers before he dips his head low and seals his lips over mine, forcing them apart and sliding his tongue into my mouth.

Jax's kiss is all consuming, full of passion and fire and it makes every nerve ending in my body sizzle with anticipation. His free hand glides over my back and he begins untying the ribbon on the corset of my dress. In contrast to my clumsy fumbling, his movements are confident and precise, and the fabric loosens as he unfastens the giant thread easily.

He slides his hands inside the soft material, pushing it down until it falls easily to the floor and I'm standing in just my cream lace panties. My nipples harden as he palms my ass in his huge hands and crushes me against him, deepening our kiss. I trace my hands over his back, feeling his powerful muscles flexing beneath my fingertips. It makes him groan into my mouth. Pressing his groin into mine, his hard cock rubs against my abdomen.

"Fuck, I need you so bad, Luce."

Suddenly all my nerves melt away. Yes, this is special, but, he's right, everything with him is special. He is the most incredible man I know. And I know that I own him as much as he owns me.

I pull back from our kiss and leave him panting for me as I drop to my knees. Tugging at his soft leather belt, I open it quickly before reaching for his zipper. The familiar sound of it opening makes him hiss out a breath as his hands fist in my curls. He threads his fingers through the thick strands of my hair as I pull down his boxers and allow his thick cock to spring free. The precum beading on the tip makes me smile. I look up at him as I dart out my tongue and lick it off.

He glares at me with dark eyes full of fire and longing. Then his teeth catch on his bottom lip as he mutters one word. "Fuck!"

I look back at his beautiful cock before I suck it into my mouth. Taking him all the way to the back of my throat the way he taught me to. Swirling my tongue over his thick shaft, I suck softly at first, moving my head only slightly back and forth because I know that it drives him crazy. His deep, husky groans roll through his body and when I wrap my arms around him, holding onto his incredible ass, he takes his cue to start fucking my mouth.

He's gentle at first, rolling his hips as his hands keep fisting in my hair.

Pulling back, I flick my tongue over the tip again and he growls like an animal.

"Not nervous now, are you, baby?" he hisses out the words as I bring him closer to the edge.

"Nu-uh," I mumble around him filling my mouth.

"That's my good girl. You love sucking my cock, don't you?" He picks up his pace, fucking me harder.

"Uh-huh," I moan as saliva dribbles down my chin.

"How wet am I gonna find you when you're done, Luce?"

I close my eyes and breathe in through my nose, aware of my soaking lace panties as the gentle throbbing in my pussy turns to a heavy ache. I swear he could make me come like this if he tried. There's something so freaking hot about making him lose control, and when he starts with the filthy talk too! Damn! I will be a hot, trembling mess by the time I'm done.

Suddenly, he's tugging my head back and pulling his pulsing cock out of my mouth. I look up at him and he wipes the spit from my chin with the pad of his thumb, before putting it into his mouth and sucking it clean.

I blink while he stares at me, wondering if he's going to let me get back to what I was just doing.

"The first time I come inside my wife, it won't be in her mouth. Stand up, baby."

Holy fuck!

I take his hand and allow him to pull me into a standing position. "Where will it be?" I breathe.

He slides his hand between my thighs. "You already know the answer," he says with a grin, but then his eyes darken again when his fingers brush over my wet panties. "Damn, baby, you're fucking soaking."

"I know, Jax. I've been desperate to have you to myself all day."

He brushes my hair back from my face, his eyes narrowed as they search mine. "I shouldn't have made you wait so long. Let me make it up to you."

Before I can respond, he scoops me into his arms and throws me onto the bed, making me laugh.

"You don't have any making up to do," I say as he crawls over me.

"What?" he scowls, but his eyes are full of mischief. "It's not acceptable for me to leave my wife in such a state. Pussy aching and dripping wet for me."

The ache deepens and I rock my hips against him, desperate for a little friction.

"Well, we were kind of busy," I whisper as I take his handsome face in my hands. "You know, getting married in front of all our family and friends."

"Still no excuse. I should have taken you somewhere quiet and made you come." He starts to trail kisses over my collarbone. "Finger fucked you in the coat room and put my hand over your mouth so no-one could hear us," he chuckles as he makes his way lower.

"You would have got us in a whole heap of trouble," I pant as his lips dust over my nipples and his hand slides over my stomach until he reaches the edge of my underwear. "Can't get in trouble for fucking your wife on your wedding day, angel. These sweet little panties would have been drenched in your cum while we did our first dance."

"They already were," I giggle and he bites my nipple,

11

making me groan instead, before his hand slips inside my panties. His fingers glide through my wet folds and onto my swollen clit.

"Ah, Jax," I cry out as he presses against it, swirling his fingertips over the sensitive bud of flesh.

I have been waiting for this from the moment I saw him in his tux this morning. I have never seen him look so handsome, and sexy. This man wears any suit like he was born in one, but a tux? Wow! My panties almost caught fire just looking at him.

"If it makes you feel any better, I've been hard for you almost the entire fucking day."

"I know," I laugh again. I felt it when we were dancing, and then he stayed sitting down for most of the rest of the day.

"You want my fingers in you, Luce?" he murmurs against my skin as he peppers kisses over my breasts.

"Yeah," I groan, bucking my hips against his hand, so needy for more.

"Yeah?" he growls, sliding his fingers from my clit until he reaches my entrance. I spread my legs wider, allowing him easier access as his large hand fills my panties. "I'm gonna need you nice and wet and loose, baby, for how hard I'm gonna fuck you. Okay?"

"Okay," I whimper. Then he slides two thick fingers inside me and stars flicker behind my eyelids as the waves of relief and pleasure roll through my body. "Oh, God!"

"No, just me, baby," he chuckles. "I'm gonna add another one. Okay?"

"Yes!" I pant as I ride his fingers, chasing the orgasm that's only a breath away.

He adds a third finger and the burning stretch stops me from falling off the edge of the cliff as he twists them inside me. My walls squeeze around him as a sudden rush of wet heat coats his fingers and makes my head spin.

"Jax, please?" I groan.

"I know," he soothes as his lips dance over my skin and he works his fingers inside me, pushing deeper and harder until I'm on the edge again. "Such a good girl, letting me stretch you wide open for me, aren't you?"

"Oh, Jax!" I groan as my climax bursts through me. It's quick and intense. The culmination of all the anticipation and the wanting, of waiting for the entire day to feel his hands on me.

"Fuck, Luce, you're shaking, baby," he says, slowly sliding his fingers out of me before he hooks them into the band of my underwear. "Let me get these off you so I can see my wet pussy."

I suck in a lungful of air, my head still reeling from the rush of endorphins racing around my body, but I lift my hips so he can wriggle my panties off me. When he's done, he presses his palms flat against the inside of my thighs, spreading me wider for him.

"Fuck, angel. You are so fucking hot. You know that?"

I look down at him and he's staring at me with such intensity that it makes tears prick at my eyes. I don't know what I did to deserve to have a man like this worship me.

"You're pretty hot yourself, cowboy," I whisper.

That makes him chuckle as he runs his thumb through my dripping pussy, coating it in my cum before sucking it into his mouth. "And sweeter than fucking honey," he says with a wink before he drops his head and runs his tongue from my opening, up to my clit, sending shockwaves of pleasure rocketing through me.

"Oh, fuck, Jax!" I moan loudly, my fingers threading through his thick, dark hair.

He wraps his arms around my thighs and then shuffles back off the bed, so he's kneeling on the floor, before he pulls me closer to his face. Then he feasts on my pussy like it's going to be his last meal.

CHAPTER 2
JAX

I swear my cock will explode if it gets any harder. I need to fuck her now, but I can't stop myself from eating my wife's delicious pussy. I've been thinking about burying myself inside her from the moment I stepped onto that red carpet at the hotel. I have never seen anything so goddamn beautiful in my entire life as her standing there waiting for me, with our little guy standing by her side.

Her dress was simple, as I'd known it would be, but it accentuated her assets perfectly. From the boned corset which showed off her slim waist and her incredible tits, to the softest silk which clung to her hips and her delicious ass. I mean, it was bordering on the obscene how closely that silk hugged her skin, but anything that clings to her ass is obscene to me. She's always complaining that it's too big, but it's perfect and I have no idea how she thinks otherwise.

When she started sucking my cock shortly after we got into this room, I was seconds away from blowing my load against her throat. I had to stop her from going any further. I want all of my cum in her pussy first.

"Jax," she groans softly as I flick my tongue over her clit.

I love the way she says my name when I'm teasing her. The way she begs me makes me want to fuck her even harder. If I make her come again, I can fuck her as hard as I plan to and know she won't be too sore later when we get to the ranch. I have a surprise there for her. I just hope my father has done what I asked him to do for once.

"I got you, Luce," I mumble against her delicate skin as she writhes and squirms, riding my face to her climax. I grab her hips and hold her still, concentrating my efforts on her clit, my teeth grazing over the sensitive nub as I rim it with my tongue.

"Oh, God! Jax!" she shouts when it hits and her cum pours out of her, coating my chin.

She's still riding the waves of it when I flip her over, pulling her down off the bed until she's bent over it with her knees on the floor. I can't wait even a second longer to get my cock in her.

I drive inside, sinking deep into her smooth, silky heat and heaving a sigh of relief once I'm buried in her. Her tight little pussy squeezes around me as she whimpers and moans.

"You feel so fucking good milking my cock like that, baby," I growl as I pick up my pace.

Slamming into her over and over. I thrust my hips against her, and her beautiful peach of an ass jiggles every time.

Looking down, I watch my cock driving in and out of her. Each time I pull out, I'm smeared in her creamy white cum. Watching that as well as her ass bounce against me while I'm nailing her tips me over the edge. With a final thrust, I rail into her and when she cries out, I lose it. My balls draw into my stomach and my hair tingles on my head as I fill her with my release, pumping every last drop of it inside her.

"That was..." she mumbles but doesn't finish her sentence, her face pressed against the duvet.

I'm still as hard as iron though, and she is about to get another pounding because my cock is screaming for her pussy.

I pull out of her and grab her waist, standing up and bringing her with me before spinning her around so she's facing me. Her perfect tits pressed against my chest and her hard nipples brushing over my shirt.

Taking hold of her hands, I place them on my chest. "You ready to finish what you started earlier now?"

Her cheeks are flushed pink, her hair mussed up and her pouty lips open slightly as she breathes hard and fast.

"Yes," she purrs, looking up at me through her thick dark lashes.

Her hands tremble again as she starts to remove my shirt, but this time I know it's not about nerves. Her nails graze my skin as she works each button loose, and when she reaches the last one, she glides her hands over my abs and chest before pushing the soft cotton over my shoulders. It gets stuck at my wrists and she frowns at me.

"My cufflinks, angel," I remind her.

Her cheeks redden further. "Oh, yeah," she whispers.

They were my wedding gift from her and Matthias. Simple platinum ones with two words engraved on each one. Husband and Dad. The two most precious roles I will ever have in my entire life.

I hold out my wrists and she removes the cufflinks before placing them on the dresser beside us. Then she pulls the rest of my shirt over my arms, her warm soft skin leaving trails of fire on mine. I rarely let her undress me, preferring instead to watch her coming down from an orgasm while I do it myself. But something about this with her tonight, now that she's my wife, I want her to take this tux off me herself.

Once my shirt is in a heap on the floor, she goes to my dress pants. My belt and zipper are already undone, so all she has to do is slide her hands in them and work them down. She tugs at my boxers too while she does, dropping to a crouching position as she pulls them over my calves.

"Damn shoes," she mutters as she tugs at the laces.

"Here, let me help," I say, kicking them off for her.

"Thank you," she whispers as she brushes a thick curl out of her eyes.

I lift my feet one at a time so she can take off my socks and my dress pants, and once I'm naked she stands tall again, brushing those hard nipples the length of my body as she does.

"You are so damn beautiful," she breathes, echoing what I say to her almost every time I see her naked, and making me grin. Her hand slides over my abs and down to my cock. She wraps her hand around the shaft and squeezes tightly, making me groan. "How are you still hard after what we just did?"

Coasting my hands down her back, she squirms as I skim over her waist because she's so ticklish. I drop my hands to her ass and squeeze. "I am *always* fucking hard for you, baby. I could fuck you seven ways to Sunday and still keep going."

She sucks in a sharp breath before I lift her by her ass cheeks and plant her down on the bed. Crawling over her, she spreads her legs wide for me and I settle between her thighs, my cock nudging at her entrance. Taking her hands, I lace my fingers through hers and pin them either side of her head as I edge inside her, sliding in easily as her juices coat the top of her thighs and my groin.

"Jax." My name leaves her lips on a breathy moan.

"You're so fucking wet, Luce. How the fuck do you get like this, baby?"

She stares into my eyes. "Because you make me come so hard," she laughs softly and I take in a breath.

She doesn't deserve the pounding I'm about to give her. She's going to be sore and swollen no matter how ready I've made her, but that's not going to stop me. When she remem-

17

bers our wedding night, I want her to remember how I felt inside her, when I molded her tight little pussy to the shape of my cock forever.

"Who do you belong to?" I ask, rubbing my nose over her jawline and inhaling her sweet, intoxicating scent.

"You, Jax," she purrs, rolling her hips so that I'll slide deeper inside her, but I pull back. She'll get all of me when I'm ready.

"Damn right you do."

"Please, Jax," she bucks her hips again, desperate for my cock even though I've only just fucked her. I love how much she wants me, even though it's nothing compared to my need for her.

"You're mine, Luce. You got that?"

"Yeah," she whimpers. "Yours."

"Mine!" I drive all the way into her silky heat, forcing her further up the bed.

I release her hands and she cries out, her nails scratching my back as she clings to me. She draws me deeper, her tight, wet pussy gripping me like a vise — like she will never let me go. She's mine, but I'm hers too. There's been no-one like this before her, and there will be no-one after her.

"Damn, Jax. You fuck me so good," she gasps out on a breath.

"I'll fuck you like this forever, baby."

"Promise?" she stares into my eyes, pleading with me even as I'm fucking her raw.

"Promise." I bury my head in her neck and fuck her until we both find our release.

CHAPTER 3
LUCIA

J ax rests his hand on my thigh as he turns the truck onto the dirt road that leads to his ranch. The only light are the headlights of the truck and the half moon overhead. His Aunt Molly and his father, Harvey, run the place, and the locals don't even know it belongs to him. It's been in his father's family for years, and when Harvey almost lost it ten years ago, Jax bought it back.

Jax doesn't have a great relationship with dad and even refused to invite him to our wedding. I kind of like him though, and his dog, Blue, who is the cutest and most well behaved mutt I've ever met.

I've only been to this ranch once before, but somehow it feels like home. It was seven months ago, when Jackson brought me here to keep me safe. This is also the place where he finally admitted his feelings for me, and then he told me that no man would ever touch me again.

The memory of that night makes me smile. I turn to look at him and he's staring at me. It makes a blush creep over my cheeks. I will never get used to the way that man looks at me.

I pop an eyebrow at him. "Shouldn't you be watching the road, cowboy?"

"No traffic here, angel," he replies with a wink before fixing his attention back on the track in front of us.

"No, but Blue might be running around."

"That dog is too old to run this far from the house," he chuckles. "Besides, he would never stray so far from Harvey's side."

"No, I suppose not," I agree. "He is devoted."

"Hmm," he murmurs and suddenly the atmosphere in the truck grows a little tense.

"I'm looking forward to getting to bed," I yawn, lacing my fingers through his.

"It's been a long day," he agrees, but he's distant, lost in thoughts of his father, no doubt.

"It's been a perfect day, though?" It sounds like a statement but it's a question and I don't know what I'll do if he doesn't answer me.

He lifts my hand to his lips, brushing them over my knuckles. "Better than perfect, baby," he whispers and I smile.

I slide across the bench seat in the old truck, until I can rest my head on his shoulder.

"Almost there. I'll have you in bed before you know it," he says as we approach the house.

"Can't wait," I sigh as I wrap my arms around his huge bicep.

Instead of stopping outside it when we get there, Jax drives straight past the main house.

"Where are we going?" I ask, craning my neck to see the house getting smaller behind us.

He winks at me. "You think I'd spend our honeymoon anywhere where I couldn't let you scream at the top of your lungs without anyone hearing?"

I stare at him in surprise. It was me who suggested the ranch for our honeymoon. I think Jax had an exotic beach, where I'd wear nothing but string bikinis, in mind, but I love it here. "So, where are we staying?"

"Not far, angel," he whispers and then he nods his head, indicating me to look out of the windshield.

I peer into the distance until I see faint, twinkling lights. "Is that the old barn?" I squeal as I lean forward in my seat, trying to get a better view.

"It sure is."

I saw the barn on our last visit. It's a beautiful old building, with oak beams and high ceilings. I told Jax what a crime it was it was sitting empty. He asked me what I'd do with the place and I jokingly said I'd turn it into a little house for us, so that we could visit with Matthias whenever we wanted and not be a burden on his aunt. For the past six months, since he proposed to me, he's been asking questions about what it would look like — letting me ramble on about my dream hideaway in the country.

Tears prick at my eyes as the building comes into view. There is a porch and a balcony now, where there was once just a huge door and a hayloft. It has giant sliding French doors so the front of the house looks like it's made entirely of glass — just like I described. Fairy lights are strung up around the outside, making the place seem even more magical. There's even a huge rocking chair on the porch like in my dream house too.

"Jax," I gasp. "How did you do all this?"

He rolls the truck to a stop. "I didn't," he says as he opens the door.

He holds out his hand and I scoot along the seat and allow him to help me out. Wrapping an arm around my waist, he stares up at the house too, and I realize this must be the first time he's seen it as well as me.

SADIE KINCAID

"Then who did?" I whisper. "Because it's exactly how I described it to you."

Suddenly, a cold, wet nose, is nudging at my leg, making me jump in surprise. I look down to see Blue, wagging his tail and looking up at me with his huge dark eyes.

Dropping into a crouching position, I scratch behind his ears. "Hello, boy," I giggle. "I've missed you."

"I hope it's what you wanted?" Harvey says as he comes into view. "I followed all of your instructions to the letter."

I stand again and Blue rubs his head on my legs. "You did this, Harvey?" I blink at him.

"No," he shakes his head softly. "I just told the expensive contractors that Jax paid for what to do, is all."

"Go see it, baby," Jax whispers, giving me a gentle nudge in the direction of the house. "It's all yours."

I smile at him before I walk a few steps ahead and step up onto the porch. The huge double doors lead to an open plan living area, with the biggest couch I have ever seen in my life. It's full of pale pink and gray cushions — just like I talked about.

I spin on my heel and run back to Jax, throwing my arms around his neck and burying my face there. "This is the best thing anyone... I can't believe..." I choke out the words as the emotion of the whole day overwhelms me. Every second of it has been entirely perfect, but this has completely blown me away.

He brushes his lips over my ear. "Anything for you, baby. Go sit on the porch and wait for me, okay?"

I step back from him and stare at his face, but he's unreadable right now. His jaw ticks as he tries to keep a lid on his emotions. Eager to explore further inside, I turn around to do as he asks, but not before I walk over to Harvey and throw my arms around him too.

"Thank you, Harvey. You took Jax's instructions and turned my dream house into a reality."

He pats my back gently and cautiously and my heart breaks for him. I know that he's trying not to be overly familiar because Jax is glaring at him right now, and he has warned him before that Matthias and I are off limits. I wish that we weren't though. I know that Harvey let Jax down badly, but I see how desperately he wants to make up for that and be a part of his son's life.

"It was the least I could do," Harvey says softly.

I kiss his cheek before I look back at Jax and then walk to the house. Taking a seat on the huge rocking chair, I watch my husband and his father intently.

Jax gives Blue a scratch on the head before he walks over to his father and I strain to hear their conversation. It's not eavesdropping if they're only standing a few yards away, right?

"I didn't expect it to look like this," Jax says.

"I followed your instructions to the letter."

"I know," Jax nods. "It's just..." He rubs a hand over his jaw.

"Is it not what you wanted?" Harvey asks. "If I got something wrong, I can call the contractors back and have them fix it. Out of my own pocket, of course."

I brush away a tear as it rolls down my cheek. Harvey doesn't have any money — well not a lot. He drank it all away. I will my stubborn husband to give his father something as he stands there waiting for some validation.

"It's... perfect." Jax finally admits and the way Harvey's face lights up makes my heart swell in my chest. "Thank you."

"It was my absolute pleasure," Harvey says, his voice cracking with emotion.

Jax stuffs his hands into his pockets and they both stand in awkward silence for a few seconds until Harvey clears his throat. "I'd better get back to the house and leave you and your new wife be."

"Yeah," Jax agrees and Harvey turns away.

"Molly will be back tomorrow afternoon," Jax says, stopping his father in his tracks. I did offer his aunt a ride with us, but she insisted on flying back coach, although I know that Jax bumped her up to first class. "Lucia and I might come to the house for dinner. If you're around?"

"I'll look forward to it," he says with a soft smile before he calls Blue and the two of them walk back to the house, disappearing into the darkness.

Jax's boots make a satisfying clunking sound on the wooden porch as he climbs the two small steps and makes his way over to me. We both changed from our wedding outfits on the plane and now he's dressed in jeans, a flannel shirt and boots — my LA cowboy. I smile at him. I'm so proud of him for allowing Harvey in a little, because I know how much it cost him.

"Hey, cowboy," I purr, kicking off my sandals onto the porch.

"Hello, Mrs. Decker," he growls, bending down and scooping me into his arms.

I giggle as I snake one arm around his neck, fingering the buttons of his shirt with the other as he carries me over the threshold. Once we're inside, he sets me on my feet.

"I love this house, Jax," I whisper. "It's the best surprise ever."

He presses a soft kiss on my forehead. "I'm glad you love it, Luce."

"Does this mean we can visit the ranch more often?"

"Yep. It's got three bedrooms too," he says with a wicked grin.

I pop one eyebrow at him. "Three? One for guests?"

"No, guests can stay at the main house," he slides his hands over my hips and onto my ass. "One for us." He kisses my neck. "One for Matthias." Kiss. "And a nursery."

"A nursery?" I giggle as he goes on kissing my neck. "You're being a little premature, aren't you, cowboy?"

"No," he murmurs, grazing his teeth over my skin. "I can't wait to put my baby inside you."

Heat sears between my thighs. We've discussed more kids, but I didn't realize he wanted them so soon. "Maybe we should just enjoy being married for a little while first?" I suggest.

"We'll see," he laughs softly.

"Where is our bedroom?" I purr into his ear, as his kissing and ass grabbing ignites the spark of desire that is always flickering when he's around me.

"Upstairs and at the front of the house. I'll grab our bags and lock up. You go on up," he says as he smacks my ass.

"You sure you don't need any help?"

"Nope. Go relax, baby, and I'll be up to take care of you soon."

I kiss his beautiful lips and then head up the stairs to explore the second floor.

CHAPTER 4
JAX

After I bring our bags in and finish locking up, I check the fridge. It's fully stocked like I asked and I also notice a bottle of champagne in there that wasn't on the shopping list I sent ahead.

I pick it up and examine the label. It's a good vintage. But, I suppose booze is an area of expertise for my father. Shaking my head, I slide it back into the fridge to save for tomorrow.

I half expect Lucia will be sound asleep by the time I get upstairs. It's almost one a.m. here, and we're still on L.A time so it's been a long day for both of us. I might just wake her anyway and fuck her back to sleep in our new bed, in our new house.

I look around the expansive kitchen with a huge island in the center, just like Lucia talked about. When she first mentioned the possibility of turning this old barn into a house for us, I dismissed it, thinking that we'd spend so little time here, it would be easier to stay in the main house. It's certainly big enough. But when I realized just how much she and Matthias had fallen in love with this ranch, I knew I had to make a home here for us. A place to call our own. A place where I can make her come as loudly as I want without her having to

26

spend the next morning blushing every time someone looked at her.

I have to hand it to Harvey, he has risen to this particular challenge. Yeah, it was the contractors who did the work, but he oversaw every aspect of it. He must have done to have the place looking like this — exactly how she described it to me. I've spent the last six months pumping her for information, under the guise of daily chit chat over our morning coffee, and then passing it onto Harvey.

I had wondered about the implications of asking him. I mean I didn't want him to get the wrong idea about me and him. Just because we were in contact, didn't mean our relationship had changed. It was all about the house, and nothing more. To his credit, he never pushed for more, and he did a great job here. And the look on her face when we pulled up outside. Fuck me! She looked like a kid on Christmas morning. I can't believe she actually thought I'd take her to my aunt's and father's house for our honeymoon. She expects so little yet deserves so much.

I grab two bottles of water and switch off the lights before heading up to bed. When I walk into the room, she's lying under the covers, her arms behind her head and thankfully not asleep.

"I was just about to come find you," she says with a smile.

I start to pull off my shirt. "Sorry, baby, I was just locking up."

"Always so security conscious," she giggles. "Even here in the middle of nowhere."

I arch an eyebrow at her. "Even here, Luce. I would never take a chance with your safety. You know that."

"I do," she grins at me. "But that doesn't mean I'm not going to ride you on that rocking chair on the porch, cowboy."

"Well, I'd be disappointed if you didn't, baby."

Sitting on the bed, I pull off my boots and toss them into the corner before taking off the rest of my clothes.

"I hope you're naked under there, Mrs. Decker," I say as I slip beneath the covers.

"Of course," she breathes as I slide my hand over her stomach and then between her thighs.

She winces when I slip my fingers between her folds.

"Are you sore, baby?"

"No," she purrs.

"Don't lie to me."

"Well, maybe just a tiny bit, but I still want you, Jax," she breathes, rocking her hips against my hand.

"What do you want?" I tease her as I circle her clit softly, careful to be gentle with her after the way I took her on the plane.

We have a whole week here and I intend to spend most of my time naked with her.

"Your fingers and your cock," she pants and my cock hardens.

I love how she asks me for what she wants. It took her a while to be confident enough to do it without blushing.

"Both?" I whisper in her ear. "So fucking greedy for me, angel."

"Yeah. You've created a monster," she giggles as she takes hold of my hand and guides my fingers lower, right where she wants me.

"Oh, you want my fingers inside you?" I ask as I slide one into her soft, wet pussy. "Not on your needy little clit?"

"I want both," she hisses as I add a second and rub that spot inside her that makes her whimper.

As I rub the pad of my thumb over her clit, her soft little whimpers turn to moans.

"Such a good girl." My teeth graze the soft shell of her ear.

"I'm gonna make you come and then you're going to show me exactly how you want my cock, angel. You got that?"

"God, yes," she groans, bucking her hips and chasing her orgasm.

I'm too desperate to fuck her to draw her pleasure out any longer. I push my fingers deeper, rubbing harder against that sweet spot while I press on her clit with the pad of my thumb and she comes apart for me, her nails digging into my forearm as she rides the waves of her climax.

As soon as she stops trembling, I slide my fingers out of her and roll onto my back. "Come ride me, baby," I groan as my cock aches to be in her pussy.

She climbs on top of me. One hand on my chest to steady herself while she grabs my shaft with the other before sliding herself onto me. Her juices slick my cock as her walls squeeze me tight.

"Fuck me, you're fucking perfect," I hiss as I reach for her tits, kneading them in my palms as she starts to roll her hips over me. "Show me how much you love my cock."

"God, Jax," she groans, milking me as she rides me.

Her cum runs out of her, slicking her thighs and my groin as she brings us both close to the edge. I slide one hand down to her clit and begin to rub before grabbing hold of her waist with my other hand. I rock my hips into her, matching her rhythm and sinking deeper inside her with each thrust.

She looks down at me through her long dark lashes. "You just can't help yourself, can you?" she purrs. "One of these days, I'm going to have to tie you up, cowboy."

"I'd like to see you try, angel," I growl.

Rubbing her clit harder, my fingertips dig into the skin of her waist while I hold her in place as I fuck her.

Her eyes roll back in her head as she comes hard for me, because the truth is she loves me being in control. I watch her fall apart around me as I grind out my own release. When we're both done, she lies on top of me and we both pant for breath.

I run my fingertips up and down her back, careful to avoid her ticklish spots and she sighs in contentment. "I love you," she whispers.

"I love you too, angel."

"You mind if I fall asleep right here, dripping cum onto you?" she giggles softly.

I pull the covers up around us both and then wrap my arms around her before planting a soft kiss on her head. "There's nowhere else in the world I'd rather you be than in my arms, baby," I whisper but she's already fallen asleep.

CHAPTER 5

LUCIA

T blink in the dim light of the room as I wake up. Looking at the windows, it seems it's still dark out, but I feel like I've been asleep for hours. It's only when my eyes adjust and I peer more closely at the enormous glass doors that lead to the balcony, that I see that it's the glass that's dark. They must be those fancy ones like we have back in LA. They can go from transparent to dark glass that blocks out the sun and the outside world at the touch of a button. The sun is shining in the sky but you would never know it in here.

I smile as I snuggle against the soft pillow. That is some fancy shit!

Jax's arm is draped over my stomach and he wraps it tight around me, pulling me closer when he feels me moving. "Good morning, Mrs. Decker," he mumbles sleepily.

"Good morning," I shift my body, turning so I can face him. "This bed is so comfy."

"It is. It's the same one we have at home," he replies, his eyes still closed.

By home, he means his fortress on the beach in LA. We still haven't found a place that we both like yet, although my father

31

tells me that one of the houses near him and my mom is about to go up for sale. And I could get used to living in the hills again.

"I should probably check in with home, actually." I stretch, trying to wriggle from his grip, but he holds me tighter. "And then I'll take a shower." My thighs are moist and tacky from last night.

"No point taking a shower yet. I'm about to fuck you in a minute," he says matter of factly.

"I'm super sticky though," I tell him.

"I like you sticky." He grins as his eyes finally open.

"Wouldn't you prefer to eat a nice clean pussy?" I ask with a flash of my eyebrows.

"Who said anything about eating pussy?"

"But you always start the day that way," I giggle as he starts to kiss my neck.

"True. So you know I don't give a shit about eating you out when you're full of cum, angel, don't you?"

"Yes," I purr. "But I'm all extra messy this morning. I fell asleep straight after."

"I know. You were drooling on my chest," he laughs as he rolls me onto my back and trails kisses over my skin.

"I was not," I insist.

"Were," he murmurs as he moves lower, his lips dusting over my stomach until he reaches my pussy. He pulls my thighs wide apart and I feel wet heat trickling out of me.

"Jax, I swear things are real messy down there," I gasp, tugging his hair to stop him from what he's about to do.

He looks up at me, his eyes full of fire and mischief. "Lucia Decker," he gives me my full title, "if you ever try and stop me from eating this sweet pussy again, I'll put you over my knee and spank your ass red. I don't care how sore you are."

His words alone make wet heat surge between my thighs

and when he dips his head and licks the length of my folds, I moan loudly, no longer caring about showering first.

AFTER HE ATE me out and fucked me, I finally got my shower and now I'm lying on the bed waiting for Jax to finish his while I check my messages.

A few moments later, he walks out of the bathroom with a white towel wrapped around him. It's slung low on his hips, revealing his chiseled abs and his new tattoo of two turtle doves, which he got just before our wedding.

"Everyone back home okay?" he asks with a nod to my cell phone in my hands as he sits on the bed.

"Yep. My mom sent me a picture of Matthias and the twins playing in the pool with my dad and Hugo. She told me in no uncertain terms that I am not to text or call unless it's an absolute emergency, apart from right before Matthias' bedtime so we can wish him goodnight."

"She'll take good care of him."

"I know."

He reaches out and brushes a strand of damp hair from behind my ear. "You miss him, baby?"

"Yeah. I mean I know he's having the time of his life and is well looked after, but I've never been this far away from him before."

Jax doesn't reply.

"Not that I don't enjoy having you all to myself," I add quickly.

"You're allowed to miss our son, Lucia," he laughs softly. "I miss him too."

"You do?"

"Of course I do. Doesn't mean I still won't enjoy every

second of having his mom all to myself though." He winks at me before he stands and starts to dry himself off.

My phone pings to signal another text message and I open it, laughing out loud when I read it.

"Who's that?" Jax asks with a frown.

"Archer," I grin at him. Archer is my best friend from college. He's a drummer in a band. One hundred percent gay and one hundred percent has a crush on my husband, which I think Jax secretly likes.

"What did he say?"

"He said that he hopes I've had so much dick that I can't walk this morning. And he also sent a meme that says, save a horse, ride a cowboy."

"Well, he's not wrong. On either front."

I gasp in feigned indignation. "I can walk just fine, thank you," I insist, even though my pussy is throbbing so much from last nights and this morning's activities that I swear I can still feel Jax inside me.

"Then maybe I need to fuck you harder next time," he whispers as he leans down and gives me a soft kiss on the cheek. "Now all of my clothes are in the bags downstairs. I'm going to go get dressed and start breakfast."

"I need some clothes too," I say, jumping up from the bed.

He looks me over as I stand here in a skimpy white towel, his eyes narrowed as he appraises me before he slowly shakes his head. "Not sure you're gonna be needing any clothes this week, angel."

"Not even for dinner tonight at the house?" I grin. "And you promised to take me riding, and help me practice my shooting."

He rubs a hand over the thick stubble on his jaw as though he's considering my request. "Hmm. I do kind of have a surprise lined up for Tuesday night too, and as that also requires you leaving this house, I'm definitely going to need you to be wearing clothes for that."

"Another surprise?" I squeal, clapping my hands together in excitement. "What is it?"

"Now if I told you, it wouldn't be a surprise now, would it?" He steps toward me, giving me a soft, chaste kiss on the cheek before he smacks my ass and grabs it hard. "I'll go bring our bags up."

CHAPTER 6
LUCIA

I hold onto Jax's hand as we stroll through the grass toward the main house. We've had an incredible day not doing much at all. He cooked us a huge breakfast and afterward we watched a movie. Then we went for a long walk and when we stopped for a rest under a huge tree, we lay in the grass for the longest time, just kissing.

This afternoon, I sat on his lap in the huge rocking chair and we just talked and watched Blue chasing a rabbit before I fell asleep. Jax carried me inside then and we both took a nap. He said it was the first time he'd taken an afternoon nap in his entire adult life.

I woke up wrapped in his arms, with the sun setting and a soft breeze blowing through doors leading to the balcony. It's been like something from a movie.

I sigh contentedly and he squeezes my hand in his.

"You okay?" he asks.

"Way better than okay." I smile at him. "You?"

"Starving," he replies.

. . .

As soon as we get to the house, Molly rushes out to greet us, as though she didn't see us yesterday at our wedding.

"What did you think of the barn, Lucia? Didn't Harvey do a great job with it?" she asks as she ushers us inside and into the large kitchen where Harvey is busy finalizing dinner.

"Yes he did. I love it. It's beyond perfect," I agree.

Harvey smiles to himself and I walk over to him and give him a peck on the cheek. I've decided that I can be nice and polite to him, even if Jax struggles to.

Jax asks Molly about her flight as they both take a seat at the table.

"Can I help with anything?" I ask Harvey.

"No, you go sit yourself down," he insists. "It's almost ready."

I do as he says and take a seat next to Jax, who hasn't even acknowledged his father's presence yet.

When Harvey has served up his delicious looking chicken casserole and Jax has his mouth full of food, I start talking.

I hate to eat in silence. Family dinners should be about laughter and conversation. I never had that growing up, not until I was adopted by Alejandro and Alana when I was seventeen, who are both into the whole family dinner thing. So now, I always make sure Jax, Matthias and I eat dinner at the table at home in LA, and that we all talk about something.

"Can I ask where you got that beautiful rocking chair on the porch, Harvey?"

He wipes some gravy from his chin and blinks at me before glancing at Jax as though he's waiting for permission to speak, and it makes me feel so sad for him.

"Did you restore it yourself?" I ask another question because he wouldn't be rude enough to go on ignoring me.

37

"Yes," he eventually replies.

"It was bright purple when you bought it, wasn't it?" Molly says with a laugh. "Gaudy looking thing."

"Well, it's not now. It's beautiful," I say with a smile. "And comfy too. Jax and I fell asleep on it this afternoon."

"No, you fell asleep, angel," he reminds me with a grin.

"It must have taken a lot of work?" I ask before I take a bite of the casserole.

"Not really. Once I stripped the paint, I sanded it down and gave it a few coats of wood oil," Harvey replies. "I enjoyed doing it. Gave me something useful to do with these old hands."

"Well, I really love it. You've done such a great job with the whole place, hasn't he, Jax?" I nudge his leg with mine.

"Yeah," he admits. I mean he can't exactly deny it. "Did you restore those oak beams too?"

"Yup. But that was much harder work. I had to ask the contractor to help me out with those," he admits, but there is a light in his eyes that wasn't there a few seconds before. It's painfully clear that Jax's approval means everything to him.

Jax nods his head as he goes on eating his meal.

"What are you going to use that spare room for then?" Molly asks with a wicked twinkle in her eye.

"A nursery," Jax replies without missing a beat, making me turn and scowl at him.

"A nursery?" Molly shrieks. "Oh, I'm going to get me some more babies around this place." She clasps her hands together in delight.

"Maybe not for a while yet though," I say before she gets too carried away.

Jax laughs softly and I roll my eyes at how sure he is of himself.

"You know what would look good in there?" he says to his aunt. "One of those old-fashioned cribs that rock."

"Like the kind you had?" she says with a huge smile.

"Well, can't say I remember that far back," Jax laughs.

"You did," Harvey says quietly. "I rocked you to sleep in it every night for a year after you were born. One time when you had croup, it was the only thing that would stop you crying. Your mom and I used to take turns rocking it all night long," he wipes a stray tear from the corner of his eye.

I sense Jax bristling beside me. I wish that I could take his pain away so that he could let his father in a little.

With perfect timing, Blue jumps up and places his fat paws on the table and makes everyone laugh.

"Get down you dumb dog," Molly chides him, before taking a piece of chicken from her bowl and hand feeding him.

Then we go on eating the rest of our meal making idle small talk and avoiding any further discussion of Jax's childhood, his mom, or nurseries.

AFTER DINNER, Jax and I walked back to the barn. On the way we looked at the stars and he told me about the different constellations and the mythology behind them. I suspect it was a way of avoiding the conversation we're about to have as I stand in the bedroom undressing.

"Why did you have to tell them about the nursery?" I ask.

He frowns at me. "Why wouldn't I? I didn't think it was a secret that we're going to have more kids?"

"It's not," I say with a sigh. "But telling Molly about a nursery, Jax? She got so excited. It just feels like there's unnecessary pressure to fill a nursery now, is all."

He walks across the room, wrapping his arms around me. "There is no pressure, angel. I'll talk to her. Okay?"

I place my hands on his solid chest. "You really want a baby so soon, though?"

He brushes my hair back from my face. "Yes. If it was up to me, I'd toss those birth control pills you're taking down the toilet and have you knocked up before this honeymoon is over."

"You know it's unlikely to happen that quickly, right?"

"Well we'll never know unless we test the theory out." His hand skates over my stomach until it's splayed over my abdomen. "So, what do you say, baby? You gonna let me put my baby in you?"

I can't deny the thought of having Jax's baby fills me with excitement, but this is a big deal. "We've been married less than two days and you already want me barefoot and pregnant?"

He arches one eyebrow at me. "I never said you had to be barefoot."

I push against his chest, but he's so huge he doesn't budge at all.

"Besides, Matthias is desperate for a little brother or sister," he reminds me, going for the jugular.

"I know. He tells me almost every day, and you encourage him."

His face breaks out into a huge grin as he pulls me closer until I'm pressed against him and I feel his hardening cock digging into my abdomen. "I support him. That's what dad's do."

"You are the best dad," I admit. He is incredible with my son, Matthias. No-one who saw them together would have any idea that Jax isn't his biological father.

"Make me one again," he whispers, his breath dusting over my cheek and making goosebumps break out all over my body.

Holy mother of God. How the hell do I refuse an offer like that?

"Okay, no more birth control pills," I agree.

"Good girl," he laughs softly before he scoops me up into his arms, making me yelp in surprise. "Might as well get started right away."

"Well, I haven't taken one for over twenty-four hours now, so..." I grin at him.

"Really?" He tosses me into the middle of the bed.

"No. You know I take them at night."

He pulls his t-shirt off over his head and climbs onto the bed, holding himself over me. "Something about fucking you and knowing that I could be getting you pregnant makes me feel like a fucking animal, baby. I want to fill you so full of my cum that your pussy is bursting with it."

"Damn, Jax," I whisper. I'm pretty sure he could knock me up with his dirty talk alone.

CHAPTER 7
LUCIA

"Damn, your ass looks good in those jeans, cowboy," I say as I follow Jax into the stables.

He turns and gives me a cheeky wink. We've had the perfect morning, sleeping late and having slow, lazy morning sex, before a huge breakfast of pancakes and bacon. After which I insisted that we need to leave the barn for the rest of the day for some sunshine and fresh air. Besides, I want to practice my riding. I learned a little when I was here last, but I feel rusty already.

"Horse is all ready for you, boss," Cody steps into view, leading Jax's horse, a beautiful black stallion named Bastian. Cody is one of the ranch hands here I met last year.

"Thanks, kid," Jax replies.

I put my hands on my hips and frown. "Horse? Just one?"

"I was only asked to get Bastian ready, Ma'am," Cody tips his hat at me.

Ma'am? I suppress a smile at his sudden formality. He's about the same age as me and has worked here since he left high school. When I was last here, he called me Lucia.

"What about my horse?" I ask Jax.

"Beat it kid," he says to Cody with a grin. Cody hands him the horse's reins, before tipping his hat at both of us and walking out of the stable.

"I thought you were teaching me to ride?" I ask, my eyes narrowed in suspicion.

"Hmm," Jax rubs a hand over the stubble on his jaw and something about the way he does it makes heat flush over my chest. He is too handsome for his own good. "Well, I don't want you overdoing it now, do I? You're not used to riding, at least not horses..." He flashes his eyebrows at me.

I open my mouth in mock indignation and he laughs softly.

"Once I teach you to ride properly, there's going to be no stopping you. I could see how you were getting the bug for it last time we were down here. And I just don't want you getting sore, angel. Not from a horse anyway."

I frown at him, crossing my arms over my chest. "So, what are we doing today?"

"We'll still go for a ride. A nice gentle one on Bastian here. Me and him will show you around all of our favorite spots," he says, reaching for my hand.

I try to glare at him, but the idea of spending a few hours on the back of a horse with Jax's arms around me while he shows me some of this beautiful country, sounds pretty good to me.

"Fine," I say with a sigh. "I can't help but feel like you have an ulterior motive though, cowboy."

"And what could that possibly be, angel?"

I put my foot into the stirrup and Jax puts his hand on my ass to give me a lift. I look down at him once I'm seated. "Like you're going to take me to some secluded spot and fuck my brains out?"

He laughs out loud before shaking his head. Then he climbs onto Bastian behind me, wrapping his arms around my waist and scooting me back a little so I'm pressed against his body. "Not today, baby," he whispers in my ear.

AFTER OUR RIDE, Jax showed me how to take off Bastian's saddle and make sure he was cooled down and hydrated before we put him back in his stable. It was almost dusk by the time we got back to the barn. We took some steaks from the fridge and Jax barbecued them while I made a potato salad and then we sat on the porch, eating dinner, drinking wine and talking.

It has been a perfect, relaxing day — so different from our life in LA.

"You think you could get used to living out here?" he asks as I stare into the darkness, watching the fireflies in the distance.

"Hmm, maybe. It sure is peaceful here, but I think I'd miss LA though. You?"

"I like it when I'm here, and when I'm in LA I think about how peaceful it is back here, but yeah, I miss home too. I really miss the kid," he says with a soft laugh as he leans back in his chair.

He and Matthias spent half an hour on a video call before dinner talking about nothing but Avengers and dinosaurs.

"Me too," I admit.

"He's gonna love this house."

"He sure is. His little face when you showed him his room here was so cute," I chuckle. "We should figure out a way to spend more time here. I mean you can do a lot of what you do from anywhere, right? As long as you have a good WIFI connection."

"Yeah," he says with a nod as he stares out across the fields.

"I like how relaxed you are out here."

He narrows his eyes at me. "You do?"

44

"Hmm. You're much less grumpy." I take a sip of my wine and stifle a grin.

"Oh, angel." He shakes his head. "Now I know you did not just call me grumpy."

I arch an eyebrow at him and bite on my lip, then I tilt my head in challenge. "Pretty sure I did."

He's up off his seat before I can take another breath, picking me up, he hoists me over his shoulder and I spill half my wine on the floor.

"Jax!" I shriek half in surprise and half in laughter.

He takes the wine glass from my hand and puts it onto the table, before slapping my ass and making me squeal. Sliding the French doors closed, he carries me up the stairs and into our bedroom before tossing me onto the bed.

I stare up at him as his eyes burn into my skin.

"Grumpy?" he asks with a low growl that vibrates through my entire body.

"Yes," I whisper, fluttering my eyelashes.

"You looking to get your ass spanked, Luce?" he says as he starts to unfasten his belt.

"God, yes," I pant as my eyes lock on his hands.

"Oh, not with this, baby. Not tonight," he laughs darkly. "I have something much better in mind for you."

Wet heat floods my pussy as fear and excitement skitters throughout my body, making me shiver. He stalks toward the bed with his belt in his hands and fire in his eyes.

"Flip over. I want you on your knees with your ass in the air and your hands holding onto to the bed," he orders.

I roll over and do as he asks, gripping onto the metal spindles of the bed-frame. A few seconds later, Jax is wrapping his belt around my wrists, pulling the soft leather tight until he secures me in place. I turn my head so that my cheek is pressed against the pillow and watch him.

45

"Grumpy, huh?" he asks me again.

"Sorry," I purr and then despite trying not to, I smile.

"Oh, Luce," he says with a shake of his head and a wicked glint in his eye.

Then he takes off his shirt and jeans until he's standing in just his boxer briefs and I lick my lips as I admire his body. All muscles and glistening skin covered in dark ink. He walks to the back of the room and I crane my neck to see what he's doing but he remains annoyingly out of sight.

The first thing I see again are his feet coming back into view as he walks back toward the bed. The soft thwack of something hitting his palm startles me and as he gets closer I see him holding a riding crop in his hands.

I swallow hard. It's just like the one I saw at the stables today.

Shit!

"I forgot to tell you I bought you this, Luce. But actually, I don't think you'll need it down at the stables. You're too sweet to use one on a horse. I didn't think I'd have cause to use it on you so soon though, angel," he growls as he crawls onto the bed.

His warm, rough hands glide over my outer thighs as he pushes my sundress up over my ass.

"So fucking beautiful," he hisses. "I wonder what this pretty ass is going to look like when I stripe it with my riding crop."

"Jax," I whimper. I have never seen him use one of those things on a horse, but I already know he can wield it like a pro.

He slips a hand between my thighs, tugging my panties to the side and dragging a finger through my wet folds. "And this pussy too," he groans and my legs start to tremble as I suck in a breath.

He rubs a firm hand over my ass. "Have I ever hurt you, Luce?"

"No," I whisper.

"You think I want to?"

I draw in another deep breath. Of course he doesn't. "No," I breathe.

"Good girl," he soothes and then he brings the crop down lightly over my ass cheeks, leaving a warm pleasant sting that makes me moan.

He does it a few more times until I'm arching my back in pleasure. "Fuck, Jax," I gasp.

"Oh, you like that, baby?"

"Uh-huh," I murmur.

He hooks his fingers into the waistband of my panties and begins tugging them off over my hips and thighs. "Let's get these panties off you so I turn that pretty ass red," he says, rolling them down to my knees.

Then he settles on the bed behind me and a few seconds later, I feel the sting of the crop across my cheeks. It's harder this time but it sends pleasure and pain skittering through my body like an electric current. My pussy twitches with need as he does it again.

"Ah, Jax!" I moan loudly.

"You're dripping wet already," he chuckles before he slides the riding crop between my folds, circling the tip over my clit before dragging it back to my entrance. He slips the tip inside ever so slightly, just for a second, and my knees almost buckle.

"Fucking soaking," he hisses as holds the tip of the crop near my face to show me that it is glistening with the cream of my arousal.

I close my eyes as my cheeks turn red with heat.

He nudges his knee between my thighs. "Spread those legs wider, Luce. I want to see that pussy dripping for me."

Groaning, I open as wide as I can while being restricted by my panties bunched at my knees.

"Such a beautiful pussy too," he growls before he spanks me with the crop. This time the tip of it flicks over my clit and I yelp in surprise.

He does it again with just the tiniest flick of his wrist and suddenly my inner thighs are tingling.

"Jax, please?" I whimper.

"Fuck, baby, I love hearing you beg for this," he growls, sliding the tip of the crop inside me again — this time a little deeper.

He thrusts it in and out of me a few times and I moan in frustration as warmth rolls through my stomach and thighs. He pulls it out and slides it to my clit again, rubbing it while he starts to spank my ass with his hand.

"Fuck, Jax, I-I," I can't take any more. I need to come. I need the ripples of pleasure that keep fluttering up my thighs to burst out of me. In that sweet spot between my thighs where he's rubbing me with the soft leather.

"You want to come?"

"Yes, please?" I pant as my climax remains frustratingly close.

He flicks his wrist again, whipping the crop against my clit over and over again until I see flashes of light behind my eyelids, my thighs and pussy contract and release as my orgasm crashes over me.

He leans over me, wrapping an arm around my waist to keep me upright. "That's my good girl," he whispers in my ear.

I nod, my face brushing against the pillow as tears roll down my cheek.

"We're not done yet, baby. What's my favorite thing to do to your ass other than spank it?"

"Fuck it," I whisper.

He laughs softly as he pushes himself back up before I feel

one of his fingers, sticky with my cum, sliding into my ass. He pumps it in and out and I lean back into him, wanting more.

The snap of a cap lets me know he has lube here somewhere too and a few seconds later, he's coated his shaft and is pressing the tip of his cock against me. He pushes in slightly and I hiss at the pain and pleasure of him breaching my opening. He's so big that it takes a few seconds for my body to adjust, no matter how much he prepares me.

Then I feel something nudging at my pussy opening. It's thick and it stretches me as Jax is pushing into my ass. "Good girl, you can take me," he grits out the words as he presses deeper inside me while he edges something into my pussy.

When I look between my thighs I see the tip of the riding crop and realize he's about to fuck me with the handle.

"Oh, God, Jax!" I whimper as he pushes it deeper inside and starts to fuck me slowly, sliding it in and out of my wet pussy.

"You like that, baby?" he groans as he presses himself in deeper too. "You like having both of your tight little holes filled at the same time."

"Yeah." I rock my hips back against him, wanting more even as he stretches me so wide that it burns.

"You feel so fucking good," he hisses as he drives all the way in.

"You feel so good," I whimper as he fucks my ass and pussy at the same time.

The complete fullness I feel is pleasure verging on exquisite pain. He knows exactly how much I can take as he fucks me a little harder.

"You gonna come all over this, Luce," he twists the crop, pressing on the spot inside me that makes me whimper and mewl, while driving his cock deeper into my ass.

"Yes," I shout as my inner walls squeeze tightly around the leather handle, making him groan loudly.

He pulls the crop out of me and slides two fingers into my pussy instead. "I wanna feel you come," he hisses. "Every fucking squeeze and tremor. Your orgasms are mine, Luce. I want to feel every fucking part of them."

He thrusts his fingers harder inside me and I come apart around him, squeezing him deeper and tighter as my climax tears through my body.

"Fuck, Luce!" he roars as he thrusts harder, pressing me flat to the mattress as he grinds his own release out into me.

When he is spent, he lies beside me, pulling me close to him so his hot breath is on my ear and his heart beats against my skin.

"Fuck, angel," he breathes.

"I know."

"You okay?"

"Yes. But did you just fuck me with a riding crop?" I giggle.

"Yep," he laughs softly. "How was it?"

"Good," I purr, "but not as good as you. Nothing feels as good as you inside me, Jax."

He smiles at me. "And nothing ever will. You just remember that."

"I will," I whisper.

He reaches up and frees my wrists from the leather and then he pulls me to lie on his chest. "Who do you belong to, Luce?"

"You, Jax. Only you."

CHAPTER 8

JAX

"Come on, Luce, we're going to be late," I shout up the stairs to her.

"Late for what though?" she shouts back. "It would help me to get ready if I knew what to wear."

"I told you jeans and a tank top is fine," I remind her.

"I'm almost ready then," she calls back and I sit on the sofa and wait, hoping that she enjoys the surprise I have planned.

A few minutes later, Lucia walks down the stairs. She's dressed in cowboy boots, tight fitting blue jeans that show off her incredible curves and a white tank top. And she looks so damn good I seriously consider cancelling our plans and staying home with her instead. But that will only lead to an all night fucking session, and we've been doing plenty of that already.

I figure she deserves a night out.

"Will I do?" she asks, giving me a twirl as she reaches the bottom stair.

I walk over to her, pulling her into my arms and burying my face in her neck. "You'll more than fucking do. You look damn edible in those jeans."

"Thank you, cowboy," she giggles. "Do you like ma boots?" she tries a southern accent.

"Sure do. Pretty sure they're gonna look good wrapped around my neck later too."

"You have a filthy mouth, Jackson Decker," she says with a grin.

"Sure do, baby. Now let's go."

Lucia talks non stop on our drive to the city. She asks constant questions as she tries to figure out where we're going.

"You're going to know in about ten minutes, baby," I assure her.

"Fine," she leans back against her seat and I slide my hand onto her thigh and squeeze.

"You remember the first time I ever kissed you was in a truck?"

She turns to me and smiles. "Sure do, but we did way more than kiss, Jax."

"Hmm. I knew the very first moment I tasted your pussy I was never gonna eat another for the rest of my life."

That makes her laugh out loud and the sound goes straight to my dick. Or maybe it's the memory of our first time, back in LA in my Hennessey Goliath. I ate her pussy before I fucked her on the back seat and I've been addicted to her ever since.

"You did not," she protests. "You told me it was just one night, remember?"

"Yeah, but when you told me no man had ever made you come before, I knew that I had to save you from a life of mediocre sex."

"You're my hero," she flutters her eyelashes at me, clutching her hands together and pretending to swoon.

"You'd better believe it, baby." I wink at her and she blushes.

We sit in silence for a few seconds before I speak again. "It's true though, Luce."

"What is?"

"That I knew. From the very first moment I kissed you, I knew there would never be anyone else."

"Jax," she whispers as tears prick at her eyes.

I brush over her cheek with my fingertips. "I just wanted you to know that."

She takes my hand in hers and kisses my knuckles. "Just when I think you couldn't possibly be any more perfect, Jackson Decker, you go and say something like that to melt my heart."

I narrow my eyes at her. "Just your heart?"

"And obviously my panties too," she adds.

"That's my girl."

When we pull up outside the stadium a few moments later, Lucia frowns as she peers out of the window.

"Are we watching a game?"

"Nope. A fight," I tell her, jumping out of the truck and opening her door for her.

"Who is fighting?"

"A friend of ours. Someone you have a bit of a crush on, maybe?"

She opens her mouth as though completely insulted by that comment. "I only have eyes for you. You know that."

"A girl crush, baby. You admire her is all I meant," I say with a wink.

"Toni is fighting tonight?" she asks with a huge smile as she takes my hand and we walk toward the stadium.

"She sure is. And she got us some ringside seats too."

"I had no idea she'd be here. Is it a sanctioned fight? Her belt's not on the line, right?" she asks and I smile at her newly acquired knowledge of MMA fighting.

Since Toni Moretti started training her about eight months ago, she's become a huge fan of the sport, and she and Toni have become friends. The fact that Toni has a bit of thing for my girl is something I don't dwell on too much. I trust Lucia completely, and Toni too. She and I have been friends for a long time.

"It's an exhibition thing. It's all publicity for her big fight next year."

"I can't wait to see her kick some ass live," she says with a grin. "I've only seen her on TV before."

"I know," I wrap my arm around her waist. "You like your surprise then?"

She places her hands on my cheeks and kisses me. "I love it. I love you."

"Love you too, baby."

Then with my hand on her ass and her hand in the back pocket of my jeans, we walk into the stadium to find our ringside seats.

I MOSTLY WATCH Lucia instead of the fight, her eyes shining with happiness as she watches the sport she's come to enjoy so much.

"Wow! They're so good," she shouts to be heard over the crowd. "It's so much better watching live."

"It sure is."

I slide an arm around her shoulder and when Toni finally comes into the ring, the crowd goes wild with cheering and applause. She is the star of the show and she knows it. She laps up the attention like she was born for it. Playing to the crowd and taunting her opponent, whom I happen to know is a good friend of hers. When she sees Lucia and me, she gives Lucia a wave and my girl squeals with delight.

"She waved at us," she says with a huge grin. "I feel so important."

I laugh and shake my head. Her father is the king of fucking LA and she's the heir to the entire Montoya empire, along with her little brothers of course, but getting waved at by Toni Moretti is what makes her feel like a VIP. At least half of the people in this room would know her family name, but she has no clue how powerful and special she really is. And that is one of the many things I love about her.

CHAPTER 9
LUCIA

My entire body is alive and sizzling with nervous energy as we walk through the stadium. I loved the whole night. All of the fighters were so skilled. I figure I picked up a few tricks I can try on Toni at our next training session — not that she wouldn't already know them all herself. Damn, hadn't thought of that!

"You enjoy yourself, baby?" Jax asks, pressing a kiss on my forehead as he slings an arm around my shoulder.

"Yes. I loved it. Thank you."

"You're welcome."

"It's a shame we couldn't go back there and speak with Toni though," I say with a sigh.

"She's busy with press and PR people and she has a few meet the fans things to do," he says with a shrug.

"I guess," I say, feeling a little deflated. "Would have been nice to see her is all."

"You'll see her, baby," he laughs softly. "She's meeting us in a bar a few blocks away when she's finished up in there."

"She is?" I stare at him.

"Yep. You think she would come all this way and not say hi to her biggest fan?" he teases me.

"I'm not her biggest fan."

"No?" he laughs again and the sound rumbles through his chest.

"Maybe one of the biggest, but not *the* biggest," I admit.

"I have to warn you, she can be a bit of an asshole after a fight. Must be all the adrenaline and the adulation going to her head or something."

"She's always an asshole," I remind him.

"True."

TONI ROLLS her glass in her hand making the ice clink against the sides. She licks her lips as she signals the waitress for a refill.

"I see you still love your bourbon?" Jax says with a smile as he leans back on the bench, his arm draped around my shoulder.

"Can't beat it." She winks at him. "Reminds me of our weekend in Cabo."

Jax shakes his head and groans.

I look between them both. "Cabo?"

"Cabo, baby," Toni winks at me.

"You two went to Cabo together?"

"We didn't go together. We were there at the same time and we..." Jax runs a hand over his jaw.

"You what?"

"We hooked up," Toni says with a shrug as though she didn't just drop a grenade into the room.

"Y-you two?" I give my full attention to Jax.

"We didn't exactly hook up. Not with each other," he says before shooting Toni a warning glare.

"So, what did you do?" I frown at him. I hate that I feel like the only person at the table who doesn't know what's going on here. Jax assured me he and Toni had never had sex together. Did he lie to me?

"Oh Jax. It was years ago. Before you even knew Lucia here," Toni says with a wicked laugh. "She knows you were a wild-card, don't you, *honey*?" she almost purrs the last word and it makes my cheeks flush pink for some reason.

"Yes," I say, narrowing my eyes at her. "But I didn't know that you two had..."

Toni pulls a face, bordering on disgust. "Oh we didn't do anything to each other. I don't dig guys that way."

"You've had way too much to drink, Moretti," Jax says quietly.

"So what did you do?" I lean forward in my seat, desperate to know what the hell she's going on about.

"You mean who did we do? What was her name, Jax?"

"I don't remember," he growls.

"Casey? Kayleigh?" She frowns as though she's deep in thought. "Can't recall her name, but damn she had a sweet pussy."

Annoyingly, I gasp out loud like a naïve schoolgirl and that makes Toni smile. I knew Jax had a varied and interesting sex life before we met. I'm pretty sure he whored his way through the entire state of California, but it's something he doesn't like talking about with me.

"I'm almost certain it can't be as sweet as yours, Lucia, because I have never seen our Jackson here so in love."

"Enough!" he barks.

"No," I shake my head. I want to know more and not because I'm jealous but because something about it sounds kind of hot. I imagine for a second being the lucky recipient who got to be taken care of by Jax and Toni at the same time. "You two had a threesome?"

"We sure did."

"How? What?" I look between the two of them again.

"Lucia, no," Jax says with a sigh.

I place my hand on his thigh and squeeze. "Please? I've never done this kind of stuff. Tell me."

He rolls his eyes so I turn back to Toni, who seems more than happy to relive their wild time in Cabo. "You'll tell me, right?"

She leans forward, signaling me to lean in too, and when I do she whispers. "I can tell you, but I'd rather show you, honey."

"Not a fucking chance," Jax says as he runs his hand down my spine and I'm not sure whether it's that, or what Toni just said, or maybe both, but a shiver of excitement skitters through me.

"Looks like you're gonna have to tell me then, honey," I say to Toni with a flash of my eyebrows. She opens her mouth and sucks in a shallow breath that makes me smile. I love to see her rattled, even if it was just for a second.

"You asked for it, princess." She glances at Jax quickly before she goes on talking. "Jackson had already hooked up with this chick when I bumped into them. We went for a drink and then back to her room. Her and Jackson were fooling around on the bed, and then..." She licks her lips before she looks to Jax again. "You want to tell the rest?"

"You're doing just fine on your own," he replies.

She laughs before her eyes fix on me again. "I bet Jackson here that I could eat her pussy better than he could and she was up for that too, so we did. It was so fucking hot, Lucia," she whispers, her eyes darkening at the memory. "She sat on his lap and he held her wide open for me while I ate her."

"Oh," I gasp as wet heat sears between my thighs. It sounds so freaking hot and I'm just listening to the story.

"And then when she was on the edge, he slipped his cock into her ass and fucked her while I made her come. Twice." She holds up two fingers.

"I don't think you can take all the credit for that," he says and she grins at him.

"I suppose not," she admits with a shrug. "We made a pretty good team. I mean how many times did we make her come that night?"

"I don't recall," he mutters.

"Quite a few," she purrs.

"Wow!" I whisper as heat creeps up my neck and onto my cheeks.

"We never did find out which one of us ate pussy better though, did we?" Toni arches an eyebrow at him.

"No. And we never will," he growls as he wraps his arm around my neck possessively and pulls me close to him.

"Aw, that's such a shame," she pouts as the waitress comes over with her drink.

"Thank you," Toni says with a smile and a wink and our young waitress smiles right back. I'm not into women, but there is something about Toni Moretti that is completely captivating. She takes a sip of her bourbon and then looks at me.

"Imagine how hot it would be, Lucia, to be sitting on your husband's lap and have him holding your legs open while he watches another woman eating your pussy and making you come?"

I squeeze my thighs together as the thought makes heat sear between them. Toni watches me like a predator watches its prey and I feel Jax's eyes burning into me too. I glance at him to see if I'm imagining it, but he's staring at me intently, assessing my reaction, and I don't know what the right one to have is. He's my husband and I adore him. He is everything I want and need, but I can't deny that the image Toni just conjured in my mind has me feeling all kinds of things I shouldn't be.

"So, I'm not flying home until the day after tomorrow. Do you two lovebirds have plans I can gatecrash?"

"We're on our honeymoon," Jax reminds her.

"I know, but you don't fuck all day and night do you?" She narrows her eyes at us. "Do you?"

"Pretty much," I say with a shrug.

"Straight people," she says, rolling her eyes and shaking her head.

"You could come for dinner tomorrow night and see our new house? If you promise to behave?" Jax offers.

She flutters her eyelashes at him. "I always behave, Decker."

"Hmm," he mumbles.

"That would be great. You should see the place. It's beautiful," I add.

"Then I'll swing by. At six?"

"Six is fine," Jax replies.

"Great," she knocks back the last of her drink and checks her phone. "My driver is outside. I'll catch up with you two fuck-bunnies tomorrow." Then she stands on shaky feet.

Jax reaches out and steadies her but she slaps his hand away and frowns at him.

"I'm fine, Decker," she snaps. "I just kicked Sonya Kim's ass. I can get out of this bar."

Then with a final eye roll, she leaves the bar, leaving Jax and me alone.

"Can we go home too?" I whisper.

He arches an eyebrow at me. "You tired?"

"Not even a little," I say, taking his hand and standing up.

He stands too, before dipping his head low so he can whisper in my ear. "You're getting fucked so hard when we get home. You know that, right?"

"I'm counting on it, cowboy."

CHAPTER 10
JAX

I drove back to the barn with my cock damn near busting out of my jeans. I all but dragged Lucia out of the truck, carried her to the porch, pulled her jeans down over her ass and fucked her right there over the wooden railing. After we both came hard, I carried her upstairs and straight to bed.

Now we're both naked while she straddles me and I'm still desperate to be inside her, like my cock has already forgotten that he fucked her ten minutes ago. But something's not right. She seems distracted.

"What's on your mind, baby?" I ask her as she bites on her lip, and not in the trying to be a brat and tease me way. Her mind is elsewhere and I don't like it.

"I-I," she sucks in a shaky breath. "Am I enough for you, Jax?"

"What the fuck, angel?"

"I mean, when it comes to sex, is what we do enough for you?" she mumbles the words as though she's ashamed or worried to say them too loud.

"Are you suggesting that our sex life isn't exciting for me?" I look down between us. My cock is as hard as iron as it nudges against the folds of her slick pussy. "If I got any more excited, I'd walk around with a permanent boner."

My fingers flex, digging into the skin of her hips as I hold onto her. I am so fucking desperate to bury myself inside her.

"I don't mean that," she whispers. "But you're used to threesomes and adventurous stuff that I've never even tried. I just don't want you to get bored with me."

"Lucia," I sigh as I wrap my arms around her waist and pull her closer to me. "There is no comparison to the sex I used to have with random women, to what you and I have."

"That's what I mean," she breathes. "Am I too... vanilla for you?"

"Vanilla?" I arch an eyebrow at her. "Last night I tied you up and spanked you until you came so hard you almost passed out. You think that's vanilla?"

"To people who are used to threesomes and stuff, probably," she shrugs.

"I'm not used to those things. So, I had a couple of experiences, but I push boundaries with you that I never have before."

"You do?"

"Yes," I brush her hair back from her beautiful face. "I want to give you everything you want and need, baby. But it wouldn't matter if all you needed was vanilla. I used to have a lot of sex. I enjoyed it. It was fun and a good way to relieve some tension and kill a few hours. I sometimes slept with the same woman more than once, but it was out of convenience and familiarity."

She blinks at me.

"But sex with you is completely different, baby. You're like a drug that I will never get enough of. My cock gets hard just thinking about you. I think about fucking you constantly. I could fuck you all day every day and it wouldn't be enough. I will never get bored of you or with you."

"Jax," she breathes as she rolls her hips over me, coating me in her juices. "I just want to be everything you need too."

"You already are, Luce, now for the love of all that is holy, let me fuck you," I plead as I grab her hips again and slide her onto me, impaling her on my cock. She hisses as I stretch her wide, pulling her onto me until I'm as deep as I can possibly get. "This right here is all I'll ever need."

"Damn, Jax. You fuck me so good," she whimpers as she rocks her hips onto me.

I sit up so I can hold her close as she rides me.

"You liked Toni talking about eating you out though, didn't you, baby?" I growl as I trail kisses along her throat. Her pussy walls squeeze me and the heat flushes across her cheeks.

"Jax," she purrs. "Stop it."

"You don't have to pretend, Luce. I could see how turned on you were."

She looks into my eyes and I see the uncertainty in hers.

"Did you think about how good it would feel for me to hold you wide open while Toni licks your sweet pussy?"

"Jax!" she groans loudly, milking my cock as she slicks me with heat.

"Even talking about it has you on the edge, Luce."

"Because you're talking about eating my pussy while you're fucking me, Jax. Of course I'm on the edge," she groans in frustration.

I flip her onto her back, sinking deeper inside her and making her eyes go back in her head. "Don't lie to me, Luce." I roll my hips so that I'm rubbing against her sweet spot inside. "Did you think about how good it would feel?"

"Can you just leave it?" she groans as she rakes her nails down my back.

"Are you pissed at me? Is that why you're bringing up this vanilla shit? Are you trying to pick a fight with me?"

She blinks at me. "I'm not trying to pick a fight," she whimpers as I keep her on the edge.

I narrow my eyes at her. She's holding something back. Wrapping my hands around the back of her thighs, I lift her slightly and drive in a little deeper. "Jax!" she gasps as tears start to roll down her cheeks.

"You're not coming until you tell me what's going on for you, Luce," I growl as I pull out of her. We stare at each other until the tension becomes too much.

"I'm jealous, okay," she snaps.

Fuck! I'm such an asshole.

"I don't mean because you did that," she wipes her cheeks with the back of her hand. "I didn't even know you then."

"Then why, baby? You know you can tell me anything."

"I'm jealous of the girl you did that with. I mean not of her as a person, but the experience she had with you. I will never have that. Yes, what Toni said sounded hot, but you're what makes it hot, Jax. You, not Toni," she sniffs and turns her head away from me. "Ignore me. I'm being silly. I think maybe I had too much to drink."

I slide my hands from behind her thighs, letting her lie flat on the bed and turn her face back to me, brushing a tear from her cheek. "You are everything to me, Luce. *Every-fucking-thing.* Do you understand me?"

She nods her head.

"You give me experiences that nobody else ever could or would, baby. I need you to believe that. There has been nothing like this for me. Ever."

She blinks at me. "I do believe you."

I lean down and kiss her as I slide back inside her. This is the only thing I can think of right now to prove to her that she is it for me. She is all I'll ever need. But what if she needs something more? She was so fucking naïve and innocent when it came to sex and then I staked my claim on her and told her no-one would ever touch her again. Was it unfair of me to deny her a chance to go out and do some of the shit that I got to do?

She wraps her arms around my neck and her legs around my waist. "I love you, Jax," she whispers.

"I love you too, baby."

"Can you just make me come so hard that I forget about being such a weirdo about this?" She gives me a faint smile.

I kiss her forehead. "You are not a weirdo and yes, baby, I'll make you come real hard, okay?"

"Okay." Her smile widens and I sink deeper, determined to give her what she needs.

CHAPTER 11
LUCIA

Standing on the deck, I squint in the fading light as I see the car headlights approaching.

"She's here," I shout to Jax who walks out to stand behind me, wrapping his arms possessively around my waist. I haven't forgotten what he said last night about Toni eating my pussy while he holds me down. The memory of the way he talked about it and the images it conjures in my head makes wet heat slick between my thighs. I hope he doesn't bring it up in front of her though, because I might just die of embarrassment.

"Hey, lovebirds," Toni says with a grin as she climbs out of the sleek, grey Audi. "How are we tonight?"

"Get your ass in here. You're late, Moretti," Jax says to her.

She rolls her eyes. "Is he always like this?"

"Always," I giggle.

She jogs up the few steps before giving each of us a hug. Then she looks inside the house. "This place is nice," she whistles.

"Come on in and Lucia will show you around while I get us a drink. Red or white for you?"

Toni winces. "White. But just a small one. I got a little bit wasted last night. I'm sorry if I said anything inappropriate."

"Nah," Jax waves his hand dismissively. "Nothing inappropriate about suggesting I hold my wife down while you eat her pussy."

Toni laughs, while my cheeks flush pink. I wonder why I'm the one who's blushing when it's the two of them who keep bringing it up, not to mention the fact they've actually done it with a woman — lucky gal!

"Besides, I'm driving anyway," she looks back at her car.

"You can stay in the house if you like," Jax offers.

Toni arches an eyebrow at me in amusement.

"The main house. Not here," he warns her.

She laughs softly as she links her arm through mine. "Come on, princess. Show me around this beautiful castle of yours."

AFTER DINNER, I refill our wine glasses and then take our drinks onto the deck where Jax and Toni are sitting. Jax is in the huge rocking chair and after I put our drinks on the table, he grabs my waist and pulls me to sit on his lap. Wrapping his arms around me, he holds me tight. My dress rides up slightly and I tug it down, conscious of Toni's eyes on me.

It's been a lovely evening. We've eaten delicious food, drank some good wine and had a lot of laughs talking mostly about Toni's dating disasters. I suppose it was inevitable that the conversation would eventually turn to sex.

"I met a woman last week who could eat pussy like... I dunno," Toni waves her hand in the air, "some kind of sex guru. I mean, she made noises come out of my body like I've never even heard before," she ways with a wistful sigh.

"So are you seeing her again?" I ask.

"Nope. She was way too high maintenance for me. Always calling and texting and wanting to know where I was." She screws her face up in disgust. "I can't be doing with all that shit. That is not my vibe," she lets the word vibe roll off her tongue. "Best damn head I ever got though."

"So you're giving up the best head of your life because she called and texted too much?" I ask.

"Oh, Lucia," she says, shaking her head at me. "There will be another. Most women give amazing head. At least the ones I know do. You ever had head from a woman?"

I feel Jax's arms tighten around me.

"No."

"You should have tried it before this one married you off for life."

"I think I can live without it."

"Think about it," she sits forward in her seat. "Women know exactly what to do down there. They have all the same equipment you do. They know *exactly* where the clitoris is. No searching around for it."

"So do a lot of guys, Toni," Jax says, his voice a deep rumbling growl.

I wonder if he's pissed at her, but when I look up at him, he's smiling. I squirm on his lap as he winks at me, because this man does not need any directions to the clitoris.

Suddenly, I'm feeling hot and a little lightheaded.

"Yeah, but it's not the same as really knowing the hardware, you know what I mean?"

"My friend, Archer, he's gay but he's dated a few women and he told me that guys give the best blow jobs because they know how everything works," I add, smiling as I think about him and some of the incredibly funny conversations we've had - usually over pancakes the morning after one of his dates.

"Or maybe that's because he's only attracted to dudes, so he just wasn't into the women who gave him head?" Jax offers.

"Also true," I admit with a giggle.

"You should feel a woman's mouth on you once, Lucia. Just for the experience," Toni says, but she's looking at Jax now, not me. "It doesn't seem fair that your husband here has got to live out all of his fantasies but you don't."

"He is all of my fantasies, Toni," I say with a smile and I mean it.

"And I respect that," she says with a nod. "Monogamy is not for me, but you two seem happy. All I'm saying is there's no reason you can't experience that. Jax could be involved. He can be in complete control."

"What?" I whisper.

"I'm not going to lie and say I wouldn't love to taste your pussy," she breathes and heat flushes over my chest and neck. "But I promise this will all be about you. A wedding gift." She runs her tongue over her full lips.

"I-I don't know what you mean," I stammer while Jax remains unusually silent. His breathing grows faster and his cock is getting harder beneath my ass.

"Don't be shy. You know what I'm offering. Jax can hold you down, like the girl in Cabo, while I eat your pussy and make you come."

I blink at her. Why does that sound so hot? I shouldn't be thinking about anyone else making me come. But being held in Jax's strong arms while she does that. Wow!

I press a hand to my hot cheek.

Jax presses his lips against my ear as he slides a hand between my thighs. He brushes his fingertips against my panties and I close my eyes when he finds them damp.

"Is that what you want, angel?" he growls.

I turn around and stare at him. Surely he has lost his mind?

He licks his lips as he waits for my answer and I open my mouth but nothing comes out.

He looks over at Toni. "Give us a few moments, will you?"

"Take all the time you need." She winks at me before she walks back into the house.

Jax pulls my panties aside and slides a finger inside my wet pussy, making me whimper. "Thought so," he says before he pulls his hand from between my thighs and wraps his arm around my waist again. "This isn't some kind of test, angel. This is a one time deal. If you want this, I'll give it to you. Do you want it?"

I look into his eyes and my breath catches in my throat. How do I tell my possessive husband that I want someone else to make me come? And why is he offering it to me?

"Talk to me, Luce. Tell me what's going on in your head."

"You told me once, when we were at his ranch, that if I let you fuck me bare, no-one would ever touch me again. Why has that changed?"

"It hasn't, angel, and I said," he presses his lips against my forehead and gives me a brief kiss before he goes on, "that no man would ever put his hands on you again. Toni isn't a man, is she?"

"No," I whisper. "But I don't understand why. I would hate to see you with anyone else — man or woman. It would kill me."

He sighs as he brushes my hair back from my face. "You haven't had as many experiences as me, and there is nothing I can do to change that. You'll never have a threesome. You'll never have anyone else inside you, baby, because you are mine. But, I can give you this. I know she's a bit much, but I trust Toni. She'll make this good for you. She won't go too far and I'm secure enough to know that having her make you come won't change one thing about the way you feel about me."

"It won't. I love you so much, Jax. But I need you to know something else."

He narrows his eyes at me. "What?"

"The reason this sounds so hot is because you're part of it. The thought of you holding me down for her... The idea that you're watching her make me come. It's not that I want her, I want that experience with you." I told him that last night, but we'd both been drinking and were right in the middle of sex. It also felt like we were on the verge of an argument. I need to know that this is about him and me, not Toni.

"I know, baby," he smiles before he kisses me softly. "You want me to tell her this is okay when she comes back out here?"

"Yes, please," I whisper.

"Good girl," he growls in my ear. "And when she's done making you come, baby, I'm gonna send her home so I can take you to bed. Then I'm going to fuck you hard all night long. Okay?"

"Yes please," I breathe, all too aware of how capable he is of keeping that promise.

A second later, Toni walks out of the huge French doors. "So, am I leaving, or...?" she lets the question hang in the air.

Jax responds by shifting me on his lap so that I'm sitting facing frontward, with my ass between his thighs. "Just your tongue, Toni. No fingers," he warns her.

She bites on her bottom lip as she stares into my eyes and heat floods my entire body.

"And not inside her," Jax goes on, sliding his hands between my thighs as he presses his lips against my ear. "I am the only person who gets to be inside you, baby. You got that?"

"Yeah," I whimper as Toni stalks toward us both.

"Can I take those pretty little panties off her though?" she asks with a wicked grin.

Jax hitches up my sundress until it's bunched around my waist. "Be my guest."

She drops to her knees, and slides her hands up my inner thighs, parting them slightly. Her skin is so soft and warm. Her fingernails are clipped sort, but she rakes them over my delicate skin making me squirm beneath her touch.

Jax keeps his hands gripped firmly on my waist, letting me know he's in complete control.

"Oh, I can smell your sweetness, Lucia," she whispers, rubbing her nose over the damp patch on my panties. "I'm going to enjoy eating you out so much, princess."

She hooks her hands into the top of my underwear and slowly starts to peel them over my hips and down my legs. Once she pulls them off my feet, Jax's hands glide over my hips and abdomen until he palms my inner thighs and spreads them wide apart for her.

"Oh, that is a beautiful pussy," she says, biting on her lower lip as she sucks in air through her nose.

Her soft fingers skate over my skin, in complete contrast to Jax's firm grip. When she slides her hands higher and they brush against his, he moves his back, hooking them beneath my knees and pulling my legs further apart, spreading me even wider for her and holding me still.

Then Toni parts my wet folds with her thumbs. "Damn!" she whispers, staring at my pussy as I look down at her.

My legs tremble in Jax's hands and she's barely even touched me yet. I lean back against his hard chest and close my eyes.

"Look at me, princess," Toni commands, but I can't look her in the eye when she's about to eat my pussy. I feel too embarrassed.

"Jax?" she says with a soft chuckle, her breath dusting over my delicate skin as she starts to pepper soft, butterfly kisses all over the inside of my thighs.

Jax presses his lips against my ear again. "I want you to open your eyes and look at her while she eats your pussy, baby," he growls.

"Okay," I breathe, tilting my head. I look down at Toni and when she catches my eye, she winks at me.

"That's my girl," she whispers.

"No, it's *my* girl, Moretti," Jax growls. "You're allowed one taste, so fucking savor it."

"Is her cum real sweet, Jax?" she purrs between kisses as she edges closer to the top of my thighs.

"The sweetest you'll ever taste," he says, tightening his grip on my legs as though to remind me that I'm only his. As if I could forget.

When Toni blows a cool stream of air over my wet pussy lips, I whimper, pushing my ass back against Jax who groans in appreciation as I rub up against his hard cock.

I bite on my lip to stifle my own moan and Jax nips at my earlobe. "Stop biting on that damn lip, Luce. If I'm gonna let someone else make you come, I want to hear every single sound you make."

"Okay," I gasp.

Toni's tongue is dancing over the skin on my thighs now and wet heat is pooling in my pussy. I try to squeeze my thighs together, but Jax holds me in place for her.

"Damn, princess, you're dripping wet here," Toni says and then she darts out her tongue, lapping at my opening and my hips almost buck off Jax's lap, making Toni chuckle while I suck in a breath.

"Good girl," he whispers as he shifts his hands slightly, pulling my knees back so that my ass drops further between his lap and Toni has even better access to me.

When she flicks her tongue over my swollen clit, I moan shamelessly. "Toni, please?"

"Fuck, baby. You feel how hard you're making me here?" Jax growls and the sound rumbles through his chest as he presses his thick, hard cock into my lower back.

"You're too damn sweet, princess," Toni murmurs against my skin before she takes my clit into her warm, soft mouth and starts to suck softly.

It feels so different to anything I've felt before. Her lips and tongue are way softer than I'm used to.

I rock my hips against her mouth for a little more friction, but I can hardly move. It makes me whimper in frustration and Toni suck a little harder as she circles the sensitive bud of flesh with her tongue.

"Hold one of her knees, Moretti," Jax orders and to my surprise, she obeys him without question. She keeps one hand pressed against the very top of my left thigh, while her other skates up and curls around the back of my right knee, replacing Jax's.

"Jax," I groan, wondering what he has planned.

"I know, baby," he whispers as he unfastens a few of the buttons on the top of my sundress before sliding his hand inside. Pulling down my bra, he cups my breast in his large hand. He squeezes softly and I moan in response. When he rolls my hard nipple between his finger and thumb, a rush of wet heat sears between my thighs. This is what I needed. His hands along with Toni's mouth.

Toni lifts her had slightly. "Your girl is soaking down here, Jax. You sure I can't slide my fingers inside her?"

"No," he snarls.

"Oh but think how she'd be squeezing me," she whines softly. "I bet she's real tight too. Does she feel amazing?"

Oh my God! Heat flashes over my chest and cheeks, but

then Toni's warm, soft tongue is fluttering over my folds and my eyes start rolling as the familiar waves start rolling through my core.

"She feels like fucking heaven," he hisses. "She would ruin you for any other woman, Moretti. I'm doing you a favor."

She doesn't respond, she's too busy holding my thighs open so she can eat my pussy. I feel her own soft moaning growing and the sound vibrates through me, making me shudder.

"Damn, you taste real good, princess," she murmurs against my delicate skin.

"Fuck!" Jax hisses in my ear as my breathing becomes harder and faster.

He squeezes my breast harder as Toni sucks on my clit again. "Oh, fuck," I gasp.

"You going to come, baby?" he asks.

"Can I?" I whimper.

"Of course, Luce. Let go. I got you."

With his permission given, my body gives in to the release it's so desperately craving and I cry out. The sound carries over the quiet night air and the thought that someone might have just heard me flutters briefly through my mind, but there's no space for it to linger.

I look down at Toni through an orgasmic haze. She rocks back onto her heels and wipes her mouth. "Wow!" is all she says as I keep on trembling in Jax's arms.

"I know I promised to take you to bed, angel, but I ain't gonna get that far," he growls as he lifts me, turning me in his arms so that I'm facing him. "I need to fuck you right now, because seeing Toni eating your pussy and feeling you come like that has made me hard as fucking iron."

"My pleasure, Decker," Toni laughs softly behind us.

"Beat it, Moretti," he says to her with a wicked grin.

"I know where I'm no longer welcome," she says breezily.

But before she goes she leans over me, titling my head so that I can look at her. "Thank you, Lucia," she whispers before she kisses me, allowing me to taste myself on her soft lips.

"Thank you," I breathe.

"Any time," she winks at me. "Thank you, Decker. I see why you married this one."

"You're welcome. Now get outta here so I can I fuck my wife."

CHAPTER 12
JAX

"Fuck, Luce, slide that hot wet pussy onto me, baby," I groan as I unzip my jeans and pull them down enough to let my weeping cock free.

I have never felt the need to fuck anyone this much in my whole goddamn life. I am so hard for her I could come just looking at her. I almost did watching Toni eat her pussy.

It was fucking hot to see her giving me complete control of her body and letting me offer her to someone else. I'm glad that I got to give her that experience but now I need to bury myself inside her so deep that she will never ever forget who she really belongs to. I need to remind her that nobody makes her come as hard as I do.

"Jax," she breathes as she wraps her hand around my shaft, squeezing me as she shifts her hips so that she can slide onto me, as though she's as desperate to feel me inside her as I am to be there.

"I need you on my cock, Luce," I bite out, grabbing her by her hips and pulling her down, impaling her onto my length. Sinking deep into her silky wet heat feels like coming home.

"Fuck, you feel so good," I sigh at the relief of having her tight pussy squeezing me.

"God, Jax," she whispers as she rests her forehead against mine. "I need you to fuck me."

"You do, baby?"

"Y-yes," she whimpers, the desperation in her voice is like music to my ears. She needs this as much as I do.

My fingers dig into the soft flesh on her hips as I roll her over me and push up, rutting into her like I will never get deep enough inside.

"Who does this pussy belong to?"

"You, Jax," she hisses, her hands wrapped around my neck as she clings on while she rides me hard.

"Who do all of your orgasms belong to?" I suck on the soft skin of her neck and bite down.

"You."

"This whole hot little body?" I thrust harder and she yelps. "Whose is it?" Wrapping my arms around her waist, I hold her in place so that I can nail her as hard as I want to.

"Yours," she cries out as her orgasm tears through her. Her pussy walls clench and release around me as her cum slicks my cock.

"Jesus, fuck, Luce!" I grit out the words. "This damn chair!"

She blinks at me, her perfect tits heaving in my face as she tries to catch her breath. "Wha-" she starts to say but I seal my mouth over hers, pushing my tongue inside as I stand up and carry her into the house.

She tightens her hold on my neck as I reach behind me, with my dick and my tongue still inside her, I fumble to close the French doors because I refuse to stop for a second.

I can't. I'm consumed by the need to taste her. Fuck her. Make her scream my goddamn name over and over again.

When the lock clicks into place, I walk to the stairs, intending to carry her to bed but we don't quite make it that far.

My cock throbs inside her and I swear to God I might explode if I don't fuck her hard soon.

I pull out of her, dropping her onto the third stair as I lower myself to my knees on the bottom one.

She pulls back, gasping for air. "What was wrong with the chair?" she breathes.

"Not enough room to do this," I growl, sliding my hands up her inner thighs and pushing them wide until I hook her feet between the chrome spindles on each side of the staircase.

Then I stare at her. Taking a good look at her spread wide open for me, her pussy dripping with her cum, while she waits to be fucked.

"Jax?" she whimpers and the sound of her desperate and helpless makes my cock weep. I grab hold of her waist and she leans back on her elbows.

She sucks in a breath, bracing herself for what's about to come, because she knows as well as I do how hard I'm about to fuck her. I stare into her dark eyes as I nudge the tip of my cock at her slick entrance.

Her cheeks flush with heat and her legs tremble. "Please, Jax?"

My heart races and my skin burns with the need to be buried deep inside her — so fucking desperate to claim her that I'm scared I'll hurt her.

"I need you," she whispers and I can't hold off a second longer.

I drive into her and she cries out in a mixture of pain and pleasure. She snakes her arms around my neck, pulling me closer as I rail into her with every single thing I have. Her back is pressed in an uncomfortable position against the edge of the stair, but neither of us care. She rakes her fingers down my spine, clawing at my shirt as I bite and suck her — her breasts, her neck, her shoulders - leaving red marks all over her soft skin.

"I hope you enjoyed Toni eating you out, baby, because no-one will ever touch you again. You got that?" I growl as I drive into her.

"Yes," she breathes, her hot breath against my neck.

"You are fucking mine. All mine."

"All yours," she agrees, her pussy squeezing me tighter like she never wants to let me go.

Pressing my lips against her ear, I bare my teeth like some kind of rabid animal. "I fucking own you," I hiss.

"I know," she whimpers, tears rolling down her cheeks.

I slide my arms around her waist, crushing her against me, pinning her body to mine as I slam into her silky, wet heat.

"You fuck me so good," she groans in my ear as another orgasm rips through her body, making her shudder and tremble, and damn if she doesn't take me straight along with her. I roar her name as I grind my release into her, rubbing out every last drop into her sweet pussy.

She cups my face in her hands and I press my forehead against hers as we both pant for breath. I was too rough with her, but we both needed it.

"Nobody but me, Luce," I whisper.

"Nobody but you, Jax."

I stand up and scoop her into my arms before carrying her to bed. She's silent as I peel off her sundress and bra, noting the bite marks on her skin as I do. They'll fade by tomorrow though.

Once she's naked, I take off my own clothes before crawling over her. I run my nose along the column of her throat as her soft fingertips trail over my back.

When she spreads her legs wide for me, I slip back inside her easily, still hard despite what we just did.

"You are always ready, huh, cowboy?" she asks with a smile as she wraps her legs around my waist.

"For you, baby, yeah."

I kiss her softly, lazily exploring her mouth with my tongue as I fuck her nice and slow.

"Thank you for tonight. It means a lot to me," she whispers, breaking our kiss.

"I know, Luce. I'm glad you enjoyed it..." I narrow my eyes at her.

"Because it will never happen again, I know," she laughs softly.

"Glad we're on the same page."

"You are all I need, Jax."

"Damn right, baby," I growl before I kiss her again, and this time I won't let her up for air unless it's to moan my goddamn name.

CHAPTER 13
JAX

"Bye, buddy," Lucia and I wave at Matthias's smiling face on the computer screen. "We'll see you tomorrow night."

"Bye." He waves and blows a kiss. "See you tomorrow."

"Love you, munchkin," Lucia says.

"Love you, Momma," he blows another kiss. "You too, Dad."

"Love you, kid," I say and then the screen goes blank as he ends the call, no doubt running off to play with the twins before bed. Technically they're his uncles, even though they're only three years old. Matthias' words cause an unexpected lump in my throat and Lucia looks at me and smiles, her eyes shining.

I still remember the day he came home from kindergarten and asked me if he could call me Dad. It was just six weeks after I asked her to marry me. Lucia and he had all but moved into my house on the beach while we waited to find a place together and as far as I was concerned, I was his father anyway. But when that cute little fucker asked me that, damn I almost fucking cried like a baby. And it still gets me every time.

"I can't wait to see him," she says with a soft sigh as she sits back on the sofa. "I'm going to give him the biggest hug."

I close the laptop and put it on the coffee table before leaning back and wrapping my arm around her shoulder. She leans into me, snuggling her cheek against my chest.

"Me too," I agree.

I knew I'd miss him, but not this much. Not that the last six days alone with Lucia in this barn haven't been absolute fucking heaven, but I'm itching to get back to him too. Our conversations about the Avengers just aren't the same over video call.

"Shall we watch a movie and have an early night?" I ask before kissing the top of her head. Damn she smells so good it makes my dick twitch in my jeans.

"Sounds perfect. I'll even let you choose," she stifles a yawn.

"You tired, baby?"

"Hmm. I thought spending almost an entire week in bed would leave me feeling refreshed," she laughs softly.

"Yeah, but that only works when you're sleeping in it," I remind her.

"Ah, yes, not much sleeping with you around, Jackson Decker."

"Who woke me up at three am this morning riding my cock?" I tickle her waist and she shrieks with laughter.

"Oh, yes, forgot about that," she breathes when she stops laughing.

"Hmm. An early night with no fucking then?" I suggest.

She pops an eyebrow at me. "I'm pretty sure that's illegal when you're on your honeymoon."

"A quick fuck and then sleep?" I say, winking at her and smiling when she blushes.

"Deal, cowboy," she purrs, the sound making a direct path to my cock as she rests her head against me again. "So choose us a movie."

THE CREDITS ARE ROLLING over the screen and I look down to see Lucia's eyes are closed and she's breathing softly. Switching off the TV, I'm about to carry her to bed when I hear the banging on the French doors. Lucia jolts awake and we both look around to see Molly standing outside.

Lucia sits straight and I jump up, jogging over to find out why my aunt just scared the hell out of us.

"Jax," she pants as I pull open the doors. Her hair is all mussed up and she's in her pajamas. My blood starts pumping faster in my veins. "It's your father. He's in the hospital. Somebody beat him up. He's in pretty bad shape."

"What? Who?" I look out behind her. Did this happen on the ranch?

I feel Lucia standing behind me now, her hand on my back.

Molly blinks at me. She's stalling. Why?

"Seems he was about to get into his truck and... they think there must have been a few of them." She wipes a tear from her face.

I frown at her. "Where was he?"

She licks her lips and then sucks in a breath. "Rocky's."

No wonder she was stalling. "He was in a bar?" I snarl. "Fucking typical."

"You don't know that he was drinking, Jax," Lucia says softly, pressing a tender kiss on my shoulder blade.

"Why are you always so quick to assume the best in him?" I turn and snap at her, my tone harsher than I intended.

"Why are you so quick to assume the worst?" she counters.

"Recovering alcoholics don't go to a bar for any reason other than to drink, angel."

"You don't know that. Maybe he was meeting somebody. A friend? A date?"

84

"Can we argue about this later? Right now we gotta get to the hospital?" Molly yells as she looks between Lucia and me.

What if I tell her that it serves him right he got beat up? If he was drunk he probably ran his mouth off at the wrong people, or picked a fight with someone he shouldn't have. Maybe I don't give a rats ass that he's lying in some hospital bed. But I do care about my aunt and right now she is anxious and worried. I can't have her driving herself to the hospital. I can't let her do this alone.

"Fine. I'll get my keys," I say with a sigh. Looks like that early night just got put on the back burner.

STARING at my father in the bed, as the machines beep and hiss, keeping him alive, I wonder if this was anything he did. What the hell could he have done to make someone so pissed they'd do this to him?

I mean, back in the day, he was a mean drunk, but now, even with a drink in him, I can't imagine he's a threat to anyone. His hands are gnarled from years of manual labor. He's six feet tall, but he's sixty-one years old and the years of drinking haven't been kind to his body. He's not in the best shape. But for some reason, some people have really done a number on him. His hands are bandaged and I wonder if they're broken. That would kill him if they were. He's always worked with his hands — even when he was drunk, he still worked. As much as I hate to admit it, he can fix almost anything — providing it doesn't talk or breathe. Things – he is good with. People – not so much.

I'm still staring at him when the doctor walks into the room. "Mr. Decker," he says to me, holding out his hand. "I'm Dr. Addison. I'm the doctor in charge of your father's care while he's with us. He's very fortunate that somebody came across him when they did. He had quite a lot of internal bleeding."

"Well, I'm sure the alcohol helped numb the pain for him."

Dr. Addison blinks at me in confusion. "There was no alcohol in his system."

"What?" I frown. They must have made some kind of mistake. "But he was in a bar."

"Well, he wasn't drinking. His blood alcohol was zero."

I'm aware of Lucia's hand rubbing over my back, reminding me to breathe. She should tell me that she told me so, but she's not that kind of person. It's true that I always think the worst of my father, but that's because that's all he's ever shown me. Until recently anyway, when I no longer need him in my life.

But if he wasn't drinking, what the hell was he doing in that damn bar?

I look at him. Machines beeping and wires sticking out of him. The only reasons he's still alive.

"Is he going to be okay?" I ask, the words unexpectedly sticking in my throat.

"He was in pretty bad shape. Like I said, if somebody hadn't found him when they did, he wouldn't have made it much longer. We've done all we can. Only time will give us the answers. His body has been through a lot," the doctor says quietly.

"They have any idea who did this to him?"

"No. The guy who called it in said he didn't see a thing. He was a college kid home for the weekend and out for a late night jog. He called the sheriff too and I expect he's on his way. We had to dispose of your father's clothes, but he had his cell and some loose change as well as the keys to his truck on him. They're all in the locker there." He nods his head toward the small locker beside Harvey's bed. Then his pager beeps and he glances down at it. "I'm sorry, I have to be somewhere. I'll check in later if you're still here, but feel free to go home and get some rest. The drugs we gave him won't wear off for a while."

"Thank you, doc," I say with a nod of my head.

My aunt Molly sits beside Harvey, holding his hand and watching his chest rising and falling. "Who would do this, Jax?" she whispers when the doctor leaves the room.

I suck in a breath through my nose. "Does he go to that place a lot?"

"No," she shakes her head and wipes away a tear. "He hasn't been to a bar in years. He avoids them as much as he can."

"So why was he at one tonight? You have any idea?"

"No. He just said he was going out and he'd be back in a few hours. I was distracted preparing dinner. He seemed pleased though, you know? Like he looked happy about where he was going."

I go to the locker and take out his cell. It's an old model and he needs an upgrade, but I've hardly ever seen him use the thing. I'm surprised he knows how to. I click the button and a picture of Blue lights up the screen with a request for a six digit passcode.

"Any idea what his passcode is, Molly?"

She shakes her head. "No. Sorry."

I blink at the screen. His birthday would be too obvious. He's not tech-minded, but he's not stupid. I tap in the digits of my own birthday but get an error message. I get two more tries.

"You know when Blue was born?" I ask. My father loves that dog more than anyone or anything.

"No idea," Molly replies.

"Fuck!" I mumble, rubbing the pad of my thumb over the cracked screen. I think of another birthday, I mean I'd be surprised if he even remembered it, but it's worth a try, right? When my mother's birthday unlocks the screen I don't know whether to be annoyed or relieved.

Molly and Lucia stare at me anxiously as I go straight to his messages. Maybe that will give us some clue as to why he was at that bar?

It does.

His last message is from a number that he doesn't have saved as a contact.

Perfect. Meet me at Rocky's on Menville at eight.

Frowning at the screen, I scroll further up and discover only a handful of messages between him and the person he was meeting. It seems like my father was arranging to buy something. Swiping my thumb, I scroll higher and the image that appears on the screen almost takes the breath from my lungs.

"What is it?" Lucia asks as she steps closer to me, her soothing hand on my back again.

"He was going to buy this," I reply, tilting the phone and showing her the image of the wooden crib, just like the one I'd spoken about at dinner a few nights earlier.

"Oh, Jax," she gasps, her hand flying to her mouth to stifle the sob that comes after.

Molly cranes her neck so she can look too. "A crib?" she whispers. "That makes sense. I've never seen him so happy as he's been these past few months renovating that barn for you both. He took so much pride in it..." she starts to cry softly as she rests her forehead on my father's hand.

I tap the screen again, calling the number of the person who was selling the crib and hold it to my ear. The number is out of service and suddenly the hairs on the back of my neck stand on end.

"Did they answer?" Lucia asks.

I shake my head. "Out of service."

"What? Already? But they just messaged him tonight?" she says, blinking up at me with her huge brown eyes.

"I know, baby," I say with a sigh, wrapping my arms around her and resting my chin on her head.

"Jax, you think this was planned? You think it was a trap?"

"I don't know, Luce," I reply, even though my gut tells me that it was. Why else would that number no longer be in use? Switched off or out of range is explainable, but out of service? "I'll go through his phone when we get home and see what else I can find."

"Did you know he was looking for a crib, Molly?" Lucia asks and my aunt lifts her head and wipes her eyes.

"No. He went into town the morning after you mentioned it at dinner though? Maybe he put an ad in Johnson's store? That was how he found the rocking chair?"

"Does Shannon's mom still own that place?" I ask.

"Yeah," Molly nods softly.

"Good. I'll go there tomorrow and ask around."

I look down at Lucia again. Fuck, I love her so damn much. "I'm gonna have to put off going home for a few days, baby. That okay with you?"

I see the sadness in her eyes. She loves the ranch and I know she'd stay longer, but she misses our boy. "But Matthias?" she whispers. "He's expecting us both home."

"I know, baby, but I can't leave here until my father wakes up and I find out what's happened. It will just be a few more days. I promise."

"I don't want to go without you, Jax," she whispers. "Maybe I'll ask my father to bring Matthias here? He'll do that for us if we ask him?"

I brush her dark hair back from her face. "Until I know what this is about, I think you'll both be safer at home in LA."

"But…" her lip trembles and I dip my head and kiss her softly.

I don't want her to go either, but I need her safe. And until I know whether this was a coincidence or part of something more, I can't be assured that she is. I can't give her my undivided attention while I'm trying to find out who almost killed my father.

"I love you so much, angel, but I need to find out who did this. You understand that, right?"

"Of course I do, Jax," she breathes. "I just don't want to be away from you. I have a horrible feeling…" she shivers and I wrap my arms tighter around her.

"There's nothing to be worried about, Luce. You go home to our boy and I'll follow you in a few days."

CHAPTER 14
LUCIA

Holding onto Jax's hand, I squeeze it tightly, reminding him he's not alone in this. I hate that he's staying here in Dallas without me, even if it is only for a few days, but I understand why. His father almost died, and while I know that Jax has a difficult relationship with Harvey, I also know the type of man my husband is. He won't rest until he finds out who did this. He may not call Harvey dad any longer, but there is still something there between them, even if it is buried deep beneath years of pain and anger.

The door to Harvey's room opens and we all look up to see the Sheriff walking inside. He tips his hat in greeting and stares straight at Jax. "Jackson Decker?"

"Yeah," Jax replies.

"Sheriff Hicks," he says with a curt nod.

"You have any idea who did this?"

Sheriff Hicks hooks his thumbs into his belt loops, his eyes narrowed as he continues to glare at Jax. "I was about to ask you the same thing."

"No," Jax replies, his jaw ticking with the effort of maintaining his temper. "I'm just here on my honeymoon."

Hicks glances at me and then back to Jax. The hostility is practically oozing out of the Sheriff's pores. What the hell is his problem?

"You have any idea what he was doing in Rocky's bar tonight?"

"No," Jax snaps. "Do you?"

"I hear you and him don't get along?"

"And who told you that?"

Hicks sucks on his teeth. "People."

I hold onto Jax's arm. It feels like every muscle in his body is vibrating with anger as he glares at the sheriff. I trace my fingertips over the inside of his forearm, trying to remind him to stay calm. The way this sheriff is questioning him, it wouldn't surprise me if he was looking for any excuse to throw Jax in a cell for the night, and that is the last thing any of us need.

"Hmm," Jax rubs a hand over his jaw. "Well, people talk in small towns. You can't believe everything you hear, Sheriff."

Hicks goes on glaring at him. Trying to provoke a reaction but Jax stays silent. He might be the most ruthless and dangerous man I know, but he is also the smartest, and he knows what pissing off the sheriff in a small town like this will do. I have no doubt my father would have him out of there by morning, but it's still precious time we can't afford to lose.

"Well, maybe your father will have some answers when he wakes up," Hicks glances at me and Molly before training his glare back on Jax. "Or should I say if..."

The muscles in Jax's forearm flex beneath my fingers. "He'll wake up," Jax insists.

"Well, if he doesn't, I suppose this will become a murder investigation, won't it? So you make sure not to leave town now." He tips his hat again and then turns on his heel.

"Asshole!" Jax mutters.

"What was his problem?" Molly adds with a frown. "I mean shouldn't he be out there looking for whoever did this?"

"I'll find whoever did this, Molly," Jax assures her. He doesn't trust the cops, and especially not after the way that sheriff just eyeballed him like he was the only suspect. "I want you two to wait here and I'm gonna swing by Rocky's and see what I can find out."

"Be careful," I say to him.

He lifts my hand to his face, kissing my fingertips. "I will, baby."

"Yes, please be careful, Jax. That jackass, Hicks, seems to be looking for an excuse to toss you into a cell if you ask me."

"Yeah, I kinda got that," Jax says with a frown as he looks out of the window where Hicks is standing talking to Dr. Addison.

As soon as Hicks leaves, Jax does too, leaving Molly and me sitting either side of Harvey's bedside.

CHAPTER 15

JAX

It's almost midnight by the time I get to Rocky's bar on Menville. I called the unknown number on my father's phone again a few times on the way here, but as I'd known it would be, it's still out of service.

The place is almost empty when I walk inside. A few guys sit at the bar and a couple sit in the corner kissing, while another group of kids barely out of college shoot pool. There is only one guy serving, and I assume it's Rocky junior. This was his old man's place, but he died a few years back from lung cancer.

He tips his chin at me when I take a seat on one of the worn leather stools. "Can I get ya?"

"You know Harvey Decker?"

"Nope," he says with a shake of his head.

I suppose he might not. I mean, back in the day when the place was owned by his old man, my father was one of their best customers, but since he got sober ten years ago, he doesn't frequent such establishments any longer.

Still, I find it hard to believe that anyone in this town hasn't at least heard of my father. It's a small place where far too many people know each other's business.

"The guy who got busted up outside your bar earlier?" I jog his memory.

"Oh, that guy?" he nods his head. "Never seen him before tonight."

"And you saw him in here tonight?"

Rocky junior smirks at me and my hand immediately balls into a fist. I am in exactly the right mood for beating the shit out of someone, and he might just be the lucky recipient. "Maybe. What do you wanna know for? You a cop?"

"Do I look like a cop?"

"Naw," he shakes his head.

"So, did you see him or not, dipshit?" I snarl.

He narrows his eyes at me, sizing me up and wondering if I'm worth making an enemy of. Even if he doesn't know my name, I have half a foot and fifty pounds of muscle on the guy. "Yeah. He sat right there. Ordered a club soda. Drank it and then he left."

"Did he talk to anyone?"

"Not that I saw, but I wasn't eyeballing the guy all night. I got customers to deal with," he says with a shrug.

"Anyone follow him when he left?"

He smirks and shrugs again and the lid blows off my temper. Reaching across the bar, I grab him by the throat. "I asked you a fucking question, fuck-face. Did anybody leave behind him?"

He shakes his head as much as he can now that I have him by the throat. "No," he croaks.

Glancing around, I see we've drawn the attention of everyone in the bar and I let him go.

"Heard some folks say it was his son responsible though," he adds, rubbing at the red skin of his neck.

"What?" I frown at him.

"Hates him by all accounts," he says.

I'm seconds away from smashing his face into the solid wooden bar when that jackass Sheriff Hicks sits on a stool beside me.

"Trouble here, Rock?" he asks, giving me a side-eye.

I glare at Rocky, watching his Adam's apple bob as he swallows.

"This guy was just asking about the incident here tonight," Rocky says.

"You remember anything else since we last spoke?" Hicks asks him.

"Nope. Told you everything I know."

"Good," Hicks says then turns to me. "This is a police investigation, son, so leave the investigating to me."

Son? He's about five fucking years older than I am. I take a deep breath and shake my head. I swear to God I'm going to get arrested for murder before the night is over.

Rocky places a shot of bourbon on the bar for Hicks and I look at it and then back at him.

"I don't see you doing much investigating, *Sheriff*," I snarl. "I know you already know who I work for, and what I do back in LA." I jump off my stool and can't help but smile when he flinches. "You ever call me son again and I will give you a practical demonstration of my talents."

He glares at me and I walk away, before I get my ass tossed in jail for threatening a law enforcement officer.

I head to the parking lot and to my father's truck. It's still open so I take a look inside. What kind of investigation is Hicks running when this is just sitting here for anyone to tamper with? If there were any evidence in here, it would be useless now.

I rummage around but there's nothing in here that offers me any clues. A half packet of Lifesavers. An empty soda bottle on the passenger seat and an old chew toy of Blue's in the footwell.

My father keeps a clean truck. It smells of him though — of wood shavings and cologne. It's a brand he's used since I was a kid. A memory of him winking at me in the mirror while I watched him shave rushes back from some deep recess in my mind.

I've forgotten that there were some good times. He was getting ready to take my mom out for dinner. They used to go on a date one night every week before his drinking got real bad. Molly would look after me. She's only nine years older than me and she practically lived with us back then.

I sit on the seat in his truck and let the memory settle over me, but then Rocky's words come back to me too. Some people said I was responsible for the attack on him — that I hate him. Do I?

I hate that he let me and my mom down. I hate the man he became. But the man before that? The guy who used to sit me on his tractor and who taught me how to shave and drive? No, that guy was my hero. It was why it hurt so damn much when he let me and my mom walk out of his lives forever.

Climbing out of his truck, I scan the parking lot quickly and then I check the exterior of the building. No cameras that I can see. Damn!

There's nothing else on this strip either. The place is all but deserted. It's the kind of place I'd choose if I was going to beat someone half to death and I didn't want to be seen or recognized.

I walk to my truck and decide to head back to the hospital to pick up Lucia and Molly. It's late and there's nothing more I can do tonight. Besides, Lucia is flying back to LA tomorrow and I intend to spend the rest of this night buried so deep inside her that I can forget about everything but her.

CHAPTER 16
LUCIA

"You want us to stay here with you tonight, Molly?" I ask as she climbs out of Jax's truck outside the house.

"No," she shakes her head and waves her hand at me dismissively. "I'll be fine. You two go get some sleep and I'll see you both for breakfast in a few hours."

"You sure?" Jax asks.

"Yes," she assures him, before closing the door and walking into the house. Blue comes to greet her, wagging his tail but looking past her for his master.

We wait until she's inside and then Jax carries on driving to the barn. "You okay?" I ask him.

"Yeah," he grunts, his eyes fixed on the road ahead.

I know he's deep in thought. Processing the information from the last few hours. It's how he works. So I just rest my hand on his thigh until we come to a stop outside the barn.

Once we're inside, he locks up and we both head straight to bed. It's after two a.m. and I figure Jax must be exhausted. We both undress in silence, moving around the same space without really touching or making any eye contact. As though we're existing in two separate places in time.

I should ask him if he's okay, but I know that he's not. He told me he didn't find anything out at the bar, and also that jackass sheriff showed up so he didn't really get the chance to talk to people. I would love to know what's going through his mind right now. I open my mouth, about to ask, but he looks up with a scowl on his face, so I stay quiet.

I pull on my tank top and climb into bed while he's brushing his teeth.

A moment later, he walks out of the bathroom and flicks off the light until the room is dark. The only light comes from the moon outside which shines through the dark glass.

He lifts the covers and crawls into bed beside me, sliding a hand over my stomach until his arm is wrapped around my waist, he pulls me close and I breathe a sigh of relief.

He presses his lips against my ear. "You tired, baby?"

"Only a little," I lie. I'm exhausted, but I don't want to sleep.

"Liar," he whispers, "but I'm gonna let it slide because I need you, Luce."

I turn on my side. "I need you too, Jax, but don't shut me out."

He brushes my hair back from my face. "I'm not, angel, I promise. I'm just dealing with some stuff I thought I'd buried a long time ago."

"About your dad?"

"Hmm. Things between me and him weren't always so bad. When I was a little kid, like Matthias, he was..." he swallows hard. "I looked up to him so fucking much."

I press my body closer to his. I need him to know that he's not in this alone.

"What if I fuck up like he did? What if Matthias, or any of our kids end up hating me one day? The thought that they might feels like someone has just put my heart in a vise."

I places my hand on his chest. "They could never hate you.

You would never let them down, Jax. Or me. I know you wouldn't."

"How can you be so sure?"

"Because you know how it feels," I whisper. "And also because you always put the happiness and wellbeing of the people you love before your own."

"I'm gonna miss you so fucking much, Luce," he whispers.

A sob catches in my throat and I swallow it down. "I'm going to miss you too, but it will only be for a few days, right?"

"A few days away from you is gonna feel like a goddamn eternity," he growls, sliding a hand onto my ass.

"Then you'd better make tonight count, cowboy," I purr, sliding my hand down to his cock which is already semi-hard.

"Why the fuck are you wearing clothes in my bed?" he frowns at me as though he's only just become aware of this fact.

Then he looks down at my panties and pulls the waistband until it snaps against my skin.

"Sorry," I whisper, biting on my lip.

"You know I gotta punish you for that?" he asks as he rolls on top of me.

"Yes," I giggle.

"Ah but no spanking for you, Mrs. Decker," he growls, nipping at my shoulder blade. "Because you like that a little too much, don't you?"

Wetness pools in my center just thinking about it.

"Hmm. So, how are you going to punish me then?" I whisper.

He lifts his head, narrowing his eyes at me as though he's deep in thought. "Maybe I won't let you come?" he suggests.

I open my mouth in horror. "You wouldn't."

"Oh, I would," he whispers.

"Please don't?" I whimper, trying a different tactic.

"Maybe I'll just see how hard I can make you beg instead."

"We both know you can make me beg real hard, Jax, but what I need you to do…"

"Yeah," he whispers, trailing kisses and tiny delicious bites over my breasts through my tank top.

"Is make me come real hard," I giggle. "It's only fair seeing as you're about to deprive me of these life altering orgasms."

"Life altering, huh?" he arches one eyebrow at me as he starts to peel my top off over my head.

"Yep," I say, shifting my hips upward so that I can grind my pussy onto his cock, which is now rock hard.

He bites on his lip and shakes his head. "Damn, baby, you know how much I want to fuck you right now?"

I wrap my arms around his neck. "No. So stop fooling around and show me."

"If that's what you want," he grins, accepting the challenge. He fists his hands in my panties and tears the material in half before driving his cock deep inside me, making me cry out as he forces me further up the bed.

"I knew you'd be soaking for me, Luce," he whispers in my ear. "You always fucking are."

"I know," I whimper as I wrap my legs around his waist.

"That's it, hold onto me, baby. Because I'm gonna fuck you so hard you'll still feel me inside you when you're back home in LA."

"God, Jax," I breathe as he nails me harder into the mattress.

"You're mine, Luce. Mine!" he growls in my ear, like I may have forgotten it somehow, or like he's trying to sear the words into my brain.

He doesn't need to. They are already there.

I am his.

Utterly and completely his.

I LIE in Jax's arms, feeling one hundred percent blissed out and completely sated. The man is a machine and I have no idea where he gets his stamina and energy because he fucked me all night long.

Hard. Gentle. Fast. Slow. He fucked my pussy. My ass. My mouth. He feasted on every part of my body like a starving man at an all you can eat buffet. He made me come so many times I feel like I must need at least a gallon of water to rehydrate. I lick my dry lips.

I shift in his arms because I need to get me some of that water I've been thinking about for the past ten minutes, but he pulls me back to him.

"Just ten more minutes, Luce," he mumbles sleepily. "Just let me hold onto you a little longer."

I snuggle back against his chest. I suppose I'm not that thirsty. And this guy right here can hold onto me forever if he wants to.

CHAPTER 17

JAX

There's a dull ache behind my eyes that grows more persistent the closer I get to the hospital. I've hardly slept since the night my father was attacked. Lucia left yesterday morning and then I spent the rest of the day chasing my tail. I even spoke to the college kid who found my dad and called the ambulance, but he had nothing to offer that was helpful. I've interrogated enough people to know that he was telling the truth about not being involved.

I avoided the hospital for the entire day because I didn't want to run into the Sheriff. When I got back to the house last night it was late. I called Lucia and then did a little digging into some of the local residents online as well as that out of service number, but I found nothing.

When I eventually went to bed after midnight, I still couldn't sleep. I couldn't settle without her soft body pressed against mine. I hated saying goodbye to her at the airport yesterday. She's only been my wife for a week and it's not right that we're being forced apart so soon, but she had to go, and I had to stay. She hugged me so tight and I know she was fighting back tears. Trying to be strong for me when she needn't be.

She's the strongest woman I know. I hugged her back just as tight because I didn't want to ever let her go.

I miss her already. Her smile. Her soft laughter. The way she makes me feel at ease with the slightest brush of her fingertips. Her soft lips. Her fine ass.

Fuck! Stop it, Jax. Getting a boner right now isn't going to help the headache that's growing increasingly stronger. This is going to be another long ass fucking day!

WALKING to my father's hospital room, I groan inwardly as I see that jackass, Sheriff Hicks walking out of it.

"Mr. Decker," he says with a sneer.

"Sheriff?"

"I'm glad I ran into you actually."

"And why is that? You finally stop playing with your dick long enough to find out something about who the hell attacked my father?"

His eyes narrow in annoyance.

"I suppose you've checked Rocky's security cameras?" I ask. As far as I could see, the cheap asshole doesn't have any, but Sheriff Hicks is about to confirm that for me.

"Rocky doesn't have cameras. He says they spook his customers," he says with a smirk that I could happily slap from his smug face.

"Convenient for him when people are getting the shit kicked out of them in his parking lot, right?"

"As far as I can tell, Mr. Decker, the only person around here who has any grudge against your father..." he licks his lips as he glares at me, "is you."

I can't help but laugh and that just makes his scowl deepen. I take a step closer to him. "You think I want my father dead?"

"Word around here is you hate his guts," he snarls.

"Maybe," I reply with a shrug. "But if I wanted him dead, he wouldn't be lying in that bed, he'd be in the fucking morgue."

Hicks has no response for that. He blinks at me. I know he's looked me up. He knows who I am and so he knows I speak the truth. I might like to lie low here, but I'm the right hand man of one of the most powerful men in the goddamn country, it's kind of hard to escape that.

"Is there anything else, *Sheriff*?" I glare at him and when he doesn't reply, I brush past him.

"Just don't leave town," he shouts after me as I walk into my father's room.

Molly is sitting by his bedside, she has a scowl on her face too. "Hicks is a jackass," she hisses.

"Tell me something I don't know."

"I think he believes you're involved in this somehow, Jackson," she whispers.

"Yeah, I kinda got that too."

She looks at my father and her face softens. They haven't always had the easiest relationship either, he let her down badly too, but she has been able to forge a meaningful and loving relationship with him. "Why would he think that?" she sniffs.

"Maybe somebody wants him too?" I mutter, thinking out loud to myself more than talking to her.

"But who and why?"

I shake my head. For once I have no clue. I spend so little of my life in this town, I have no idea who I could have pissed off enough. Or maybe blaming me is Sheriff Hicks's easy out?

"No idea, Molly. But I know where to look next."

THE OLD-FASHIONED BELL rings above my head as I walk into Johnson's store. The place has barely changed since I was a kid. It's like walking back in time. People still place ads in the window, buying and selling and offering services. Like they haven't heard of this thing called the internet. It still smells the same too – of candy and newspapers. Suddenly, I feel like I'm twelve again, here to spend my allowance.

"Jackson Decker, is that you?" Hannah Johnson says as soon as I walk through the door.

"Sure is, ma'am," I say taking off my hat like a good Southern gentleman.

She comes from behind the counter, tossing her long blonde hair up into a ponytail. Her daughter, Shannon, looks just like her.

Shannon and I were fuck buddies for a long time. She's ten years younger than me, making her mom, Hannah only eight years my senior. She flirts with me every chance she gets, just like her daughter. At least just how her daughter used to. Even before I started dating Lucia, she met her husband, Ed and we've kept our relationship purely platonic since. They only got married last year, six months before Lucia and me.

"Hey, Mrs. Johnson. How are you?"

She snort laughs at my formality. "Now there will be none of that. How many times have I told you to call me Hannah? I mean I was almost your momma in law." She nudges me on the arm.

"Momma!" Shannon scolds her as she comes out of the store room at the back. "If Ed heard you saying that."

"Oh, shush. He's nowhere around, is he?" Hannah says with a roll of her eyes.

"Yeah, well Jackson and I were never going to be anything serious, were we?" she says, shooting me a look that I can't

106

quite figure out. "How is your daddy?" she asks, changing the subject.

"Of course," Hannah exclaims, her hands covering her flushed cheeks. "That was terrible what happened to him."

"He's not good."

"Has he said anything about what happened?" Shannon asks, her face full of concern. Fuck, why is she even here? I hate having her pity me. She's busted my ass for years about my relationship with my father.

"He hasn't woken up yet," I reply, surprised that they don't already know this. News travels fast in a small town.

"Such an awful thing," Hannah says sympathetically as she places her hand on my arm.

"Yeah, that's kind of why I'm here. Do you remember the ad he put in the window a few days back?"

"Yes. For a crib," she nods her head. "I told him that we had one just like it. It was Shannon's when she was a baby and then her little brothers' too."

"You do?" I frown at her.

"Did," she corrects me. "Shannon and Ed took it. For when they have babies."

"Momma!" Shannon hisses, nudging Hannah in the arm as her cheeks turn pink.

I look between the two of them. *What the fuck? Something feels off here.*

"The delivery guy needs you, Momma," Shannon says to Hannah.

Hannah rolls her eyes, bids me goodbye and then disappears into the store room.

"You going to be in town much longer?" Shannon asks me.

"A day or two, probably."

"Your wife not with you?"

I frown. "No. She had to go home to our son."

"*Our* son?"

"Yeah. He calls me Dad. I married his mom. He's my son."

"Okay," she snaps, holding her hands up in surrender. "I was only asking."

I've known this woman for eight years and I've never had cause to doubt her before. She knows things about my childhood and my past that I've only ever told Alejandro and Lucia before. Not that I told her any of it, but she gleaned it from working at the ranch all these years. I didn't mind though, because I considered her a friend. But she is hiding something from me.

"Everything okay, Shan?"

"Of course. Why wouldn't it be?" she replies with a frown.

Maybe we're both just on edge? I haven't seen her since either of us were married. Maybe she doesn't know how to be around me now?

"You still have that crib, Shan?"

"Yeah. My mom would kill me if I ever sold it," she whispers behind her hand and then she starts laughing. And there is the woman I know.

The sound of my cell ringing interrupts the conversation.

Taking it out of my pocket, I see Alejandro's name on the screen. "I gotta take this," I say to Shannon as I hold the phone to my ear.

"Hey, amigo."

"My plane is going to be at the airport in four hours, Jax. Get your ass on it," he snarls and my heart immediately starts to race. He's either pissed at me, pissed because something bad has happened, or both.

"Why? What the fuck is going on?"

I hear him draw in a breath, as though he's trying to keep a lid on his raging temper. I'm not often on the receiving end of it, but when I am it's usually to do with my wife – his daughter.

"Just get your ass on the fucking plane, because if I have to, I will come drag you back here myself."

"Then tell me what the fuck is going on" I snarl. "Is Lucia okay?"

"No," he barks and my racing heart kicks up a gear.

"What?"

"She's not hurt. She's safe," he quickly adds, because while he might be pissed at me for God knows what, he wouldn't let me have a heart attack from worrying about her. "But if she finds out... So, get back here and clear up the fucking mess you have created. Now!"

I swear my heart is about to hammer through my ribcage. "What mess? Stop speaking in riddles. What the fuck is going on over there? Let me speak to Lucia."

"No," he snarls. "You do not tell her about this. Not until we know what to do."

"For fuck's sake, amigo, you're killing me here. Tell me what's happened."

"This isn't the kind of thing I want to talk about on the phone. I fucking trusted you to take care of her..." I hear the crack in his voice and it takes the breath from my lungs. "Just get your ass on the damn plane."

Then he ends the call and I stand in the store with my heart damn near in my throat.

What the hell has happened during the last hour since I spoke to her?

I walk out of the store, hearing Shannon calling after me but I don't hear what she says. My blood is pounding in my ears as adrenaline races through my body. Lucia is safe and unhurt but not okay? What does that even mean?

I dial her number and she answers on the fourth ring.

"Hey," she says breathlessly.

"Hi, angel," I try to sound calm while my head spins with a

million questions, but I ask her the only one that really matters right now. "Are you okay?"

"Yeah, just doing some yoga with my mom, sorry. I thought it was supposed to be relaxing. Do I sound out of breath?" she laughs softly.

"Just a little. How is Matthias?"

"He's fine. I just got back from dropping him at school," the tone of her voice changes. I mean I only spoke to her an hour ago and everything was fine then. "Why is something wrong?"

I close my eyes and take a breath as I prepare to lie to her. "Yeah, I just miss you, baby. I wanted to hear your voice." Only a half lie.

"I miss you too."

"I should let you get back to your yoga before your mom yells at me," I say. "I'll call you tonight. Okay?"

"Okay. Be careful, Jax."

"Always, Luce. I love you."

"Love you too."

I end the call and put my cell back into my pocket. Speaking to her has calmed my racing heart at least, but I still have no idea what the hell is going on that I can't even talk to her about it. I suppose there's only one way to find out.

THE FLIGHT from Dallas to LA has been the longest of my life. I've never felt so agitated, and nervous in my entire thirty-seven years, and given the life I've lived that's saying something.

There's a car waiting for me on the runway. I climb inside and see the familiar face of one of Alejandro's longest serving employees, his driver, Jacob.

"Mr. Decker," he says with a polite nod.

"What the fuck, Jacob? What's going on?" I ask as I sit back against the seat.

He shakes his head.

"Come on. I've known you since I was fourteen. What the hell is it that you can't trust me?"

"I don't know anything," Jacob insists. "Something happened this morning that made Mr. Montoya as mad as hell. I haven't seen him so angry in a long time. Alana was doing all she could to calm him down, but..." he shakes his head. "Then Lucia arrived back from taking Matthias to school and it was like they were pretending nothing had happened."

I close my eyes and take deep breaths, wondering what the hell I'm about to walk into.

CHAPTER 18
JAX

J acob's car hasn't even fully stopped when I open the doors and jump out, running to the front door of the house. It's opened before I reach it, by one of Alejandro's security detail.

"Where is he?" I ask.

"In his office," he says with a curt nod.

"And my wife?"

"In the pool with her mom and the boys. He's asked that you don't speak to them and go directly to his office."

"Fuck that," I snarl as I push past him.

"Jax," the guard hisses. "I have my orders. You are not to go back there. Please don't make me take you down."

"You think you could?"

He glares at me. "There are a dozen more men who would stop you before you get back there."

"A dozen?"

He nods solemnly and I swallow hard. He never has that many men at his house. What the fuck is this? "Fine. I'll go see him."

"Thank you," he replies and then he steps aside before he escorts me to his boss's office.

I mean Alejandro is technically my boss too, but I never really think of him as that. While he might give me my orders, he also treats me as his equal. The guard opens the door for me and I walk inside. Alejandro is staring out of the window, but at the sound of the door closing he spins around. His eyes lock on mine and I swear I haven't seen him this pissed since I told him I was in a relationship with his daughter.

"What the hell is going on?" I ask.

He grips the back of his office chair, his knuckles turning white with the effort of controlling the rage that is clearly coursing through his body.

"I fucking trusted you, Jax," he snarls. "She's my fucking daughter and you... you..." he puts a hand over his face and sucks the air through his teeth, as though he can't even bear to say the words.

Meanwhile, I stand here wondering what the fuck I could have possibly done that would make him think he couldn't trust me with his daughter's safety. Like her and Matthias aren't always my number one priority.

"I what?" I snap.

He nods to a brown envelope on the desk. "That came this morning," he hisses.

I frown as I pick it up and pull out the contents. And as soon as I do, I realize why he's so pissed at me. In fact, I'm surprised he hasn't punched me in the mouth yet. No father should ever see his daughter like that. But I think he could shoot me right now and I wouldn't feel a thing because I'm filled with a burning rage and anger, the likes I've only ever felt once before and that was when she was taken from me by some psychopath who was obsessed with her.

Bile burns my throat as I think about the sick piece of shit who must have taken these videos of her. There are five photographs in the envelope but they are clearly stills from two separate video clips.

Two of them are from when I fucked her on the porch of our barn. She's wearing her tank top and the fact that her jeans are pulled down, as well as what I'm doing with my hand is obscured by the wooden rails, but it's clear we're having sex.

In fact that particular still image they used, is obviously the point when she was coming. The realization that anyone but me has seen that makes me want to go on a murderous rampage of epic proportions. My blood boils in my veins as I look at each one. Each violation of our privacy, not that I care much about mine, but I do about hers. That someone has seen her like this is like a knife in my heart. But losing my shit and raging at the world is not going to help us right now. It's not going to find out who took these videos and pictures, or why.

But I suspect, that the images of me and her alone are not the images Alejandro is pissed at me about.

I slide the photographs back inside the envelope. I don't need to see them again to have them burned into my brain. I mean I was there. I know exactly what happened.

"What do they want?" I ask as the anger burns through my veins.

He picks up a piece of paper lying on his desk and tosses it at me. "Five million dollars by noon tomorrow."

I scan the single piece of paper. There is nothing distinguishable about it. Plain white copy paper with four lines of printed text. But the words sear into my heart like a hot poker. If he doesn't pay, they upload the videos to every free porn site and send stills to any gossip website that doesn't care about a law suit or two.

"I am going to find out who took these and peel their fucking skin from their flesh," I hiss out the words through clenched teeth. My teeth grinding and jaw aching with the effort.

"Who is the woman?" he snarls.

Fuck! He's not going to like the answer. But then I wonder if anything can piss him off more than the image of his daughter being eaten out by a woman while I hold her wide open for her. "Toni Moretti."

"Toni fucking Moretti?" he shouts so loud that even though his office is soundproof, it wouldn't surprise me if Lucia heard him out by the pool. "Are you out of your goddamn mind?"

I glare at him. Photographs of my wife in her most vulnerable state, not to mention having her pussy eaten, are potentially about to be released onto the web and he's worried about who else was involved.

"You want to start a war with the Morettis now too?" he growls, glaring at me.

"It's not like Toni's one of them."

"I think Dante would beg to differ," he replies with a scowl, referring to the middle Moretti sibling, and the man who took over the reins from his father. "Salvatore Moretti is her father, which makes her one of them. If this gets out that she is the woman in those photographs."

"Then what?" I snarl. "It's not like we took them, is it? Whoever did is their enemy. Not us. Besides, Toni won't give a damn. She does what she does in spite of her brothers. She's never been one of them."

"I hope you're right, amigo, because if you bring a war with the Italians to my door..."

I scowl at him "You think I want anyone seeing my wife like that? You think I would willingly let this happen? Some sick fuck has filmed us on our goddamn honeymoon, doing things that husbands and wives do. If we go to war with the Italians over this, you will have my fucking back the way I've had yours for the past twenty-four years."

He scowls back but he doesn't answer.

"Besides, I don't give a fuck about a war with the Morettis. I will take every single one of them on myself if that's what it takes. I can't believe you're thinking of anything right now other than finding out who is behind this and making sure that these images never see the light of day."

"Maybe you should have thought about that before you let someone..." he swallows. He can't say the words and I don't blame him. "And out in the open. On the fucking porch? Where anyone could see?" He's shouting again now.

"No-one should have been there. The ranch is private property. Our barn is set way back from the house."

"Well somebody was there, Jax!" he yells. "Someone watched you fucking my daughter and then when you allowed someone else to violate her."

I slam my hands on the desk. "She was not being fucking violated," I snarl. "At least, not by Toni. Whoever took those was the only person who's done that."

"You're telling me that was her idea? Don't forget I know who you really are, Jax."

"Yeah, because you were with me for half the shit I did when I was younger. It's exactly the kind of man you used to be before you married Alana," I remind him. "You think I forced her to do that? If you'd actually looked at the pictures you'd see that she was having a pretty good time."

That's the final straw and I know it was a step too far, but I'm just as pissed as he is and I need to let some of it out before I see her. He launches himself over the desk at me. His right fist comes straight at my face, but I duck it and he stumbles before turning and barreling into my chest, knocking me on my ass until we're brawling on the floor of his office.

I have him in a headlock and he elbows me in the ribs. It winds me but I don't let him go because the rage is making me feel invincible. But then he says the words that hit me harder than any blow he could have landed. "You don't fucking deserve her," he hisses.

My arms go lax and I release him. He pushes himself up, ready to attack, but when he sees me sitting on the floor, my shoulders slumped in defeat, he stops. He's not about to hit me when he knows I won't defend myself.

"I know I don't, amigo," I whisper as I put my head in my hands. I let her down. Forgetting my rage for a second, I think about how she's going to feel when she finds out and my heart breaks for her. How could I have allowed this to happen? "We need to tell her now."

"No. We can fix this before she finds out."

I look up at him. "I know she's your daughter, but she's a grown woman, Alejandro. She can handle this. You at least need to give her the opportunity to."

"I can't bear to see her face when she sees them," he says with a shake of his head.

"I know. Nor can I, but she deserves to know. She needs to be part of this conversation, Alejandro. As hard as that's going to be for you, but this is her life."

He nods his head in agreement.

"Does Alana know?" I ask.

"Yeah."

"What did she say?"

"After she picked her jaw up from the floor, she said the same as you, that I need to tell Lucia. But she agreed to let me wait until I'd spoken to you."

"That woman always did speak sense," I say, standing up

and straightening my shirt.

"Let's go tell her you're back then," he says, gesturing to the door.

CHAPTER 19
LUCIA

"Watch me, Momma," Matthias shouts as he cannon-balls into the pool, splashing me and my mom in the process.

"Well done, baby," I laugh, clapping my hands.

"That was so good," my mom adds as I grab a towel and dry off my face while Matthias and my twin brothers play.

I got back to LA yesterday and I didn't want to stay at Jax's house on my own so Matthias and I are staying with my parents until he's back. I know that Jax prefers it that way too, and my son loves spending time at this house, where all but one of his favorite people in the world currently are.

He cried last night after he spoke to Jax on the phone and my heart broke for him. I told him that Harvey was sick and Jax had to stay and help look after him for a few days, but it's hard for a kid to understand, I suppose. All he knows is that he misses his daddy and wants him to come home. I played it down to Jax though when I spoke to him later. I know he has enough to worry about trying to find out who hurt Harvey and wondering whether he's going to pull through.

I got straight back to work to try and take my mind off

things and I could see how grateful my father was for a little help. He's been so distracted today though. I think he misses Jax almost as much as Matthias and I do.

"Dad!" Matthias shrieks and I turn around to see Jax walking out of the house with my father and my heart almost bursts at the sight of him.

"Hey, buddy," he shouts as our son scrambles out of the pool and runs to him. Jax scoops him into his arms, not caring that he gets soaking wet in the process.

"I missed you," Matthias giggles.

"Missed you too, little guy. Have you been good?"

"Sure have," Matthias beams with pride.

I walk over to them both with a huge smile on my face. "What are you doing back so soon?" I ask as I reach them.

He glances at my father and something about the look they share makes my heart sink. He's not back here for something good. "Is it Harvey?" I whisper.

"Why don't you go play with Hugo and the twins?" Jax says, kissing Matthias on the forehead before placing him back on his feet. "And then we can all have some dinner?"

"Can we have ice-cream?" he asks with a grin.

"Sure."

"Okay," Matthias says with a shrug before running back to the pool.

"What is it?" I ask as my mom walks up behind me.

"We should go to your father's office," he replies.

"Here you go, sweetheart," my mom says as she hands me my sundress.

Taking it from her, I pull it over my head as my stomach flutters with anxiety. "What's going on? Why are you back? Is something wrong?" I fire questions at all three of them but none of them answer.

"Come on, angel," Jax says, wrapping an arm around my waist. "We'll explain everything."

I walk with him to my father's office, fighting the urge to throw up the entire time.

Once we're inside the room, Jax guides me to a chair and then he sits beside me while my mom and father sit opposite.

"Why do I feel like you all know something that I don't?" I whisper.

"Your dad got something this morning. He asked me to come home so we could deal with it, baby. I only got here a half hour ago."

"You've been here for a half hour and you didn't come see me?" I whisper. "What were you doing?"

"Talking to your dad," he says and then he looks at my father who nods his head, as though giving him permission to do something. "About these." Jax hands me a brown envelope.

I take it from him with trembling hands. "What is it? Is somebody sick?" I look between the three of them.

"No, nothing like that," Jax says as he brushes my hair back from my face. "Just take a look and then we'll figure out how to fix it."

"Okay," I swallow hard as I pull the contents out.

The image that I'm confronted with makes me want to curl into a ball and die. My cheeks burn with shame as tears sting my eyes. It's Jax and me with Toni. Somebody took pictures of us. Why would somebody do that?

"Have you all seen these?" I ask, my voice not even a whisper.

"Yes," my father replies.

I swallow down the sob that is lodged in my throat. "You both saw these this morning and you never said anything until now?" I look to my parents.

"I wanted to speak to Jax first," my father replies.

"Why? Why did you need to speak to Jax? Why didn't you come straight to me?" I ask, finding my voice now as feelings of anger slip in between the cracks of the shame and guilt.

"I wanted to know if we could deal with them without you being involved," he replies matter of factly, while my mom sits silently by his side.

"You weren't going to tell me?"

Jax reaches for my hand and squeezes it, but it doesn't offer me the comfort that it usually does. I have never felt so humiliated in my life and the fact that they were all going to deal with this without even telling me makes me feel like a silly little girl. "How could you even think about not telling me about this?"

"Your dad was trying to protect you, angel," Jax says, and I turn my anger on him.

"Don't defend him. I do not need protecting from the truth. How many times do I have to prove myself to you all before you stop treating me like a child?"

"You will always be my child," my father snaps. "How do you think I felt seeing those pictures?"

"How do you think I feel knowing that you've seen them? You and mom? That was a private moment that nobody should have ever seen," I snap.

"Clearly not all that private," he snaps back. "Because it's not just you two on there, is it?"

"Alejandro!" my mom hisses.

"Enough!" Jax snarls at my father as he laces his fingers through mine.

"We need to tell Toni too," I say to him as another rush of shame almost overwhelms me.

"We will," he nods.

"Well, tread carefully. I'd rather her brothers never found about this."

"Her brothers?" I blink at him.

"Dante and Lorenzo Moretti? You grew up in Chicago, *mija*, surely you've heard of the Morettis?"

I look between Jax and my father. "Wait? Toni is a Moretti? Like a Chicago Moretti?"

"Yes. A genuine pure blood Moretti."

"She's their half-sister," Jax adds. "She moved to LA with her mom when she was fourteen. She and Dante have always stayed in touch though. The oldest brother, Lorenzo isn't her biggest fan."

"I had no idea she was one of them," I say, hanging my head. "I'm so sorry, Papi."

I keep my head bent low, too ashamed to look any of them in the eye and pick at a stray cotton on my dress while Jax squeezes my other hand in his. Then he cups my chin with his other hand, turning my face until his eyes meet mine. "You have nothing at all to be embarrassed about, angel," he assures me.

I offer him a faint smile.

"Jax is right, sweetheart," my mom adds.

But my father can't let it go yet, and his anger at Jax is obvious to anyone in the room. "I trusted you to take care of her," he barks.

"He does, Papi," I insist. "This isn't his fault."

My father rolls his eyes at me but at least it stops him glaring at me.

"Do you have any idea who sent them or what they want?" I ask.

"We don't know who it was yet, but we'll find them, angel," Jax says.

"And as for what they want — money? Plain and simple greed," my father adds.

"How much?"

"Five million dollars by noon tomorrow or they upload the

videos to every free porn site there is and send the stills to anywhere that will print them."

I cover my eyes as the thought of that makes me want to throw up.

"We won't let that happen, angel," Jax assures me.

"Can you find out where this has come from? Take down any videos if they do get posted?" I ask him.

"I can take anything down. Hell, we can even get a legal injunction to do that. Filming people having sex without their knowledge or consent is still against the law. I can find these fuckers too..."

"But?" my father asks.

"Once something is out there, it's out there. I can't guarantee we'll remove every trace of it. There are screenshots and the dark web. I could spend the rest of my fucking life hunting this down once it's released. We need to find the source, and I can't do that by noon tomorrow."

"You're saying I should pay them five million dollars? Let some piece of shit use my beautiful daughter to blackmail me?" my father growls.

"I'm saying you should buy me some time. Pay the money. I can follow its trail."

"Always follow the money," I say. It's something Jax says often and he winks at me.

My father narrows his eyes at him. "Rolling over isn't like you."

"Yeah? Well I've never had someone threaten to post pictures of my wife having sex before, amigo. I'm not on my fucking A game here. I still don't know what happened in Dallas. This could all be linked for all we know," he snaps, rubbing his hands through his hair in frustration. "Besides, I'm not rolling over. This is the easiest way to find them. I'll get you your money back."

"I don't give a shit about the money, Jax, but if we look like we're weak. If we give in at the slightest hint of pressure."

I fidget in my seat. This is all my fault. "I'm so sorry, Papi," I whisper.

"You did nothing wrong," Jax reminds me, but my father doesn't reassure me. A few words to ease my guilt, but he refuses to say them. Jax turns back to him. "This isn't pressure. This is your fucking daughter, amigo."

"You think I don't know that? But this is about more than my daughter. More than you. This is about my family's legacy. I will not be the weak link in the fucking chain."

I sigh because he's right. He can't afford for our family to appear vulnerable. He is the head of the entire organization and sometimes he has to make difficult decisions. I don't envy him that.

"You're really going to risk that video being leaked?" Jax snarls at him. "Because if you do, you're not the man I thought you were and I'll find the goddamn money myself."

I smile at my husband. He doesn't have that sort of cash just lying around. None of us do. But Montoya Inc. does.

My father sighs heavily as he sits back in his chair. "Of course I won't. Arrange to have the money transferred and make sure you can follow it."

"I'll get it sorted," Jax says.

"When we find these sick fucks..." my father snarls.

"Yeah, I know," Jax agrees and it seems like they are finally on the same page.

I look down at my lap. The guilt and humiliation feels like an elephant sitting on my chest. I cling to Jax's hand as I struggle to breathe.

Jax leans close to me, his lips brush my ear. "It will be okay, baby," he whispers. "Just breathe."

My father pushes his chair back and walks around the desk

to me. Cupping my chin, he tilts my head. "Jax is right, *mija*, you did nothing wrong. Don't you ever hang your head in shame again, you hear me? You are Lucia fucking Montoya!"

"Decker actually," Jax reminds him and it makes me laugh a little. My father frowns at him but then he winks at me.

"He's right," my mom says as she walks up behind him. "You have nothing to be sorry for or ashamed about, sweetheart." Then she places her hand on my father's shoulder. "Let's go get the boys out of the pool and leave Jax and Lucia alone for a few minutes," she suggests and I offer her a smile of gratitude.

"She'll always be a Montoya, amigo," he says to Jax, only half joking, as he leans down and kisses my forehead.

Once my parents have left the room I feel like I can breathe again. Being here alone with Jax, I let out the tears I've been holding back for the past ten minutes. "Oh, my God, Jax," I cry and he pulls me into his arms.

"I'm so sorry, baby," he says as he smooths my hair. "I'll fix this. I promise you."

"I know, but what if you don't fix it in time?"

"I will," he insists. "Have I ever let you down?"

"No," I sniff, wiping tears from my cheeks. "But no matter what you do, someone still saw us. My parents saw us, but even worse they saw what I did with Toni."

"What we did with Toni," he reminds me. "You're not in this on your own, Luce."

"I know, but it's not you who's half naked with someone's head buried between your legs," I snap, regretting my tone when I see the hurt on his face. He's hurting just as much as I am.

"I know," he says softly.

"Do you think Toni has anything to do with this?" I ask, searching his eyes for my answer.

"No," he says firmly. "I told you, I trust her. I would never let her anywhere near you if I didn't."

"We'll have to tell her too," I say as a fresh wave of guilt washes over me. "What will she do? What if she kicks my ass?" I laugh, only half joking.

"Toni won't care. Not about herself anyway. She's not bothered by that kind of stuff. She even did a few adult films in her early twenties."

"She did?"

"Yeah."

"Have you watched any?"

"No," he smiles at me.

"Still, I don't look forward to the conversation."

"I can speak to her if you'd prefer," he offers.

"No, we both should."

"We'll talk to her tomorrow, okay? I'll set up the payment in a few minutes and then we can have some dinner and try to forget about it all until the morning."

"You think my parents will be able to forget it?" I cover my eyes with my hands. "And what if my father pays and that video still gets out? I mean the pictures are bad enough, but the video, of the three of us?" Heat creeps over my skin as I literally burn with shame, from my chest up to my cheeks.

"It won't, Luce. I promise."

"I can't believe my mom and dad saw them, Jax. I mean the ones of you and I are bad enough, but to see another woman eating my..." I can't bear to finish the sentence and instead I bury my head against his chest.

"I shouldn't have let it happen like that. I didn't think anyone would be able to see. I thought the ranch was safe. I'm so sorry, baby."

"It's not your fault," I say, wrapping my arms around him. Just having him here makes me feel better. His solid presence is so reassuring. He wraps his arms tightly around me again. "God, I feel so bad."

"None of this is on you, do you understand me? It's on whichever sick piece of shit took those videos of us."

"You have any idea who it might be?"

"No," he kisses the top of my head. "But I will find them. I swear to you."

He takes my hand and we stand up.

"I'm sorry we dragged you all the way here for this when you were dealing with everything in Dallas."

"No," he shakes his head. "You don't get to be sorry about that, baby. You are always my priority. Always."

"Did you find anything more about who attacked your father?"

"Not much. Nobody saw the guys who did it."

"Any luck tracing the person with the crib?"

"No, I was chasing that up today when your dad called me."

"I'm so.." I start to say but he frowns at me. "Anything I can do to help?" I ask instead.

"Yes." He leans in and kisses me softly, sliding his tongue inside my mouth and lazily exploring. I lean further into him as his hands slide onto my ass and he pushes our groins together. The familiar tingling is already building in my core. How does this man make me a trembling wreck with just a kiss?

When he breaks our kiss, I gasp for breath. "So, what is it I can do?"

"You just did it, angel," he says with a wink.

"Is it wrong that I wish we were in our own place so you could just take me to bed right now?" I whisper.

"That's exactly what I was thinking," he grins at me. "We can go home after dinner if you like?"

I chew on my lip. "I kind of promised my dad I'd stay here

while you were away, and now with this going on…. I don't want to upset him any more than I already have."

He closes his eyes and takes a deep breath before he replies. "That's okay. It makes sense for you to be here. I'll be going back to Dallas when this is taken care of. So, I'd rather you were here while I'm away anyway."

"How long will you be gone for?" I whisper. I hate that he's going to leave again, but I know that he has to.

"Not long, angel. As soon as I figure out what the fuck has gone on there, I'll be straight back here. Then I will take you home and we will spend all of our free time in bed if that's what you want."

"Sounds good."

"Come on, let's go face the world," he says with a wink as he takes hold of my hand in his.

"Ugh," I groan but I follow him through the house and we head to the kitchen, where the boys will surely be soon when they're dry from the pool.

Realizing we're alone for the time being, I wrap my arms around Jax's neck and trail soft kisses over his jaw. "I really missed you," I murmur against his skin.

"You're going to make me hard in your parent's kitchen if you don't stop that and aren't I in enough trouble already?" he laughs softly just as my mom walks into the room.

I step back from him as though he's given me an electric shock.

"You can hug your husband, Lucia," she says softly in my ear as she reaches me. Then she looks up at Jax. "Alex asked if you could see him in his office."

"Sure." he kisses me softly. "Be back soon."

I watch his fine ass walk out of the door as my mom makes herself a tea. "You want one of these, sweetheart? They're supposed to be soothing?" she laughs softly.

"Then I guess you'd better hit me up, Mom," I say with a roll of my eyes. Although I think it will take more than tea to soothe me.

When she's done, she brings them to the counter and sets them down before perching herself on a stool.

"I'm sorry, Mom," I whisper.

She looks at me, deadpan. "What for?"

"For the video. I feel like I've brought shame on the family."

"The Montoya family?" she arches an eyebrow at me. "Sweetheart, nothing you could do would ever bring shame on this family. The Montoyas have had worse scandals than this, and they're just the ones they didn't cover up."

"But Papa was talking about his legacy..."

"He doesn't want to appear weak in front of his enemies. You know how stubborn he is. Giving into blackmailers is not in his nature."

"Do you think he shouldn't pay them?"

"I agree with Jax. He needs more time and he can use the money to trace whoever did this."

"Is that the only reason?" I ask. "Don't you care if those videos of me get out there?" I whisper.

She reaches out and places her hand over mine. "Of course I do, sweetheart, but your father paying that money isn't the key to making that happen. Blackmailers don't stop once they get what they want. They keep asking for more. But I think he should pay it so that it gives him and Jax a chance to find them, and then they deal with it in their own unique way. That's the way to ensure nobody ever sees those images."

"What if they can't though?"

She raises one eyebrow at me. "This is your father and Jax we're talking about."

She's right. They are the best at what they do. If anyone can find out whoever took those videos, it's those two.

"Anyway, what's the worst that could happen, Lucia? So they do get out there? You were engaging in something private with your husband."

"Mom!" I blush at the mere thought.

"Is there anything worse than having your father see them?"

"Grandpa Matteo?" I offer.

"He wouldn't look at stuff like that. Your grandma would kill him."

"Mathias?"

"By the time he's old enough, they won't even be a memory," she says with a wink. "All I'm saying, sweetheart, is that you are not the only person in that video. You did nothing wrong, and only small minded people would judge you for it, and you don't need those kinds of people in your life."

"Hmm," I murmur, still not quite convinced.

"Or you could just front your way out of it. With the right PR?" she rests her chin on her hand and grins wickedly at me.

I sometimes forget that before she married my father, my mom was part of a well-established political family. Her father is Foster Carmichael, a prominent politician, and between the ages of fourteen and twenty-five, my mom worked his campaign trail every spare second she had. She is an actual PR wizard.

When one of Montoya Inc's restaurants was shut down last year because a couple of gangs decided to have a shoot out during bottomless brunch, she managed to spin it somehow, so it became the new edgiest place to be in LA – like people were genuinely scared they were missing out on not being there. My father dealt with the gangs in his own special way, and there has been no trouble since. It has never been so busy.

"And how would you spin this?" I ask her.

She sucks on her bottom lip as she appears deep in thought.

"We could make you the poster child for gynecological health?" she suggests. "Toni is your gynecologist and she was making a house call?"

That makes me giggle. "Mom!" I protest.

"Okay, if you don't fancy that, how about you were bitten by a snake and she was sucking out the poison?"

"No!" I laugh out loud now. "That's even worse. I'd rather people thought the truth than that."

"See, I told you it could be worse," she says with a wink.

"So, you're not embarrassed by me then?"

"Embarrassed? Me? Your father threatened to gouge out one of the other kid's father's eyes at a birthday party last week because he thought he was looking at my boobs. The guy was there with his husband. He said it in front of most of the other parents too, but I still walked into that house with my arm linked in his," she says with a shrug. "It takes a lot to embarrass me, sweetheart, and I don't think anything you could do would ever do that."

"Thanks, Mom."

CHAPTER 20
LUCIA

Despite everything that's happened in the past twelve hours, we managed to have a nice family dinner. Jax and my father played with Matthias and the boys while they spoke to my mom and me in code about who they think might be behind this. We didn't come to any conclusions, but Jax has paid the money and has done whatever technological wizardry he does to ensure that he will be able to track where it eventually winds up.

It's almost midnight and we've been talking non-stop since the boys went to bed a few hours ago, but still, we have no answers. I try to suppress a yawn but fail miserably.

"Time for bed, angel," Jax says, wrapping an arm around me and kissing my forehead.

"Us too, princess," my father says to my mom.

A few moments later, we're all standing at the top of the stairs. I hug my parents goodnight.

"Night, amigo," my father says to Jax.

"Night," he replies, and then with a wicked grin, he adds. "Just remember, if you hear Lucia shouting Daddy, she ain't calling for you."

It's clearly a joke, but my father doesn't see it that way.

At all.

His face turns a deep shade of purple and his hands ball into fists. He bounces on his toes, like a boxer ready to strike, but sensing he's about to punch her son-in-law in the throat, my mom puts a hand on his chest.

"Let's go to bed, Alex," she purrs in his ear, working her magic on him in the way that no other person on this earth can.

He falters for a second as he glares at Jax. "You're lucky my wife is here, Decker, because if she wasn't, I would shoot you in the fucking head."

"Papi!" I say.

But Jax simply chuckles beside me. "Night, amigo."

He takes my hand and we walk to our room. "Why did you have to provoke him when he's only just calmed down?" I ask him with a nudge to his ribs.

"I'm sorry, angel, I couldn't help it," he laughs harder.

We go into the bedroom and close the door.

"Besides, I don't ever call you daddy," I say with a grin.

"I know." He winks at me.

"You want me to?"

He grabs me by the waist, pulling me close and sliding his hands to my ass. "I'd rather you made me one."

"Oh," I whisper as the familiar fluttering builds in my abdomen.

He was only away from me for a day but it felt like so much longer. Chewing on my lip, I stare into his dark brown eyes as heat pools in my core.

"You know that biting that lip drives me crazy."

"I do," I purr. "So, what are you going to do about it?"

He narrows his eyes at me. "Take off the dress. Now," he orders before he walks to the bed and starts to undress.

"So bossy," I pout as I peel my dress off over my head and toss it onto the floor. "Now what?"

"Lie down."

I do as he says, looking up at him as I watch him undressing. He shrugs off his shirt, revealing his hard, tattooed body that I love so much, before he pulls off his boots and socks. Then he crawls onto the bed, holding himself over me.

"I've missed you so fucking much, Luce," he whispers, brushing my hair from my face.

"I missed you too."

"You're gonna need to make up for depriving me of your hot pussy now though," he growls.

"I think you deprived yourself, cowboy," I purr.

He scowls now. "Did you just talk back to me?"

I bite on my lip again. So, he's in that kind of mood? "Sorry, Sir," I whisper.

He flips me over until I'm lying on my front. "And you rolled your eyes at me when we were eating dinner earlier." His hand glides over my back and he unhooks my bra with deft, expert fingers.

"Well, you probably deserved that," I say, even though I don't remember the alleged eye-rolling.

He slaps my ass hard, making me yelp.

"I think you deserve to be spanked hard, angel. To remind you who you belong to."

I angle my head so I can look him in the eye. "I haven't forgotten."

"So who owns you?" He spanks me again.

"Ah!" That one stung.

"Who, Luce?" He brings his palm down again in exactly the same place.

"You, Jax," I whimper.

"Yeah I do."

"Who owns you, Jax?" I challenge him.

"You, baby. Only you." He spanks me again before he crawls on top of me and starts tugging off my panties. I lift my hips to help him.

He rubs his palms over my stinging ass cheeks. "This ass is getting fucked tonight too, baby," he growls as he slides his hands lower and spreads my thighs wide apart, dragging two fingers through my folds. "But I'm taking this hot pussy first."

"Please?"

"You ready for me?" he asks as he lines his cock up at my wet entrance. "Because I don't want to wait any longer to be inside you."

"Yes," I gasp. His spankings always make me ready.

"Good girl," he groans as he drives his huge cock into me.

Taking my hands, he presses them flat against the bed on either side of my head, lying on top of me with his hot mouth against my ear, he nails me into the mattress.

"Your pussy loves my cock. I feel you squeezing me," he growls. "So fucking tight."

"Harder, Jax," I pant, needing more from him.

"Fuck, baby," he groans, thrusting his hips and forcing me up the bed. "You feel how fucking hard you make me?"

"Yes," I whimper as pleasure rolls through my body, converging between my thighs. Every time he drives back inside me, my entire body trembles.

"This pussy is mine," he says against my ear, his teeth grazing my earlobe before he bites on it and tugs gently.

"Yours."

"You make me feel like an animal when I'm fucking you. You know that? I can't get deep enough inside you," he growls, his deep voice rolling through my body.

"Please, Jax?"

"You want to come, baby?" he laughs darkly as he takes my

hands and raises them above my head so he can pin my wrists with one of his huge hands, while the other slides beneath me and he starts to rub my clit.

"Oh, fuck!" I hiss out on a breath and he rubs harder as he rolls his hips inside me. I come with a loud cry of his name as my body bucks beneath him like a rodeo horse.

CHAPTER 21

JAX

W e're eating a late breakfast on the patio, having dropped Matthias off at school, when the email alert comes through on Lucia's work cell. It's one of dozens she gets on a daily basis and I take no notice, but she glances at the screen and frowns.

"What is it?" I ask her.

"It's from an anonymous address and it has images attached," she says with a tremor in her voice.

"Open it, angel, and we'll see what it is," I tell her.

I paid the blackmailers last night and was wondering if they would make further contact.

She opens the email and her face pales as she looks at the screen.

"What is it, Luce?"

She blinks at me, tears in her eyes.

"Lucia?"

"I-it's you," she stammers.

"What?" I frown at her, reaching for the phone but she pulls it away as she flicks through the rest of the images. Tears start to roll down her cheeks and I sit staring at her, wondering what fresh hell is in store for us now.

As though staring at my wife's brokenhearted face while she looks at whatever is on that phone isn't bad enough, her father comes storming out of the house with a look of fury that makes yesterday's meltdown pale in comparison.

"Let me see the phone, Luce," I hold my hand out to her.

She blinks at me, in a daze, so I reach over and take it from her.

"I'm going to fucking drown you in a pool of your own blood," Alejandro snarls.

I check the email. It simply says.

You should be careful who you trust.

And then there are half a dozen images of Toni and me. Heads huddled together and deep in conversation. They look like they were taken in LA, but I have no idea when. It's only when I come to the next one that I realize I have no idea when they were taken because they're one hundred percent fake. It's a picture of me and Toni and in this one we're kissing — and it ain't no friendly peck on the cheek either.

"Angel, these are fake," I insist as her father reaches us.

"Even the last one?" she snarls.

I frown as I scroll to the last one on the email. It's not fake, but it's old. It's a photograph of me nailing Shannon at the stables back at the ranch. She's naked with her legs around my waist as I fuck her against the wall with my head buried in her neck.

Fuck!

I look at her, ignoring her raging father beside her.

"Lucia, that's from years ago."

"Do you ever fuck women somewhere normal, like a fucking bed?" Alejandro shouts, like he can talk.

"It's years old," I insist.

"Papi, can you please let me handle this?" she snaps at him and he backs off. "And the ones with you and Toni. They have a date and time stamp, Jax. It was four weeks ago."

"They're fake, baby. Before last week, I hadn't see her for months-"

"You're kissing her!" she yells at me,

I reach out to take her hands but she pulls back from me and the look of disgust and pain on her face almost breaks me. "Luce, you know how easy it is to manipulate photos. That is not me, angel. Let me prove it to you."

"Did the two of you plan this?" she whispers, ignoring every word I just said. "The video and the money?"

I frown at her. I can't believe she would even consider that for a second. "What?"

"What the fuck were you two doing then?" Alejandro barks as Lucia sinks back into her chair looking utterly defeated. I have to convince her that someone is trying to set me up here, but she won't even look at me.

"We weren't doing anything!" I shout at him. "That is not me."

"Is that why you were so keen on me paying so quickly?"

I jump up from my chair and it falls to the ground as I do. "You're suggesting I would fuck you over, not to mention my own wife, for money? I have known you for twenty-four fucking years."

His Adam's apple bobs as he swallows. Deep down he knows I'd never do that. "You've broken my daughter's heart," he snarls instead. "Now get the fuck out of my house."

I look down at Lucia who stares at me with her mouth open,

her lower lip trembles and all I want to do is carry her to my truck and drive us a million miles from here so we can escape all of this bullshit. If she would just give me some time, I can fix everything.

"Luce?" I plead as my world starts to fall around down my ears. My chest is tight and I can't breathe.

Then my damn cell phone starts ringing. I take it out and my aunt Molly's name flashes on the screen. With a heavy sigh, I answer the call and press the phone to my ear.

"Jackson, he's awake," she says with a deep sigh.

"Good," I breathe again, thankful for some good news.

"But, he said…" she sniffs as though she's trying not to cry, "he said the men who attacked him told him that you paid them to do it."

The phone almost drops from my hand. "What?"

"That's what he told me."

"Has he spoken to the sheriff?" my jaw ticks as I wait for her answer. Being arrested and thrown in jail by that asshole is the last thing I need.

"Yes, but he didn't tell him anything. He said his memory is still fuzzy."

"Fuck!" I sigh, running a hand through my hair.

"We know it wasn't you, but we need you back here, Jax. He wants to speak with you."

"I'm kind of in the middle of something in LA," I say, even though after this morning, I suspect the entire fucking thing is connected. But who the hell is trying to ruin my life, and why?

"I'm worried, Jackson," she says and this time she cries.

Fuck! My aunt isn't scared of anything. I hate that I've taken the darkness of my life here in LA home to her peaceful ranch.

"I'll be back by tonight," I tell her and then end the call.

Alejandro is glaring at me but Lucia won't even look at me.

"I have to go back to Dallas…" I say to her.

She stands, wiping the tears from her cheeks. "So, go."

Then she turns away from me and walks away, tearing my heart out as she does. How can she be so quick to believe that I would betray her like that?

I look to her father. My closest friend. My brother in all but blood. "You know that's not me in those photographs, amigo. Someone is trying to fuck up my life." I shake my head in annoyance that I never saw it coming.

I'm always so fucking careful. Life as his right hand man has always taught me to be security conscious, but I've taken my eye off the ball. I used to be a workaholic, and now I spend every spare second I have with Lucia and Matthias. How do I find the balance to be able to do what I do and have a family? Maybe that's not meant for men like me.

"Whoever attacked my father told him that it was me responsible," I add, because I have to tell someone. He is the man who would usually work things through like this with me. He'd be the one at my side figuring out what the hell is going on, but by marrying his daughter, I've put him an untenable position. How did I become an actual member of his family and at the same time become less like family to him than ever?

That at least provokes some reaction in him and his brow furrows in confusion. "What?"

"Someone is fucking with me, Alejandro."

"The photographs? They're not all fake though?" he asks.

"No. The one of me and Shannon in the stables is real, but it's old. I would never..."

"How old?" he snaps.

I rub a hand over my jaw. The last time I went to the ranch before I started dating Lucia, Shannon and I hooked up. "It's gotta be at least eighteen months."

"So you were being watched or followed for the past eighteen months then?" he scowls. "How haven't we known about this?"

"Maybe it was just while I was in Dallas?" I suggest. I'm more relaxed while I'm there. It's the place where I allow myself to switch off a little. "If someone had been following me, watching me in LA, I would have known. Someone would have seen something. I'm sure of it."

"I sure fucking hope so."

"They must have been watching me on my last few trips," I say, thinking out loud. I look past him at the house. "I have to go figure out what's going on. I don't feel like she'd be safe at the barn house on her own."

"I'm pretty sure she doesn't want to go anywhere with you right now, anyway," he says, the cold edge in his tone still there.

I suck in a breath. She's my wife and her place is at my side. But I can't get the image of her walking away from me out of my mind. She didn't even give me a chance.

My head is spinning with it all. I feel like I can't breathe with the weight in my chest. I need answers and I'm not going to find any here.

"She belongs here with her family," he adds and it feels like the final fucking nail in my coffin.

CHAPTER 22
LUCIA

Jax left for Dallas a half hour ago. He tried to say goodbye, but I refused to speak to him. He stood outside my bedroom door and told me he was leaving. Then he asked that I tell Matthias he'll call him tonight and wish him goodnight. My heart broke when I heard his footsteps walking away, but I can't even look at him without seeing that image of him screwing Shannon in the barn.

Then there's the photographs with Toni. He says they're fake, but how do I know for sure? I thought I trusted him implicitly. How can that be rocked so easily by some pictures? All I do know is I can't sit around here feeling sorry for myself.

I take my car keys from the kitchen counter and start to walk down the hallway when my father's voice stops me in my tracks. "Where the hell do you think you're going, *mija*?"

I roll my eyes before I spin around and face him. "To see Toni Moretti."

"Not on your own," he says as he walks toward me. "Let's go."

"Papi, I can handle this," I tell him, my hands on my hips.

He narrows his eyes at me. "I know that you can, but you are

143

not leaving this house without a bodyguard, and I want to make sure that this isn't going to cause problems with her brothers in Chicago."

"So, you're being my bodyguard for the afternoon? Is that it?"

He nods. He and Jax are the only members of our family who seem to be allowed to go anywhere without a security detail. I must speak to them about that when things are a little calmer. Surely I've proven myself capable of looking after myself now? "And we can take my car," he says with a wink.

I arch an eyebrow at him, "The Bugatti?"

"Yes."

"Can I drive?"

"No," he shakes his head and then walks past me to the front door.

An hour later, my father and I are standing at the entrance to Toni's private gym. Her trainer, Benji opens the door and his face breaks into a smile when he sees us.

"Hey, Mr. M. Hey, Rocky," he says, winking at me.

"Is Toni in?" I ask.

"Of course." He opens the door wider and we step inside and out of the bright LA sunshine.

Toni is at the back punching hell out of a bag. Sweat glistens over her skin and a fresh wave of shame washes over me. I have to tell her about the videos too, and my father is here.

"Can I speak to her alone first please, Papi?"

He sucks on his top lip, considering my request. "Fine. But I need to speak with her too. You got any decent coffee in here?" he asks Benji, who nods his agreement and then the two of them walk into the small kitchenette, leaving me watching Toni alone.

I let her finish her set before I interrupt her.

"Hey, Toni," I say, my voice cracking with the nerves.

She spins around and faces me, her face lighting up in a smile.

"Hello, princess. To what do I owe this pleasure?" She looks behind me, no doubt looking for Jax. Looking for her accomplice?

"I wanted to show you something," I say.

At the sound of voices, she looks over to the kitchen and frowns. "Your father's here with you?"

"Yeah."

"What's going on?" she says and the change in her tone is instant.

"I told you I wanted to show you something." I pull my cell phone out of my pocket and open the email with the images of her and Jax. I scroll to the one of them sucking each other's faces and hand it to her.

The reaction on her face is of shock and disgust, and it seems genuine, unless she's an amazing actress. Maybe she is?

She peers closer at the screen. "Is that supposed to be me and Jax?"

I flick to the next image, which is the two of them sitting in the same restaurant, but their faces are much clearer. "You tell me."

"What the hell? Who? Where?" she snarls as she glares at me. "You know that's not me, Lucia. Me and Jax. We've never... Where the hell did you get those?"

"Toni, please?" I beg her. "Is there something going on with you two?"

Her face softens a little. "No, Lucia. There is only one person in your relationship I have any interest in that way, and we both know who that is," she whispers and my cheeks flush pink.

"But these pictures?"

"I don't know what magic fuckery someone has pulled, but I'm telling you that is not Jax and me. Why the hell would someone want you to think that it was?"

"They were sent to me and my dad. I think the sender wanted us to doubt Jax. To think that you and he were trying to extort money from us. I dunno," I shake my head. None of this makes any sense to me, and the one person who could make sense of it all is on the other side of the country.

"I don't follow," she says with a frown. "Extort money how?"

"That's the other thing I need to tell you about," I say as I pull the brown envelope from my purse and hand it to her. "Somebody took videos of us in Dallas."

I watch Toni's face as she flicks through the still images of her, Jax and me. I didn't bring the other ones of just Jax and me. She doesn't need to see those too. Her pretty features are pulled into a frown of disgust and anger. "Sick fucks," she hisses. "How fucking dare they!"

"I-I'm sorry," I mumble. "We had no idea anyone was watching."

"I know," she shakes her head. "I bet Jax is pissed? Is that why he's not here? Is he currently tearing people apart as we speak?"

"It's a long story," I say with a sigh. "But my father saw them too."

"Oh, Lucia," she puts her gloved hand on my arm. "I'm so sorry."

"Yeah. It was kind of awful. I mean..."

"I get it. Fuck!" she hisses. "So what did they want?"

Toni listens intently as I tell her about the demand for money and how we paid it. "Jax is hoping to find the source of the videos so they never see the light of day," I finish.

"He will," she gives me a reassuring nod. "That's kind of his thing, right?"

"Yeah. So, I'll let you know if they make any more threats or if the video is leaked anywhere," I say awkwardly, not sure what the correct etiquette is for such situations. "And I'm sorry, Toni."

"Hey, it's not on you to apologize. I hope you find who did this and that your husband and father deal with them in their own special way, but don't worry about me. I don't give a rat's ass who sees me eating a hot girl's pussy. Okay?" She winks at me.

"Okay," I can't help but laugh at her. She is both the one of the most laid back, and at the same time, aggressive, people I know.

"Hey. Is that why you've brought your father? Were you two planning on stuffing me into the trunk of his car or something?" She arches one eyebrow at me and grins, but I know she's only half joking.

"No, he brought the Bugatti anyway. Not sure you'd fit."

She nods her agreement just as my father is making his way over to us. "You two all done?" he asks with a smile.

"Yeah," I say.

"Good. Can I have a word?" he says to her, and suddenly he's all business. The atmosphere in the small gym changes in an instant.

She narrows her eyes at him. Toni Moretti is nobody's fool.

"Is this going to be a problem, Toni?" he asks.

"Not for me," she replies coolly.

"And for Dante and Lorenzo?"

"You know I've never lived my life by their rules. They won't be overly happy if it gets out," she admits. "Lorenzo won't be a problem because he still hates me, but Dante might try and do the whole protective big brother thing."

147

"And if he does?"

"I assure you it will be the man, or woman, behind the camera who will incur his wrath. Besides, I would never allow anyone to hurt Lucia or your family. You know that."

"Hmm," he rubs a hand over his jaw. "You know I needed to make sure that was still the case."

"I understand, and it is. I owe Alana my life. I'll never forget that."

I look between her and my father. This is a new development I had no idea about.

"You have my assurances Jax and me will do everything in our power to destroy those videos and whoever took them," he says.

I smile at him. Something about the way he talks about him and Jax as though they're still a team gives me hope. An unexpected sob gets stuck in my throat as I think about my husband. Alone in Dallas, thinking that everyone he loves is against him. What a huge cluster fuck this has all turned into.

"PLEASE, CAN I DRIVE HOME?" I ask my father as we reach his Bugatti Veyron.

"Nope. Nobody drives the Bugatti."

"Mom does," I remind him.

"Very occasionally, and only when she..." he grins wickedly and shakes his head. "Well, you don't need to know that, *mija*."

"Eurgh." I pull a face, feigning my disgust. "Fine. I won't ask again."

I climb into the passenger seat and try not to think about why he allows my mom to drove his pride and joy sometimes. "So, Toni and mom?" I ask instead, trying to change the subject.

"Yeah?" he replies with a frown.

"Toni said that mom saved her life."

"Hmm," he says with a nod.

"Are you going to tell me how?"

"It's not my story to tell, *mija,* or your mama's. You should ask Toni."

"Well, now you have me even more intrigued. Come on, Papi, how did the sweetest woman I know save Toni Moretti's life?"

He turns in his seat and frowns at me. "Your mom might be sweet, Lucia, but she is the strongest person you will ever meet."

"I know that too. It's just, Toni is so..." I shake my head.

"Strong?" he offers.

"Yeah. Super strong. Like she's invincible."

"Nobody is invincible, *mija,*" he says with a sigh. "And even the strongest of us need someone who will be there to pick us up when we fall. Your mom is the kind of person who sees things that other people don't. And when she knows that somebody is in trouble, she will do whatever it takes to help them. As much as that irritates the hell out of me, it's also who she is, and why I love her."

I can't help but smile at him. My parents are so very different in lots of ways. My father is ruthless, stubborn, tough and impulsive. He acts first and asks questions later. My mom is kind, compassionate, always willing to see the best in people, she is tough in a different way to him. But they are always a team. Together – they are invincible.

I thought that was Jax and me too. I wonder what he's doing right now.

"He'll find out what's going on, *mija,*" my father says as though reading my mind. "It's what he does."

"I shouldn't have let him go alone," I whisper.

"Yes, you should. He needs to do this with no distractions.

He would only worry about having to keep you safe if you were there," he says matter of factly.

I turn back to the window, wondering if my father is right. Jax does need to focus, but I'm pretty sure he needs me and Matthias too.

I sit at the large dining table, picking over the lasagna that Magda warmed through for me for dinner and feeling like my world has imploded.

How is it that less than two weeks ago I was getting married to the man of my dreams and so insanely happy that I couldn't stop smiling? Now my new husband is on the other side of the country alone. My father hates him and he can hardly bear to even look me in the eye. Not to mention that I'm potentially about to have the whole world see pictures of me naked and even worse, having my pussy eaten by Toni Moretti.

Jax swears he won't let that happen but how will he stop it when he's in Dallas trying to find out who tried to murder his father?

I swallow the lump in my throat. I've wasted too many tears already on this whole sorry mess.

I close my eyes and will myself not to cry when I feel a soft hand smoothing over my hair. "Are you okay, sweetheart?" my mom asks and that's my undoing.

I turn in my seat and bury my face against her. "No, Mom," I sob.

"It will all be okay," she soothes as she goes on smoothing my hair.

I cling to her and she lets me cry until my eyes and throat are raw and I have no more tears left. I pull back from her and wipe my wet cheeks with the backs of my hands. "Sorry," I whisper.

"Lucia!" my mom scolds me as she sits beside me, brushing away a stray tear with her fingertips. "Stop apologizing for everything. You are entitled to a few tears."

"What am I going to do, Mom?" I sniff.

"What do you want to do, sweetheart?"

"I just want this to all go away. I want to go back in time and never let anyone have a chance to take those stupid videos. I want Papi to be able to look at me again and not see... that!"

"He will," she insists.

"No," I shake my head. "He's so ashamed of me."

"He is not ashamed of you. Not even a little bit."

"But he saw..." I shake my head as it starts to spin.

"Yes, he saw something no father wants to see, but you weren't doing anything wrong, Lucia. The person who took those videos is the only person at fault here. Not you. Not Jax." She reaches out and takes my hand in hers. Her skin is so soft and warm. How is it that she always feels like home to me?

"But he was so mad at Jax. What if they can't get past this?"

She waves her hand dismissively. "You know how he gets. He's angry and he's upset. He won't take that out on you because you are his little girl, and I would give him hell if he did." She gives me a wicked grin and despite everything, I laugh. "So he took it out on Jax, but they will both shake hands when this is all over, and they'll go back to being the best of friends again. I promise you."

"You think?" I sniff.

"I know."

"What would you do if you were me, Mom? Go to Dallas or stay here and help Papi?"

She takes in a breath and then she smiles at me. "The same thing you would do, sweetheart. Be with my family."

CHAPTER 23
JAX

S itting on the chair beside his bed, I watch my father sleeping. It's after 2 a.m. and he hasn't woken since I arrived eight hours ago. The doctors tell me he'll wake up again as soon as the drugs they gave him wear off.

I listen to the beeping of the machines all around me and all I can think about is her and how I've abandoned her when she needed me the most. I tried to call her a couple of hours ago and her phone went straight to voicemail. How have I fucked everything up so quickly?

I shouldn't have left without forcing her to speak to me. Does she think I chose my father over her and our son? Did I?

I feel guilty that it's my fault that he almost died. I feel guilty that I assumed the worst of him and the thought that I might never get to tell him that makes me feel like I can't breathe.

But nothing hurts me more than the look on her face when she told me to go. Having to walk out of that house and leave her behind almost killed me. I suppose she's a Montoya first and my wife second and I'll have to get used to that, because I can't fucking live without her. Knowing that she doubts me makes me feel like my heart has been ripped out of my chest, leaving a gaping black hole in its place.

As soon as my father is awake, I'm going to hear what he has to say about his attackers and then make my peace with him. Then I'm on the first plane back to LA to take my wife back. I'll carry her out of that goddamn house if I have to.

I put my head in my hands and close my eyes. I miss her so much I swear I can even smell her damn perfume. I figure I must be dreaming when I feel her soft fingers in my hair.

"Hey," she whispers and now I know for sure I've fallen asleep and I must be dreaming. But I look up and she's standing right there. Right in front of me.

"Lucia?" I blink at her, still not sure that she's not a figment of my imagination.

"I'm sorry I let you leave without me," she whispers, a fat tear rolling down her face.

I spring from my chair and wrap her in my arms, pressing her soft body against mine. Fuck! She is real.

"I'm sorry I left you, baby," I whisper in her ear. "It will never happen again. I promise."

"I should never have doubted you, Jax. I know that you would never betray me like that."

I close my eyes and squeeze her tighter as the relief washes over me. When I finally release her from my embrace, she's smiling up at me. Suddenly the reality of her being here with me instead of safe in her father's mansion hits me.

I frown at her. "Did you come here alone?"

She rolls her eyes and despite where we are, it makes me want to spank her ass. "No. I had my own personal security detail." She indicates her head toward the door. Alejandro is standing there with a sleeping Matthias in his arms.

"Now that you're with Jax, I'm going to get this guy to bed. Okay, *mija*?"

153

"Yes, Papi. I'll see you all in the morning."

"In the morning," he replies with a nod of his head.

"All?" I say to her as he walks out of the room.

"My mom and the twins came too. As well as Hugo, Raoul and another eight of his men. It's like a whole family trip," she says as she bites on her lip. "I'm sorry. I did ask Molly and she said it would be okay for them to stay at the house."

"Matthias *and* the twins at the house? Molly will be over the freaking moon," I say with a laugh, thinking of my aunt and her fussing. "I'm surprised your dad left LA with everything that's going on though."

"Hmm. Well, when I reminded him that the only man who could get us out of this mess was in Dallas, and that said man could work his magic from anywhere in the world, he decided that this is where he should be right now too."

"You're incredible, have I ever told you that?"

Her cheeks flush pink. "No," she whispers.

"I'm pretty sure I have, but I'm telling you again anyways." I kiss her forehead and she leans into me, wrapping her arms around my waist and sending all kinds of signals to my groin area that I could do without right now.

"You're more than incredible, Jax," she whispers. "You and Matthias are everything to me. Wherever you are is where I am. You don't get to rush off trying to save the world on your own anymore, even when I'm being an ass and tell you to leave. You got that?"

"Yes, ma'am."

She looks up at me and she looks so fucking beautiful that I can hardly believe that she's mine. "I love you," she whispers.

I don't say the words back to her. I show her instead, sealing my lips over hers and sliding my tongue into her mouth. I kiss her like I might never get the chance to again, until she's clawing at my back and whimpering into my mouth and I'm wondering whether there is a supply closet somewhere I could take her to.

"You two wanna get a room?" a voice croaks behind us.

I break our kiss and grin at her and she wipes her mouth. "We just got busted by your dad," she giggles.

"Better than being busted by yours." I wink at her before I spin around and see my father trying to reach for the water beside his bed.

"Here, let me get that," I say as I hand him the plastic cup.

He accepts it gratefully and takes a few sips before handing it back.

"I wasn't drinking, son," he says as he looks up at me.

"I know."

Tears fill his eyes and I have to look away, but Lucia is by my side, squeezing my hand reassuringly. "It's so lovely to see you awake, Harvey," she says with a huge smile. He grins back at her. I mean she's pretty hard not to smile at.

"They told me it was you," he coughs.

I sit beside his bed. "What exactly did they say?"

He licks his dry, cracked lips. "Jackson wants you gone, o-old man. He paid us good money to do the j-job."

"What?" Lucia gasps, covering her mouth with her hand. I forgot she doesn't know about this latest development. She was too pissed at me to allow me to tell her.

Fuckers! "I didn't..." I shake my head.

"I know that, son," he laughs and coughs at the same time. "If that were true, you're man enough to do it yourself."

"I can't believe somebody would say... that it was you?" Lucia looks between me and my father and then her eyes settle on my face. "Why?"

"To get me thrown in jail? To cause a bigger rift between me and my family here. I don't know yet, angel, but I'm damn sure going to find out." I turn back to my father. "Can you describe them? How many of them were there?"

His eyelids flutter closed and he takes a deep breath.

"Jax, he's exhausted," Lucia whispers.

"Yeah, I know," I agree with a sigh.

"You want me to give you two some time alone?"

I shake my head. "No. You can hear this too."

I have so many questions about what happened that night, but his eyelids are already drooping again. I know that if he knew who did this, he would tell me straight away. That doesn't mean he can't point me in the right direction, but I guess I can wait a few more hours.

I take a deep breath before I speak. "I did think you were drinking," I admit. "It was the first thing I thought when they told me you'd been at that bar."

"I know."

"I know why you were really there though. To buy that crib?"

"Yeah," he nods as his eyes flutter closed. "Was gonna fix it up real nice for them babies of yours."

"I'll find you another one to fix up if you'd like?"

"Uh-huh," he murmurs.

"Maybe one day you can rock your grand-babies to sleep in it too?"

His eyes are closed and he doesn't speak, but a single tear rolls down his cheek. My hand is on his bed and he reaches for it, curling his fingers around mine. I don't think I've allowed him to touch me since I was a little kid, but I hold his hand in mine until he drifts back off to sleep.

"DID you mean what you said in there?" Lucia asks as we walk down the hallway to the parking lot. My father is asleep and we'll call back to see him in the morning. "About your dad and our babies?"

"Yes," I say, lifting her hand to my lips and kissing her knuckles.

"You'll really let him be a part of our lives, Jax?" she asks, her eyes shining with happiness.

"Yes. As long as he stays sober and that's okay with you."

She throws her arms around my neck. "It's better than okay," she squeals, peppering my jaw with kisses and earning us a stern glare from one of the passing nurses.

Which reminds me of our other problem. The fact that someone has videos of my wife being fucked makes my blood boil. But, just for tonight I want to forget about all of our problems. She's right here in my arms and she's mine.

I pick her up and toss her over my shoulder caveman style before I slap her ass, making the disapproving nurse's eyes almost roll out of her head.

CHAPTER 24
LUCIA

As the main house comes into view, I can't help but smile. Even after all that's happened, I do love this place. This ranch has always felt like home to me, from the first moment I stepped foot on the soil here. I can see two of my father's security personnel are stationed outside the house, and I know there are at least two more on watch nearby.

"A guy I know has a security company in the city. I have two men patrolling the ranch perimeter at night until I get a better security system set up. We're getting some more ranch hands in during the day too, to make sure all the fences are properly maintained. The barn is secure, angel. It always has been as long as we're inside it," Jax says to me, his face full of concern. "But I understand if you'd rather stay at the main house for now."

I reach for his hand and lace my fingers through his. "I love our barn. Even after what happened there. It's ours and it always will be. Besides, I feel safe anywhere with you, Jax."

"You want to go home then, angel?"

"Yes, please," I say with a smile and the way he smiles back at me makes me almost melt into a puddle on the seat.

As soon as the truck comes to a stop outside the barn, Jax jumps out and runs to the passenger side, opening the door for me. Taking his hand, I step out and as soon as I do, he hoists me over his shoulder like he did at the hospital.

"Hey," I giggle as I beat my fists against his fine ass. "I can walk."

He ignores me and carries me straight into the house, locks the door behind us and takes me up the stairs, flicking on the light switch before he sets me down on my feet. I look into his deep brown eyes, but suddenly an image of Shannon's legs wrapped around his waist and his head buried in her neck while he was fucking her invades my thoughts and it makes me falter.

He sees it too. He slides a hand to the back of my neck. "What is it, angel?"

"I can't stop picturing you with her... with Shannon," my voice trembles.

I feel the deep sigh rolling through his chest.

"I recognized that look on her face, Jax. It's the same one I have when you're with me."

He narrows his eyes at me. "No, Luce." His hand slides from my neck and down over my ribs until he reaches the edge of my sweater, gripping it with both hands, he starts to work it off and over my head. I lift my arms in compliance, only breaking our gaze when the soft cashmere is over my eyes. "That picture was just two people fucking." His hands skate down my sides to the waistband of my jeans as he presses his lips against my ear. "Two bodies responding to each other on a purely physical level." He tugs open the button. "What you and I do is so much more."

"Jax," I shiver as he slides down my zipper before fisting his hands into the denim as he slowly pushes the fabric over my hips.

"You are the only woman I've ever loved." He kisses my neck. "The only woman I've ever wanted to marry." One of his hands coasts over my lower abdomen. "The only woman I have ever wanted to fuck a baby into."

Tears prick at my eyes. "I know," I whisper.

He stops kissing my neck and wipes a stray tear with the pad of his thumb. "You are everything, Lucia. I may have fucked other women, but there has been no-one before you and there will be no-one after you. You are it for me, angel."

The deep, soothing timbre of his voice permeates every cell of my body, making warmth pool in my core.

He drops to his knees and presses a soft kiss on my stomach as he starts to pull my jeans down over my thighs and calves. He takes off my sneakers without untying the laces, followed by my socks and jeans. When he stands tall again, he glides his hands over my back, unhooking my bra with one deft flick of his fingertips before he pulls it off my arms. I am in awe of how quickly this man can get me naked. No doubt another skill he's honed over the years. *Stop it, Lucia!*

I will all thoughts of him with other women to leave my head as his hands slide over my hips until he's palming my ass. Then he lifts me, wrapping my legs around his waist and walking us to the bed before he lays me down on it. His hot mouth is on my neck, covering my throat with kisses that send pleasure skittering up my spine.

It's not enough though. I need to feel his skin against mine. "Why are you still wearing all of your clothes?" I whisper.

"Because you haven't taken them off me, baby," he says with a smile.

I reach for the edge of his t-shirt and he helps me to pull it off over his head before he lies over me again. My pebbled nipples press against his hard chest and when he moves, he causes a delicious friction there that makes my toes curl.

"Jax," I moan as I rake my nails down his muscular back, making him shudder.

He nips at my shoulder in response, making me moan softly as his lips trail lower, dusting over my breasts and my stomach until he reaches the edge of my panties. Hooking his fingers into the waistband, he pulls them off quickly before tossing them onto the floor, but all the while his hot mouth is on me. Sucking and licking my stomach and my thighs, but purposely avoiding that spot where I need him the most.

"I want your mouth on me. Please?" I beg him.

He moves lower, swirling his tongue over my clit and making me arch my back in pleasure.

"My good girl, always ready for me," he murmurs against my skin before he pushes himself up onto his knees, unfastening his belt and sliding it off.

Wet heat sears between my thighs and I whimper, making him laugh softly.

"Maybe later, baby," he says as he throws the belt onto the floor. He unfastens his jeans before pulling out his cock which glistens with precum. He wraps his hand around his shaft. "See how hard you make me, Luce?"

My breath catches in my throat as he leans over me again, resting his weight on his forearms. Every cell in my body is screaming for him. My pussy aches with a deep need to be filled. When he presses the tip of his cock against my entrance, I moan so loudly, I'm sure everyone in the main house must have heard.

I wrap my legs around him, trying to pull him all the way inside me, but he resists me, teasing me until my need grows into desperation.

His lips dust over the shell of my ear. "No-one ever made me as hard as you do. I might have fucked a lot of women, Luce, but I never did this with anyone but you." When the final word has left his lips, he sinks deep inside me, showing me exactly what he means. "Jesus, fuck!" he hisses.

The relief at being full of him sends waves of euphoria rolling through my body.

"Oh, fuck!" I groan as I cling to him, not wanting him to pull out again.

I feel his thick cock throbbing inside me as he fills me so completely. So perfectly — as though we were made for each other. Then he slides out slowly, so I feel every single millimeter of him as he pulses against my inner walls. "How do you make it this good, Jax?"

"It's not me, angel. It's all you. You make it good," he growls in my ear as he fucks me so deliciously deeply and slowly that I feel like I'm on another plane of existence.

He doesn't just make me come, he gives me the longest, most intense orgasm I've ever experienced in my life. It builds quickly, but it doesn't detonate and fizzle out. Every time I reach the edge, I don't fall back down and come up again. Instead another edge stretches out before me, and on and on, until tears are rolling down my cheeks and my nails are sinking into Jax's shoulders as I beg him to stop and keep going at the same time.

"I got you, angel. Just let go," he groans in my ear as he continues his slow, rhythmic movements.

"I can't," I whimper. I don't want this feeling to end but my body craves the release. I need that final explosion of starlight and ecstasy to settle into my bones.

"Yeah, you can. Come for me," he commands and I couldn't hold on any longer no matter how hard I tried. It's like my body is hardwired to obey him.

"Oh, Jax!" I cry out, clinging to him as he rolls his hips against me, rubbing at the sensitive spot inside me as he grinds out his own climax.

"Fuck, Luce," he breathes in my ear as he slows to a stop.

I gasp for breath as tiny specks of light flutter behind my eyelids. The places where are bodies are joined are slick with cum and when he pulls out of me, the wet popping sound is so loud it makes me giggle softly.

"You soaked us, angel," he whispers as he rolls onto his back, wrapping his arms around me and taking me with him so that I'm lying on his chest.

"It was your fault though."

"Damn right it was," he laughs softly as he runs a hand through my hair.

"I'm sorry I doubted you, Jax. Even for a second."

He grabs my jaw, tilting my head so we can look into each other's eyes. "I know, Luce. I know that it's hard not to trust what's right in front of your eyes."

"I need you to know that I trust you, Jax. I do. It was just a shock and I-I," I stammer.

He grips my jaw tighter. "Stop apologizing. You reacted how anyone would, Luce. The fact that you believe me and you're here now is all that matters."

"What if it had been the other way around? If you'd seen photographs of me with another guy?"

"I'd have lost my shit and cut off his cock before I asked any questions," he says with a scowl.

I roll my eyes and shake my head.

"Hey, at least I admit it, right?" he gives me a wicked grin.

"So, you wouldn't even listen to me? Because you know the pictures would be faked too. You know I would never do that?"

He laughs softly before giving me a quick kiss on the lips. "I know, baby. I'm just teasing you. I would lose my shit though. But I'm sure you could calm me down." His hand slides to my ass and he squeezes.

"I could, huh?"

"You could make me do anything you damn well want to, and you know it," he says, all the laughter gone from his face now. He stares at me, his dark brown eyes full of fire.

"I didn't know that," I admit.

Almost before I've finished the last word, he flips me over, pinning me flat to the mattress. "Don't play innocent with me, Lucia," he growls, pressing his groin against me. *How the hell is he hard again already?* "You know exactly what you do to me."

I trace my fingertips over his jawline. He is so goddamn handsome and intense. I love him so much I feel like my heart might burst. "And what's that cowboy?" I whisper.

"You have me in the palm of your hand. I am nothing without you, angel. I would kneel at your feet if you asked me to. I would do anything to make you happy."

He rubs his nose along the column of my throat, inhaling deeply and making me shiver.

"You make me happier than I ever even imagined was possible." I slide my fingers through his hair, pulling his head back so I can look at him again. "No more time apart, okay? Wherever you are is where Matthias and I belong."

"Deal," he says before he seals his lips over mine.

As he's kissing me, he turns us onto our sides and hooks my leg over his waist. Then he slides deep inside me again and I moan into his mouth.

"This is where I belong, angel," he breathes as he starts to fuck me again. "I can't keep the fuck out of you."

Pleasure rolls through my core as he finds the perfect angle to rub my clit while he fucks me. Then he sucks a finger into his mouth and grins at me because we both know where that's going.

"God, Jax," I whimper as he slides it into my ass a few seconds later.

"I love filling you up, baby," he groans softly. "I wonder if

I'm going to fill you with a baby too when I pump all my cum into you?"

"Are you going to kiss our child with that filthy mouth?" I gasp as a wave of pleasure rocks me.

"I kiss our other one with it, so..." he replies with a wink. "Now stop talking and let me fuck you."

I melt into him, pulling his face back to mine so I can kiss him again.

CHAPTER 25
JAX

When I wake the following morning, with her perfect ass nestled against me, I bury my face in her hair and smile. This right here is where we both belong. I can't wait to show Matthias his room here in the barn too. Having them both here is exactly what I need.

She wiggles her ass against my cock and it twitches against her. I wrap my arm tighter around her and kiss her neck, making her squirm.

"Morning, cowboy. I see you're already up," she giggles.

"I'm always up around you, angel." I slide my hand between her thighs and she moans. "You think we have time before breakfast?" I whisper in her ear.

"Yes, definitely," she breathes as I rub her clit softly.

"And what exactly do we have time for, baby?" I tease her, because she knows how much I love it when she asks for what she wants.

"We have time for your fingers in me. Your hot mouth on my pussy and then some super lazy morning sex," she purrs.

"You want soft and slow this morning?" I murmur as I push her onto her back and pepper kisses over her body.

166

"Uh-huh," she whimpers as I slide two fingers inside her.

"Fucking soaking, baby. Just how I like you."

I thrust deeper and watch in satisfaction as her eyes roll back into her head. "Forget slow," she pants, her breathing already ragged as I finger fuck her. "Just give me everything you got, cowboy."

"Everything?"

She rakes her nails through my hair and pulls. "Everything!"

I GAVE her everything I had twice over before we showered and locked up the barn to head to the main house. We pass a few of Alejandro's men on the way and they nod to Lucia and I in greeting. Unlike the security I hired, these are Alejandro and his family's personal protection and I accept that they'll be here as long as he, Alana and the twins are. The company I hired don't set foot near the house. I want them in the shadows. Our place in LA is a fortress and while I accept that's the way things have to be there, I want things to be different here.

When we get to the house, we walk into the kitchen and I swear the smile on my aunt Molly's face could light every room in this place.

Lucia's twin brothers are sitting on the floor with Blue playing with dinosaurs. Matthias is helping my aunt make pancakes while Hugo stands beside her chatting. Alana and Alejandro are sitting at the kitchen table drinking coffee and smiling at each other like there is nobody else in the room. I know that this is the kind of atmosphere in a house that my aunt always longed for but never had.

"Morning," Lucia says and everyone looks up and greets us.

"Hey guys," Matthias says as he turns around and smiles. I

head straight over to him. I've missed this kid so much. I hate that I left without saying goodbye yesterday.

"Hey, buddy," I say when I reach him, leaning down and kissing the top of his head.

"Hey, Dad," he holds up the wooden spoon in his hand, covered in chocolate. "You want to lick the sauce?"

"No. You do it."

He grins at me before he sticks out his tongue and licks the spoon clean. I love that he has no idea of the drama going on around him and I make a silent promise to him that he never will.

"You want to see your new bedroom at our house later?"

"Yeah," he squeals. "I wanted to come look this morning, but Molly told me you'd be sleeping."

I look at my aunt and smile gratefully.

"Can I sleep there with you and Momma tonight?"

"Of course you can. It's gonna be our house when we come visit the ranch now."

"Cool! Can we ride the horses too?" he asks, and I laugh. This kid lives his life at one hundred mile an hour.

"Not today, buddy. I have to go see my Dad for a while, and then I have to do some work with your Papa."

"Can I come see Harvey too?"

I look over at Lucia. I'm not sure if seeing him in that state is the best idea, but she nods her approval. "Sure, buddy. For a while."

"Yes!" He does a mini fist pump and then he unexpectedly throws his arms around me. "Momma said that we're staying here with you until Harvey is better and you can come home with us? Are we?"

I hug him tight to me. "Yeah. I'll miss you too much if you go back to LA without me."

"I'd miss you too, Dad," he whispers. "Momma doesn't play Avengers like you do."

Fuck! This kid gets me right in the feels.

"Matthias, put your father down. I need to talk to him real quick," Alejandro says, getting up from the table and heading out into the hallway. He signals me to follow him.

"I'll be back for some of those pancakes and chocolate sauce as soon as they're ready," I say, giving him a final kiss on the head before I follow his grandfather out of the room. As I pass her, Lucia, reaches out and squeezes my hand while she remains deep in conversation with her mom. I lift it to my lips and kiss her fingertips before I head out after Alejandro.

When I walk into the hallway, he's leaning against the wall with his hands stuffed into his pockets.

"Thank you for bringing them out here," I say as I cross my arms over my chest.

"Well, it seems my daughter can be very persuasive when she wants to be, but I guess you already know that?"

"I sure do."

"And anyway, where else would they be, amigo? They're your family."

I stare at him, my eyes searching his face and waiting for the inevitable but that must be a part of that sentence. He and I haven't been the same since I started dating his daughter, and even though I understand that, it still hurts like a motherfucker.

"Fuck, you're *my* family too, Jax. You always have been..." He runs a hand through his thick hair. "I'm still trying to figure how we fit now that you're married to my daughter, but I need you to know that I have always got your back. Apart from Alana, I trust you more than anyone in this world."

Fuck! This was not what I was expecting at all. "Thanks, amigo. That means a lot."

"Yeah, well, I know you've had some shit going on with

Harvey and everything, and if that had been me, you'd have been moving heaven and earth to fix it. Alana, the boys and I can stay here as long as you need us, amigo. We will find the *hijo de putas* who are trying to fuck with you and make them regret that they even know your name." He steps forward and wraps me in a bear hug. "Just tell me what you need, okay?"

"Breakfast's ready," Matthias shouts, interrupting the moment.

"Looks like we better get back in there," Alejandro says with a flash of his eyebrows.

"Yeah, and thanks, amigo. It means a lot to have you at my side."

"Where else would I be?" he says with a wink and then he walks back into the kitchen.

I follow him but I hover in the doorway for a few seconds. It seems like my entire world is in this one room. I feel a pang of guilt as I think about my father lying in his hospital bed and I realize perhaps there is room for him in it too.

Now that Alejandro is here, we can focus on finding out who attacked Harvey and who was behind those damn videos. I have a hunch that when we follow the different trails, they'll lead us to the same people.

CHAPTER 26
LUCIA

After the breakfast things are cleared away, we settle the boys in the den watching cartoons with Hugo while Jax, my parents, Molly and I sit around the table to figure out the fastest way out of the mess we all seem to be stuck in the middle of.

"So, let me get this straight," Molly says, brushing a thick lock of blonde hair from her eyes. "Not only did somebody beat your father half to death and tell him that you were responsible, they also videoed you and Lucia with another woman, black-mailed Lucia's father and then tried to make it look like you were conspiring with the other woman to get your hands on the five million? Is that about it?"

I gasp in a breath. She pretty much nailed it. Everything that happened does seem to point to Jax being the real target here. "Don't forget the picture of Jax and Shannon too," I add. "That was taken at least a year and half ago."

Molly frowns but she nods her head in agreement. "You think it was someone we know? Here in Dallas?"

"Well, whoever took those pictures of me and Shannon had to have known about the two of us…"

"It wasn't exactly a secret, honey," Molly says with a shake of her head. "The whole town knew about you two."

"Could Shannon be behind this?" I ask.

"That's exactly what I was thinking," my mom adds with a nod.

"She couldn't have taken the picture of the two of them though," my father says.

"No, but she could have had someone else take it," I offer.

Jax nods his head. "She also has a crib like the one my dad went looking for on the night he was attacked, and he placed the ad in her mom's store, so she knew all about it."

"But she's happy with Ed now," Molly says with a frown. "Why would she do that?"

"Beats me," Jax rubs a hand over his jaw.

"Who is Ed?" my father asks.

"Ed Sawyer. Local vet. Moved here four or five years ago. He and Shannon got together about eighteen months ago..."

"Before or after that photograph was taken?" I ask.

"After," Jax insists.

My father looks between Jax and Molly. "And where was he before he came here?"

"I have no idea," Molly says with a shake of her head.

"I'll find out by the end of the day," Jax says.

"No, I can deal with that," my father replies.

Jax arches an eyebrow at him. "You sure?"

"I think I've learned enough from you over the years to find out a little more about Ed. Besides, I need you tracking that money, because I see why we're looking into the possibility of Shannon or Ed being involved here, I mean jealousy is the oldest motive there is, right? But, I feel like this is bigger than that. This is deeper than a spurned ex-lover or a jealous husband."

"I agree, amigo," Jax says with a nod. "There's something bigger going on here."

"Where is that money right now?" my father asks him.

"As we suspected, sitting in offshore accounts. It bounced through eight in total and now it's spread across four," Jax replies.

"But you can trace those accounts eventually?"

"Yes. But it will take a few days."

"We need to find whoever has those videos too," I remind them. "They could still be right here in town. I mean if they've been here all this time anyway."

"Yes, we do," my father agrees. "Who has access to this ranch, Molly?"

"Well, it's private property, but it's huge and I suppose anyone could sneak in here under the cover of night. We don't have fancy security systems because we've never really needed em."

"Yeah, well that's gonna change," Jax mutters.

"But you have workers here, right?" my father goes on. "And regular visitors."

"Yes. We have ranch hands. I've had the same six for the past three years, two of them for much longer than that. Four of them live in the bunk house and the other two live with their wives and babies in town. We have delivery trucks. A horse trainer. Shannon and Ed also come here a lot to check on the horses. She's a veterinary nurse, that's how she and Ed met. They were friends for a long time."

"Well, we already have Shannon and Ed in our crosshairs. What about the ranch hands? They have free access to the whole property, right? Any of them a problem?"

"No," Molly insists with a shake of her head. "They all came to work here straight from high school. They're good boys."

"We can't rule anyone out, Molly," Jax says to her and she sighs but she nods her head.

"I'll go speak to them this morning while you're at the hospital," my father says.

Jax arches an eyebrow at him. "They're just kids, amigo."

"So? I can be diplomatic," he insists.

"Kind of like using a jackhammer to crack a peanut though, Papi," I chuckle.

My mom laughs softly too. "I have to agree with our daughter on this one."

"I'll take Molly with me. She'll keep me in line, right?"

My mom puts her hand on his shoulder. "I still think there's something not right about Ed. How about you and I look into him, and Hugo can go with Molly to speak to the ranch hands. If they did see anything that might help, then we don't want to scare them off, do we? And, whilst you are the most incredible man I know," she places her hand on his cheek, "you're also kind of terrifying."

He shrugs his shoulders, pleased with her assessment of him. "Fine. Hugo and Molly deal with the ranch hands."

Molly's cheeks flush slightly but she nods her agreement.

"You and I will look into Ed and Shannon while Jax and Lucia are at the hospital. Anything else you need me to do, amigo?" my father asks Jax, making me smile.

This is his way of making things right between them, of showing him that he would still do anything for him. I have to admit, the guilt I feel at coming between the two of them still weighs heavy on me. But as they sit across from each other now, working together, it's clear they have nothing but love and respect for one another, and it makes my heart swell in my chest.

"If you get time, you could look into those photographs of Toni and me. If you can figure out the restaurant, then you could get their CCTV and cross reference the dates to prove they're fake."

"We know they're fake. We don't need proof, Jax," I tell him and my father nods in agreement.

Jax sighs deeply, taking my hand and squeezing it in his before he turns back to my father. "See if you can dig up some CCTV from anywhere in town that might help then? Or better still talk to the bar owner," he suggests. "Now, if there was ever a situation where a jackhammer was needed to crack a peanut, that would be it."

"Why? Is he an asshole?" my father asks.

"Kind of. When I went to speak to him, the sheriff arrived not five minutes after, which was a hell of a coincidence if you ask me. And that guy is looking for an excuse to toss me into a cell, so I had to back off."

"I'll drop by and see what he has to say then."

"Be careful," my mom warns him. "That goes for all of you," she adds as she looks at the rest of us. "We have no idea who we're dealing with yet, but we do know they're willing to go to extreme lengths to get what they want."

"I always am, princess," my father says before kissing her forehead and making her blush. I swear they are like a pair of lovestruck teenagers.

"We will be, Mom," I assure her.

A LITTLE OVER AN HOUR LATER, I'm walking down the hospital corridor with Jax's hand in mine while he carries an overly excited Matthias in his arms.

"Does this kid ever stop talking," he whispers in my ear while Matthias goes on talking about how cool it is to have his very own bedroom at the barn house and whether he thinks Harvey will allow Blue to sleep there sometimes.

"Nope. You already know that, cowboy. You sure you want to add another one into the mix so soon?"

He lets go of my hand and wraps his arm around my waist instead.

"One hundred fucking percent," he growls and my insides flutter.

"Are you guys even listening to me?" Matthias says with a sigh, and I realize somewhere in his incessant chatter he must have asked us a question.

Jax winks at me before he turns his face toward our son. "Of course we are buddy."

"So can we just get our own puppy instead, a Dallas dog?" Matthias asks with a cheeky grin.

"A Dallas dog?" I ask.

"Yeah, for when we're here. A puppy just like Blue?"

"But won't he miss us when we're in LA?" Jax says. "And wouldn't you miss him too?"

Matthias's face falls. "Oh, yeah," he whispers.

Jax tickles him, making him laugh again. "So, if we did get a puppy like Blue, he'd have to live with us in LA and Dallas, wouldn't he?"

At this, Matthias squeals with delight. "Yes, he would. Can we get a puppy then? Please, Momma?"

I roll my eyes at my husband. "Did you just promise our son a puppy?"

"No," he grins at me. "I said if we got a dog, is all."

"We'll see, munchkin," I tell him.

"Okay," he pouts and Jax whispers something in his ear that makes him giggle.

"You just promised him a puppy, didn't you?" I nudge him in the ribs.

"I would never," he says with a chuckle as he pulls me tighter.

"Is this how it's going to be, cowboy? You teaming up with our kids against me?"

He gives me a kiss on the cheek. "I will always be on your team, angel. Promise."

"Why is Harvey in here, Dad?" Matthias asks as he looks around at the strange surroundings. I realize he's never been in a hospital before, not even when he was born. He arrived quickly and unexpectedly at my parent's house back in LA.

"He got hurt, buddy. But he's going to be just fine and he'll be able to come home real soon."

"How did he get hurt?" he asks, his eyes wide and innocent as he looks into his father's face. God, I want so much to protect him from everything that is bad in this world.

"He was doing something nice for me and somebody didn't like it so they hurt him."

"But why?"

Jax looks to me and I nod for him to go on. I would love for our son to think that the world is only full of good and kind people, but the reality is that it's not. In our family, he's going to learn that sooner than other kids, but he needs to know that not everybody is a good person. "Sometimes people hurt other people. Because they're scared, or greedy, or just plain mean. Or maybe because they hurt someone they care about."

"Did Harvey hurt someone?"

I feel the tension in Jax at that question. Harvey hurt him and his mom so badly. "No, buddy," he whispers. "And your mom and I would never let anyone hurt you. You know that, right?"

"Yeah," he rolls his eyes.

"Good," Jax puts him on his feet as we reach Harvey's room. "Now there's gonna be a whole lot of machines in here and things that you've not seen before, but they're all just making Harvey better, okay?"

"Okay," Matthias smiles as he curls his fingers around Jax's.

I follow the two of them into the room. Harvey is awake and the smile on his face when he sees Matthias almost lights up the whole room.

"Look out, here comes trouble," Harvey chuckles as he beckons my son toward him.

Matthias runs to the bed and clambers on.

"Be careful," I shout.

"Leave him be. He's fine," Harvey insists.

"Does your face hurt?" Matthias asks as he gets himself comfortable on the bed.

"Naw," Harvey shakes his head. He looks so much more alert that he did in the early hours of this morning.

"When are you coming home?"

"Soon as I can. Maybe a few days. Hey, have you been looking after Blue for me?"

"Well, I only got here yesterday, but yeah, I took him out for his pee this morning, and then I helped Aunt Molly with his food. He slept by my bed too. I think he's kinda sad. He misses you."

"I miss him too," Harvey says as tears prick his eyes. "But he has you here now, so I'm sure he won't be too sad."

"Hey, I made you something," Matthias says as he reaches into the pocket of his jeans and pulls out a pebble.

"Did you know about that?" Jax whispers to me.

"Nope," I say, watching intently as Harvey examines the small rock. It has something painted on it in red, but I can't see it from here. But suddenly Harvey's eyes are brimming with tears and he puts a hand over his face.

"My nana helped me make it. It's okay if I call you that, right?" Matthias asks.

Harvey's chest starts heaving as his body is wracked with sobs.

"What the fuck does that say?" Jax mutters as we both walk to the bed.

Harvey is clutching the stone in his hand while Matthias stares at him.

"Did I do something wrong, Dad?" he asks Jax who puts a hand on his shoulder.

"No, son. But, what did you paint on your rock?"

Harvey wipes his eyes and opens his mouth to speak but his words are choked by another sob.

"Grandpa," Matthias whispers. "Harvey is your daddy, and you're my daddy, so he's my grandpa like Papa, right?"

"That's right," Jax replies before he plants a soft kiss on the top of our son's head.

Harvey takes Matthias's hand in his. "That is the best gift I've ever gotten." he sniffs. "Thank you."

At this praise, Matthias beams proudly and I watch the three of them. Three generations. I'm happy that my son has another grandparent in his life. As far as I'm concerned, the more people that love him, the better. But mostly I'm happy that Jax is allowing his father back into his life. He deserves to be surrounded with people who love him too.

WHEN MATTHIAS HAS ASKED Harvey at least two dozen questions and told him all about his and Jax's plan to get a puppy just like Blue, I take him with me to get him a juice box and the rest of us a coffee. I know that Jax needs to speak to him without Matthias around.

"That was a really sweet thing you did for Grandpa Harvey," I say as I hold his little hand in mine and we walk through the hallways to find the cafeteria.

"I wanted to make him something he could keep forever," he says with a proud smile. "Rocks last forever, you know?"

"They do, huh?"

"Yup."

"You know what else lasts forever?" I ask him.

"What?" he blinks up at me.

"A momma's kisses," I pick him up and smother his face with kisses, making him giggle.

"No they don't," he squeals.

"Oh yes they do." I insist. "Once a momma kisses her child, she creates a special kind of magic. You can still feel it forever."

"You can?" he asks, his eyes wide.

"Yup. Whenever you want to feel your momma's kiss, you just close your eyes and put your hand right here," I place his little hand over his heart. "Then you remember real hard and you'll feel it."

He scrunches his eyes tightly closed and I press a feather light kiss on his cheek. "Wow. I do feel it," he says.

I hug him tighter and smile. Yep, I could definitely handle a few more of these.

CHAPTER 27

JAX

"That sheriff was in here asking questions again this morning," my father says as he struggles to push himself into a more upright position in the bed with his busted hand.

"Here let me help you, old man," I say as I tuck my arm under his and hoist him up.

"Less of the old. I'm in the prime of my life here."

"Yeah, you look it," I laugh as I sit back down.

"He's itching to throw you in jail, son."

"What did he say?"

"Asking me all kinds of questions about you. Why you don't visit more often. What you do back in LA. Is it true that you and I don't get along. Did I think you held a grudge for all my drinking and pushing your mom away."

"What did you tell him?"

"I told him that I didn't remember anything about the night of the attack, and that anything else was none of his goddamn business."

His loyalty to me almost makes me choke up. "Do you remember anything?"

"I waited in the bar for thirty minutes. I saw a few faces I recognized and I said hi to Jimmy Bird. We spoke about some new mares he just bought. Then I figured the guy with the crib wasn't showing and I left. I was walking to my truck and they came out of nowhere. They just started beating on me and telling me that you wanted me gone."

"Can you describe any of them?"

He shakes his head sadly. "Not really, son. It was dark. I had my arms over my head, trying to protect myself. But you know, they never went for my head. Now ain't that strange? They said you wanted me gone. And the easiest way to kill a man is a blow to the head. So, why not do that? You break a man's arms and legs, well he's gonna be in a whole lotta pain, but he's not going to die."

I nod my agreement. "You don't think they wanted you dead then?"

"Nope. I think they wanted you in jail. Who the hell have you pissed off that much, son?" he asks, but he's grinning at me.

"Way too many people to count, Dad," I admit.

"You know, one of them had a red cap on with something on it, though. Motor Oil or something?" he squeezes his eyes shut as though he's desperately trying to remember. "I'm sorry I'm not a lot of help."

"Yeah, well I'm sorry I got you stuck in the middle of all this."

He stares at me and sucks in a deep breath before he speaks. "I haven't been a part of your life for such a long time."

"I know..." I start to say but he holds up a hand and I stop talking. I got to say my piece to him and I suppose I should allow him the same.

"And I didn't deserve to be, son..." he says, his voice thick with emotion. "But all I could think about when those assholes were beating the hell out of me, was that you never knew how truly sorry I was for everything. It is my greatest regret in life that I didn't get sober for you and your mom. And now, I get to tell you to your face that I'm sorry." He holds a hand over his heart. "That even though I have no right to be, I am so proud of the man you've become."

"Thanks, Dad," I whisper.

He nods his head and a tear rolls down his face. "I thought I'd never hear you call me that again. I'd let those punks kick my ass every damn day to hear you say that word."

I don't speak because I can't. There is so much hurt and pain between us. So many things that have been left unsaid for too long. Right now, words aren't needed. We both know.

So, we sit in silence, easy in each other's company while we wait for Lucia and Matthias to return.

WE LEFT my father resting and with a supply of candy and comics that would keep a kindergarten class busy for a week. He loves comics. I didn't know that about him, but Matthias did. He's an amazing kid and the fact that he calls me Dad is a fucking honor. I see now why it means so much to my own father that I finally call him dad again. In my head, he's always been Dad, but I refused to give him the satisfaction of saying it to his face for so long.

As we reach my truck, a huge SUV pulls up beside us. The window rolls down to reveal Alejandro's face. I mean, of course he hired a giant black SUV. No truck for him.

"I have a lead, amigo," he says and then he opens the door and climbs out.

"From the bar?"

"Hmm," he flashes his eyebrows at me. "The owner was a little more receptive without his buddy, the sheriff around."

"And your boot on his face," Raoul adds as he climbs out of the back seat.

Alejandro shrugs before he stoops and picks up his grandson. "You want to go back to the house with your mom? I think that dog needs a walk. And Tomás and Dario are desperate for you to show them around the place."

"Yeah," Matthias agrees. "What about you, Papa?"

"I just got to go somewhere with your Dad, but we'll be back before dinner. Okay?"

"Okay," he agrees and then hands Matthias to Raoul, who straps him into the child seat in the back.

"Your mom is still looking into Ed back at the house, but she could use a little help," he says to Lucia.

"I'd rather come help you two," she says, popping an eyebrow.

"No, angel," I say, pulling her close and kissing her forehead. "I need you and Matthias safe. Please go home."

"We're only going to scare a few red-necks, *mija*, we'll be just fine," her father assures her.

She rolls her eyes. "Please be careful. Both of you," she hugs each of us in turn before she climbs into the back of the car with our son.

Alejandro and I watch the SUV pull out of the parking lot. "Am I gonna get my suit dirty in your beat up truck?" he asks me.

"Hey, Darlene might be old, but she's clean," I tell him.

"Darlene? You named your truck Darlene?"

"Yup."

He frowns at me in disgust. "Who the fuck are you and what have you done with my best buddy?" he asks with a shake of his head as he starts walking toward the old Ford I drive when I'm down here. "I mean in LA you wear good suits and drive a fucking Goliath. I mean it's a truck, but it's a beast."

"And your point is?" I ask as I open the driver door.

"Here you wear jeans and cowboy boots and drive an old jalopy that you've named Darlene."

I laugh at the look of horror on his face, but before I can come up with a snappy comeback, the sound of someone shouting my name makes us both turn.

"Jackson," she shouts again as she jogs across the parking lot.

"Who the fuck is that?" Alejandro snarls.

"Shannon."

"Ah, I didn't recognize her with her clothes on."

I narrow my eyes at him. "Just don't."

He holds his hands up in surrender.

"I've been wanting to speak to you," she says, slightly out of breath when she reaches me.

"Here I am."

"I kind of wanted to catch you on your own." She looks over at Alejandro who crosses his arms over his chest and glares at her.

"There's nothing you can't say to me in front of him," I tell her. It's the truth, but also he would roast my balls on a skewer if I asked for a minute alone with her.

She licks her lips as she looks at him and then sighs. "I did something kind of stupid," she finally says.

Well, now she has both of our attention. "How stupid?"

"Like, I may have gotten you into some trouble, stupid. I'm sorry, Jackson, you know how sometimes my mouth runs away with me."

"What did you do, Shan?"

She chews on her bottom lip, looking up at me through her thick, dark lashes and I feel the anger radiating from Alejandro like the heat from an open fire.

"Shannon?" I snarl.

"I was talking to the sheriff. He came to the store asking about the ad your daddy placed, and then he was asking about the two of you..."

"And?"

"I kind of told him that you hate him and haven't spoken to him properly in years," she breathes.

"For fuck's sake, Shan."

"I know, Jackson," she sniffs. "I'm so sorry. You know I'd never get you into trouble on purpose, I just didn't think."

"You have no right talking about me and my business to anyone."

"I know," she nods. "I'm so sorry. If there's anything I can do to fix this, I will. I should have kept my big mouth shut, but then Ed was talking to the sheriff and they were talking about you and then they asked me..." she starts to babble.

"Ed was talking to the sheriff about me?"

"Well, they were talking about your daddy being in hospital is all. The whole town is talking about it."

"Yeah," I say with a frown.

This whole thing is fucked up and it's driving me crazy. I feel like the answer is right in front of my face but I can't connect the fucking dots right. I wonder if I should tell her about the photograph of the two of us. I hadn't even considered that if she's not involved in any of this, she's as much a victim as the rest of us.

But, I don't know that she's not involved yet. And I definitely have a feeling in my gut about Ed. I've met him half a dozen times or so. He seems like a nice enough guy. She says he's not the jealous type, but who really knows, right? If Lucia was friendly with a guy she used to fuck, I'd be pissed as hell and I'd be ready to slit his throat if he so much as smiled at her again.

The irony of that doesn't escape me. Maybe it's time to put an end to this friendship Shannon and I have too.

"Hey, we have somewhere to be," Alejandro reminds me.

"Yeah, I gotta go, Shannon. Anyone else asks about me and my father, you tell them it's none of their business. You got that?"

She looks down at the ground. "Yeah. I'm sorry."

I don't say anything else. Instead, I climb into the truck, start the engine and drive away.

CHAPTER 28
JAX

"So, who are these guys? Any idea?" I ask as I drive toward the address Alejandro gave me.

"Nope. That asshole who owns the bar said he's seen them a couple of times but he didn't know their names. They were there the night your father was beaten up. They had one beer each and then left just before he did. They're known to be trouble and people generally stay out of their way."

"So, how does he know where they live?"

"His girlfriend used to buy a little pot from one of them."

"So we're looking for some pot dealers? If this is where they keep their stash, they're probably armed."

"Isn't everyone in Texas armed?" he says with a shrug. "Besides, I don't think they're big time, else they wouldn't need to beat people up as a side hustle, would they?"

I nod my agreement and keep driving.

When we finally pull up at the house, I shut off the engine and take a look around. It's an old wooden house set on a small plot of land. There's nothing else nearby, which makes it kind of perfect for us. There are motorcycle parts on the front lawn and an old tin bathtub full of rainwater.

"You ready to do this?" Alejandro asks, tucking two guns into the waistband at the back of his trousers.

"Yup," I jump out of the truck.

The smell of smoke hangs in the air and the thick black plume of the stuff coming from the back of the house makes us bypass the front door and head around to the rear of the property. As we draw closer, we hear talking, laughing and then someone hollers something that makes them all whoop and whistle.

"Sounds like they're having a party?" Alejandro says with a frown.

"Sounds like they're assholes," I suggest, and he laughs softly.

"How you want to play this, amigo?"

"Let me do the talking?" I ask. It's usually him who'd do that.

He narrows his eyes at me. "Like a reverse Jacksonville?"

I nod my head. A few years ago, we went to Jacksonville to deal with a bunch of rednecks who had assaulted Alejandro's cousin, Lauren, while she was working a case in Florida. She's a lawyer but she lives in London now. He started with the talking and when he didn't like what they had to say, I shot one of them and we made the others fight until there was only one left standing, before I put a bullet in his head too. "Exactly like that."

We walk into the yard and see four guys standing around a bonfire, each of them holding a bottle of beer in their hands.

"You think they got any women here?" Alejandro asks, looking around the yard.

"I hope not," I hiss, because that would sure complicate matters.

As we draw closer, I notice one of them wearing a red cap with a Motor Oil logo on it, like my father said.

"Who the fuck are you?" the one with red cap snarls.

"I hear you might be looking for work?" I say, holding my hands up in surrender.

"Fuck you!" one of them spits tobacco into the fire.

"What kind of work?" red cap asks.

"We need someone taking care of," I say, narrowing my eyes as I take in my surroundings.

The one with the chewing tobacco has a gun in his waistband. The two standing on the opposite side of the fire look unarmed and also stoned. Red cap seems to be in charge.

"You seem like you're capable of taking care of people yourself," Tobacco snarls.

"Yeah, but you did such a good job on that guy in Rocky's the other night."

That makes them bristle in suspicion and they stand glaring at us.

"Fuck. I don't have time for this," I sigh.

"Jacksonville?" Alejandro says.

"Yeah. Take out Tobacco first."

While the four men stare at me, wondering who I am and whether I'm fishing for information or genuinely looking to hire their services, Alejandro takes his gun and pops a bullet straight into tobacco guy's neck. He clutches his throat as blood pours through his fingers before he falls face first into the fire.

The two who appeared stoned suddenly wake from their trance, the adrenaline pumping into their veins as they realize they're in danger. They start to look around like frightened animals.

"What the fuck?" Red cap shrieks as he looks at his fallen comrade currently roasting on the bonfire.

Alejandro points his gun at him. "Shut the fuck up," he snarls and Red cap closes his mouth and glares at us instead.

"Come here," I say to one of the frightened ones.

He blinks at me.

"You want to end up like your friend there?" I nod to the guy in flames.

He shakes his head.

"Then come the fuck here."

He walks over to me, his legs shaking. These guys aren't professionals by any stretch. Just a group of bullies who prey on people weaker than them. When he reaches me, I spin him around to face his buddies. "Only one of you is walking out of this house. You got me?"

"Y-yeah," he stammers.

"How are you going to make sure that it's you?"

"I-I don't know. W-what d-do you want?"

"Fuck, he's pissing himself," Alejandro snarls.

I look down at the crotch of his jeans to see the light denim turning dark blue. "Jesus, maybe it won't be you after all?"

"Don't tell them nuffin, Caleb," Red cap hisses.

"Oh, he's not going to tell me. You are," I snarl at him.

"The fuck I am," he snarls back. "Not if you're killing me anyway."

I frown at him. "Oh, I won't be killing you." I push his buddy, pressing my palm between his shoulder blades and making him stumble forward. "He will."

I press the barrel of my gun against the back of Caleb's head, making him whimper. "Take this," Alejandro says, handing him his gun.

Caleb takes it with a trembling hand while his two buddies look on.

"Shoot him in the face or I shoot you in the head," I snarl, close to his ear.

"Don't you fucking dare, Caleb!" Red cap shouts.

"I gotta, Big dog," he wails.

Big Dog? Fuck me!

"Yeah, he's gotta," I say with a shrug.

"Shoot him, Caleb. Turn around and shoot him," the guy on the other side of the fire shouts.

"Well, I mean you two could try and take the gun from him," I offer just as Alejandro pulls a second gun from his waistband, pointing it at Dog as I push Caleb forward and away from us.

Survival instincts kick in and the two of them look at each other and then begin to edge forward.

"Fuck you, Aaron," Caleb snarls. Then he aims the gun at his buddy's head and pulls the trigger. Aaron screams but he's not hurt. The gun only had one bullet in and the guy in the fire took that.

Caleb pulls the trigger again.

"Fucking asshole," both Aaron and Dog shout as they round on him now, jumping on him and bringing him to the ground. "You were going to fucking shoot us, you goddamn fuck!" Aaron screeches as he jumps on Caleb's head with such force that his eye pops out of its socket.

"Ouch," Alejandro winces.

Both Dog and Aaron start to beat the shit out of him as Caleb curls up into a ball on the ground, trying to protect himself from their vicious assault. I see now why they get paid to beat people up — they're kind of good at it. Vicious little fucks once they're all nice and riled up. But the thought that the four of them beat up on my father like that makes the blood boil in my veins.

"I know, amigo," Alejandro says quietly. "But with that sheriff on your ass, we gotta try and keep this clean. Okay?"

"Okay." I grumble. He's right. Making this look like these four assholes turned on each other is the best play. It's exactly what we did in Jacksonville.

Sensing my annoyance, he turns to me. "They were just the

pawns, Jax. Save your fire for whoever paid them to do it. And the sick fuck took those videos of you and Lucia."

At the sound of her name, a fresh surge of anger sears through my chest. When we find out whoever that is, that is where I'll take my vengeance.

Aaron and Dog continue punching and stomping on their former associate until he lies motionless and unrecognizable. No longer a person, but a lump of blood, meat and bone.

"I think he's dead, boys," I shout out to them.

"Not enough," Aaron snarls.

"Well, I suggest you save your energy for fighting each other though."

They both stop and look at me. Their faces full of their buddy's blood. Teeth bared like rabid animals. "No," Dog snarls.

"Well, like I said, only one of you is walking outta here," I say with a shrug. "After you tell me what I want to know."

"What the fuck do you want to know?" Dog hisses. "Is this about that old timer at Rocky's bar?"

"That old timer is my old man, asshole," I snap.

Realizing his mistake, Dog holds up his hands. "We just did what we were paid to do. We have no beef with you or your father."

"Well now you do," I remind him.

"We just did what we were asked."

"By who?"

"We don't know the guy's name," he insists.

"Then it looks like neither of you will be walking out of here," I say, raising my gun and aiming it at his head.

Aaron ducks behind Dog as though that might save him. I shake my head in annoyance. What a pair of fucking clowns. I could take them both out before they take their next breath.

"I can give you his number. He texted us," Dog says.

I narrow my eyes at him.

"It's in my phone," he nods to the leather jacket near the bonfire.

Alejandro steps forward and picks it up.

"Left pocket," Dog says and Alejandro reaches gingerly inside before pulling out an old Nokia phone. He hands it to me.

"What's your password?"

"One eight four six," he says, wiping some blood from his cheek. "Check my last messages. They're from your guy."

I open the phone and scroll to the messages and sure enough there are a number of texts discussing my father's attack, including the instructions to make sure that he survived and that he was told I was the man responsible.

"How did he pay you?"

"Cash. Left it in a plastic bag on our porch," Aaron replies.

"But you didn't see him?"

"Nope," Dog says with a shake of his head. "If you text him, though, tell him you have something you need to talk to him about, he'll meet you. I'm sure of it. Guy was getting twitchy as hell these past few days. He even called to make sure we'd told the old guy about his son beating him up."

"You spoke to him?" I frown as I continue flicking through the messages.

"Yeah. Couple of times."

"What did he sound like?"

"I dunno. A guy?"

"Did he have an accent?"

"No he spoke English, just like we do," Dog says with a shrug. Fuck me, he is thick as pig shit.

"I'll be keeping this," I say, pocketing his phone.

"Take it, man," he insists.

"Now it's just the matter of you two deciding which one of you gets to see the light of another day," I remind him.

"What the fuck, man? We gave you what you wanted," Aaron wails.

"Yeah, but you also nearly killed my father, and you caused me and my family a whole lot of pain and trouble. And I am not the kind of man who takes these things lightly."

Dog and Aaron frown at each other.

"You beat the shit out of each other until one of you is left standing, or me and him beat the living fuck out of both you." Alejandro snarls, cracking his knuckles for effect and I suppress a smile.

"And believe me, neither of you will be breathing by the time we're done. We'll make it hurt too."

"A lot, because I am fucking itching to some break some bones," Alejandro adds. Damn, I love this guy.

Aaron and Dog give each other the side eye, assessing each other and deciding whether the other is capable of making the first move, but they both know the answer and so do we. They just beat their other buddy to death.

Dog moves first, dropping and kicking Aaron in the knee, causing him to drop to the floor. Then the two of them go at it in a literal fight to the death. There's something raw and primal about watching two men fight for survival. Each of them thinking they've topped the other, only for their opponent to get a surge of adrenaline and come back even stronger.

As Aaron overpowers Dog for the third time, he scrabbles around in the dirt for some kind of weapon. His fingers curl around a small rock, about the size of a tennis ball. He raises his fist and brings it crashing down on Dog's temple. Over and over again until he bashes straight through his skull and the soft brain tissue is peeking out.

"Fuck!" Alejandro murmurs as he leans back against the porch and watches the action. I swear the only thing missing for him is a bucket of popcorn.

When Aaron is satisfied that Dog is dead and he's not getting up for a third time, he pushes himself up onto shaky legs. He's covered in blood, both his own and Dog's. He hobbles toward us, a bone protruding from his shin and his jaw hanging slack as though it's broken. Do I think he's been through enough hell yet?

Maybe.

"To the victor go the spoils," Alejandro says with a smirk as Aaron reaches us.

"It's over?" he mumbles, spit dribbling down his chin as he struggles to talk.

"Yup," I press my gun to his forehead and he frowns at me in confusion. "All over."

I pull the trigger before he can blink and he drops to the ground at our feet. Alejandro pulls on some rubber gloves he has in his pocket, taking the gun from my hand and wiping it clean of our prints. Then he walks over to Dog, places the pistol in his hand and squeezes off a round into the dirt so that the powder residue will be on his fingers.

He tosses the rubber gloves into the burning bonfire, where tobacco guy is still roasting like a hog, and then walks back to me. We survey the scene before us, pleased with our day's work. I take the cell from my pocket.

"You going to text this mystery man then?" Alejandro asks.

"No time like the present," I say, tapping out a text message. I copy the speech patterns and terrible spelling from the texts that Dog has previously sent him, and tell him that I have something urgent to discuss that he's going to want to know about.

Now all we can do is wait.

CHAPTER 29
LUCIA

I keep glancing at the door, anxious to see Jax and my father walking through it. I know that they are more than capable of handling a few thugs on their own, but what if this is a trap? Someone went to a whole heap of trouble to set Jax up. Who the hell is behind it? Because while I have an uneasy feeling about Ed and Shannon, it feels bigger than them.

"Would you like another tea, sweetheart?" my mom asks, snapping me from my thoughts.

I know that she's worried about them too, but she hides it much better than I do. I suppose she'd had a lot more practice. She's only eight years older than me, and most of the time she feels like my best friend. But it's times like now, when I'm worried and anxious and it feels like the world is against me, that she is every bit my mom.

"Yes please. How are you doing looking into Ed?" I ask.

She walks to the counter and fills the old fashioned copper kettle before placing it on the stove. "Okay, I guess, but he's not the easiest guy to track down. I think he may have used a different name at one time. I'm sure Jax would have more success," she says with a soft sigh.

"Hmm," I say, chewing on my thumbnail.

"He'll be back soon," she says with a reassuring smile.

"How do you know that though, Mom? How do you do this all the time and not go out of your mind with worry?" I ask her.

I work with Jax and my father and I realize it's so much easier when I'm with them, because I know they're safe, and I'm too focused on the task in hand. Which also makes me realize that most of the time, my mom has to worry about me too.

"An unshakeable belief that your father is made of titanium and he would never let anything happen to the people he loves," she says with a shrug. "It's the only way."

She turns back to the stove and I feel a pang of guilt for all the times I've made her worry. My father might be the toughest man I know, but she is the strongest person I have ever met. He is the King of LA, but there is no doubt he wouldn't be the man he is without his queen.

"Hey, Molly and Hugo have been gone a while," I say, trying to take my mind off where Jax and my father are.

"Hmm, they have, haven't they?" and there is an amusement in her tone that makes me roll my eyes.

"Mom?"

She spins on her heel and faces me. "What?" she asks innocently.

I narrow my eyes at her. "Are you matchmaking?"

"No," she protests. "They just seem to get along really well is all."

"She's fourteen years older than he is," I remind her.

"Lucia Montoya!" she says, her mouth open in horror. "And how many years older than you is your husband?"

"Sixteen," I whisper, "but it's different for guys."

"Yeah, but it shouldn't be."

"I know you're right," I admit. Double standards when it

comes to dating and sex really tick me off, but Molly and Hugo have so many differences. He's become a part of our family and I wouldn't want him to get hurt again.

"Kelsey will never forgive you if you set him up with Molly and he falls in love. I mean I know she broke his heart, but still…"

"I am not setting them up. Jeez," she says with a shake of her head. "They're only talking to the boys down at the bunk house."

"Hmm," I say, my eyes narrowed in suspicion.

The sound of voices in the hallway makes both of us look to the door. A few seconds later, Jax and my father walk through it and I breathe a sigh of relief. They both appear unharmed.

I wrinkle my nose. "You smell of fire?"

"Oh, that will be from the bonfire," my father says.

"The bonfire?"

"Oh, it wasn't ours," Jax says as he walks toward me. "But it did come in pretty useful." He slips his arm around my waist and kisses me softly. "I'll go take a shower soon. How about you join me?"

"As fun as that sounds, we have more important things to focus on right now," I remind him and take a step back. "Did you find anything?" I ask loudly, but my father is distracted kissing my mom. It's not a peck on the cheek either and I roll my eyes.

"You two need some privacy here?" Jax says and they stop and look back at us.

"Just saying hello to my wife, amigo," my father says with a grin.

"Yes, we did find something. The guys who beat my dad up were paid by someone. They never met him and everything was done over the phone, but they did give us a contact number.

They said he only responds to text messages, so we took their phone and sent him a text."

"What if they give him the heads up?" my mom asks.

"They won't," my father says matter of factly.

"You sure?"

He narrows his eyes at me. "One hundred percent, *mija*."

"Oh," I whisper. I suppose beating Harvey up like that and trying to frame Jax for it was only going to end one way for the people responsible.

"What about you two? Find anything on Ed?" Jax asks.

"A little," my mom says with a frown. "But nothing out of the ordinary. I couldn't access his bank records or anything like that. You or Alejandro would need to do that."

"Okay," he nods.

"But you found out something?" my father asks.

"Yes. He moved here from Idaho, but he was only there about six months."

"And before that?" Jax asks.

"Virginia," she says. "Seems like he lived there for all of his life, except for college."

Jax frowns. "Virginia?"

"Yes. Does that mean something to you?"

"Only been to Virginia once in my life, but I wouldn't forget it," he says, sharing a look with my father that makes the hairs on the back of my neck stand on end.

"No way," my father frowns at him before he walks over the open laptop. "Where did he go to college?"

"Columbia."

"What did he do in Virginia, Alana? Was he a veterinarian?" Jax asks.

"Yes," she nods. "And he was also the deputy coroner."

"The vet was the deputy coroner?" I ask.

"Yes. As long as they've done the required training, anyone

can be a coroner in most states. I suppose as long as you know your way around cutting bodies open, it would make sense?" Jax replies and then he looks at my father again who glares at him.

"It can't be that, Jax."

"He was the deputy coroner, Alejandro. He went to Columbia just like the coroner did. They're around the same age. They worked together. I guarantee he helped him cover the whole thing up."

"Cover what up?" my mom and I say at the same time.

My father looks at my mom and opens his mouth to speak but for once he seems lost for words. "Princess, I..." is all he says.

"Alex! Jax! What is going on?" She looks between them both.

"I think you should sit down," Jax says to her.

I frown at him now. What the hell is happening here?

"I don't want to sit down until one of you tell me what the hell you're talking about and why you're both looking at me like that."

"Alana!" my father barks and she glares at him. But then she sits at the kitchen table and my father, Jax and I follow suit.

Once we're all seated, my mom clasps her hands in front of her, her knuckles white as she tries to keep a lid on her emotions. I don't feel much less anxious myself. Clearly something is going on here that involves her somehow. My father looks particularly nervous.

Oh, God. What has he done? What could be so bad that he doesn't want her to know? She knows everything about him. He keeps nothing from her. At least that was what I always thought — and I know that she did too.

"So?" she asks as her eyes burn into his so fiercely, he could well burst into flames any second.

"You remember that night at the restaurant back in LA, not long after we were married, when that guy put a gun in your face?"

"Yes," she whispers.

"His name was Layton Cooper."

"I remember. He said that it was for my father. For something he did."

"It was," my father swallows. Wow! I have never seen him looking so uncomfortable.

"You said it was just some guy with a grudge and that you didn't know what he'd done?" she says accusingly.

"I lied, princess."

She stares at him, waiting for him to explain himself.

He licks his lips and then he carries on speaking. "Layton Cooper had a daughter named, Bethany. She was sixteen years old and pregnant when she allegedly killed herself. The coroner ruled it as a suicide but Layton believed she was murdered. She told everybody the baby's father was her high school boyfriend, but it wasn't."

"Who was the baby's father?" she asks as her face turns pale. Because we both know the answer.

"Your father," he says.

She blinks at him as tears form in her eyes. "No," she whispers.

"After Layton told me his suspicions, I had Jax go to Virginia and look into it, and he verified everything Layton said, including the coroner helping your father to cover up her murder. I'm sorry, princess."

My mom looks at Jax. "You're sure it was true? You had proof of this?"

"Yes, Alana. She met your father when Cooper's construction company was doing work on your father's lake house."

"I remember that house," she whispers.

"She used to go to work with him sometimes," Jax says.

Alan's hand flies to her mouth. "Oh, God. I remember her too. I met her. She wanted to go into politics and I told her to choose another career if she wanted a life," she sniffs as a tear runs down her cheek. "But they were never alone there. I was there the entire time. And my mom."

"No. It seemed they slept together when she was on a school trip to New York. She was only fifteen," Jax replies.

"Sicko," I snap, forgetting that I'm talking about my mom's dad. I clamp a hand over my mouth.

"That poor girl," she breathes. "Why did he? I mean he could have paid her off. Wasn't that his thing? Buying and selling people was his deal. Not killing them?"

"Alana," My father says softly, reaching for her hand but she snatches it away.

"I can't believe it," she shakes her head and then glares at Jax and my father. "You must have missed something."

"I didn't, Alana," Jax insists, and I know he's right. He's a bloodhound when he goes after someone.

"You can't believe it of a man who would sell his only daughter to a monster? For a mere three million dollars?" my father snaps.

"Why did you lie to me?"

"Because I didn't want you to be burdened with what he did. I knew how much this would hurt you."

Her face turns a deep shade of pink. "You don't get to decide what truths I get to know. I decide that." She bangs her fist on the table. "You had no right to keep this from me. She was having a baby, Alex," she shakes her head and then drops it into her hands.

"Shall we go?" I whisper to Jax.

"No," my father says. "Your mom and I will deal with this later, but right now, we need to find Ed."

He pushes back his chair and walks around the table to her. Dropping to his knees beside her, he takes her hands in his. "I'm sorry, princesa," he whispers. "I should have told you."

She turns her body slightly and he wraps his arms around her, pulling her close to him until she's sobbing on his shoulder. He whispers something in her ear and a few moments later, she stops crying. She sits up straight and wipes the tears from her eyes. "Sorry," she mouths to me.

"Don't be," I say, reaching over the table, I squeeze her hand in mine.

"So, is this all about revenge for Ed then? Because you found out what his friend did?" my mom says as she regains her composure. I sense my father is not entirely forgiven, but like he said, they'll deal with it later.

"Seems a little extreme," I say.

"Yeah," my father nods his agreement. "But the Virginia connection is no coincidence."

"But what has this been about all along?" Jax says as his jaw ticks and I can almost see the synapses in his brain firing. "Not revenge. Not obsession. Not jealousy." He looks at my father. "You told Foster Carmichael that three million dollars was way too small a price to pay for his daughter. You remember that?"

"Yes," he replies, his face pulled into a scowl.

"So how much are you willing to pay to protect your own daughter, amigo? Five million?"

"Fucking *hijo de puta*," my father snarls.

It takes a second, but the shock quickly ripples around the room. "You really think he is behind all of this?" my mom asks.

"It makes sense. He's been struggling financially since he lost the backing of Montoya Inc. He has Ed in his pocket already. He hates Alejandro for stealing you away from him. He hates me for uncovering his secret. He hates that you chose your new family over him. But we're all just pawns in his game. Collateral damage. He loves one thing above all else, Alana..."

"Money," she says, closing her eyes,

"It's always about the money," I whisper, wishing I could take away some of the guilt and pain that is written all over my mom's face. We are not responsible for the actions of our parents.

Jax wraps an arm around me. "It makes the world go round, baby."

The sound of a text message interrupts the silence and Jax pulls an old cell phone from his jeans pocket. He sucks in a breath.

"It's him," he says to my father.

"Ed?" I ask.

"I think so."

"Do you think Shannon was in on this too?"

"I doubt it," he says with a shake of his head. "He must have taken those photos of me and her before they even got together and hung onto them. I don't think she'd have allowed him to keep them. Besides, she always kind of had a soft spot for my dad. I don't see her agreeing to go along with paying four guys to beat him up."

"No," I reluctantly agree. The few times I've spoken to her, she's seemed nice and genuinely happy for Jax and me.

"He's asked to meet at the diner on the edge of town," Jax says, slipping the cell phone back into his pocket.

"So, let's go," I say about to stand up.

My father catches my eye and I sit down again. "I'm going with you to meet him," I insist. "He..." I swallow hard. I hate thinking about what he did and the shame and guilt still eats away at me. "I am not sitting this one out."

"No-one expects you too, *mija*?" my father says.

"You don't?" I sit up straighter in my seat.

"If he is the man who took those videos of you, then it only seems fair you get to look him in the eye when you make him pay for it. You go with Jax."

He's right, and I love him for it, but I also suspect he doesn't want to leave my mom right now. I feel a little deflated. I was expecting much more of an argument with him and my husband about it.

"Okay, baby?" Jax asks, his face full of concern.

"Yes. I agree, obviously. I'm just surprised you two are letting me do this, is all." I look at Jax now. "You've both been kind of uber protective lately."

"Only because we love you so much."

"You'll look after her, Jax?" my mom says.

He arches an eyebrow at her in response.

Meanwhile my father laughs softly. "Better than anyone I know," he says and Jax winks at him.

And now I know that whatever struggles they've been having are done with. I suppose killing some guys with your best buddy isn't everyone's idea of male bonding, but it sure works for these two.

CHAPTER 30
LUCIA

"You think this guy we're meeting really is Ed or are we walking into something bigger?" I ask Jax as he pulls the truck to a stop across the road from the roadside diner he arranged to meet us at.

"I suppose we'll find out soon enough, angel," he says as he stares out the window, his eyes scanning the area. "But meeting at a diner tells me it's a safe bet this isn't a trap at least."

"Why suggest meeting somewhere so public though?" I ask, noting the half a dozen cars in the parking lot across the street.

"It's not that busy. Easy exit routes to the North and South. And a chance meeting in a diner is easily explained away."

Damn, I love watching him work. He's the smartest man I know.

"You think he's in there already?"

"Probably. No doubt he's sitting at one of those booths with a coffee or a soda, so that when one of the local asshole pot dealers sits at his table, he can pretend he doesn't know them. Different if he has to walk over to them."

"Hmm, I suppose."

"Trust me, angel," he says with a wink. "Let's go."

We jump out of the truck and cross the street to the diner. Jax pulls open the door and we walk inside.

"Bingo," he mutters as we both spot Ed at a booth near the back.

Ed's eyes lock on Jax's. At first he goes to smile, as though Jax and I might just be stopping by for some pie or a burger, but not even a second later, he realizes what we're there for. Ed wipes his hands on a napkin and then he stands up and begins walking quickly toward the restroom.

"Asshole," Jax mutters. "Do me a favor, angel, and go bring the truck over to the parking lot," he says, taking hold of my elbow and guiding us both back out of the door.

"Why? Where are you going?"

"To catch the asshole who's about to climb out of the restroom window." He gives me a soft kiss on the cheek before he jogs around the back of the diner.

I make my way over the road and drive the truck across to the diner parking lot, just in time to see Jax pulling Ed from the tiny restroom window by his ears. Ed's face is twisted in pain as Jax tugs him free. I can't hear him but he's red in the face and his tongue is flapping wildly like he's screaming. The image would be funny if Ed wasn't such a disgusting pervert — or actually maybe that makes it even funnier?

I'm smiling anyway when I roll down the truck window. "You okay there, cowboy?"

"Sure am, angel," Jax says as he pulls a shrieking Ed into a standing position. He slaps him across the face. "Shut the fuck up or I will pull out your tongue with my fucking bare hands," Jax snarls.

It has the desired effect and Ed clamps his mouth firmly shut.

Jax opens the passenger door of the truck and tosses Ed inside like he's a rag doll and not a man. As Jax climbs in beside him, Ed shuffles awkwardly along the bench seat, his thigh bumping against mine for a fraction of a second. But even that slight contact makes me wince and my stomach twists. This guy filmed me and my husband at our most intimate moments. Did he watch it back? Did he get himself off?

"Did you just fucking touch her?" Jax snarls.

"I I, y-you..." Ed starts to babble, but Jax elbows him in the temple, knocking him out cold.

"Sick fuck," he hisses as Ed slumps sideways until he's resting on Jax's shoulder like he's just taking a nap. I imagine anyone looking in would think they looked kind of cute. "We'll wake him up when we get there."

"And where is there? Where shall we take him?" I ask.

We didn't discuss this part of the plan, but I'm pretty sure Jax has known all along.

"To my work shed back at the ranch."

I'm shocked that we're heading to the ranch, but I suppose it makes perfect sense. Jax owns all the land. It's private property and he can do whatever he likes there without worrying about people hearing. Because I imagine Ed is going to be screaming in agony before the day is through.

ED IS STILL unconscious as Jax carries him into the tool shed. He only starts to stir as Jax wraps a huge steel chain around his wrists.

"W-what?" he screeches, trying to wrench free from Jax's hold but failing.

"You see that hook over there, angel?" Jax asks me, ignoring

209

Ed's noise and nodding toward a huge steel hook beneath his workbench.

"Yep."

"It goes on that beam there, see?" He nods now to one of supports that runs across the roof of the shed, and which has another thick metal chain dangling from it.

"Okay," I nod my understanding and grab the hook before fixing it in place.

All the while Ed watches me. He's stopped crying now and instead I think he's paralyzed with fear. I mean, we both know where he's about to go, and the thought of what Jax might do to him while he's hanging like a pig on a butcher's hook has me feeling a little queasy too.

When his wrists are securely bound, Jax carries Ed to the dangling hook and hangs him from it. It's at the perfect height for his toes to just about reach the floor.

Jax picks up a knife with a serrated blade from his tool box and holds it to Ed's chest.

"P-please don't," Ed snivels.

"Oh, I'm not going to cut you with this," Jax says with a scowl. "It's far too sharp and that would be way too easy." He pops one of the buttons off Ed's shirt with the tip of the blade. "This is just so I can do this," he adds before he starts to cut off Ed's shirt, pants and socks. Once he's done that, he takes hold of the waistband of Ed's briefs.

"No!" Ed wails, twisting on the chain like a fish on a hook.

"Yes," Jax snarls as he cuts them in one swift slice of the blade. He looks down Ed's flaccid dick, which is shriveled in fear. "I hope you're a grower not a shower, Ed, because there's not much meat for me to work with there."

I snigger at that but Ed just keeps crying. His wailing has turned to soft sobs now. It would be pitiful if he wasn't such a piece of shit.

Jax picks up a huge pair of shears and hands them to me.

"Now, here is how this is going to go," he says to Ed, his tone calm and steady now. "I'm going to ask you a whole heap of questions, and if you don't tell me the truth, I'm going to tell my girl to cut off a body part. Okay? I mean she's a nice person so she probably won't start with your cock. But your hands are pretty high for her to reach, and you only got ten toes."

Ed nods his head in understanding.

"You okay there, baby?" Jax asks while keeping his eyes fixed on Ed.

"Yep," I say as my heart races while adrenaline thunders through my veins.

"Now don't worry, Ed. I'm gonna start with the easy stuff first. Like how long have you been following me."

"I haven't," Ed mumbles.

"For fuck's sake," Jax hisses and then he turns to me. "Pick a toe, baby."

I take a step closer and fix the tip of the shears around Ed's big toe because it's the easiest to grasp as my hands tremble slightly. Then I feel Jax's strong hand on the small of my back. Reminding me that I got this. This man tried to destroy us.

"Wait!" Ed shrieks but it's too late.

I clamp the shear tightly shut and Ed's toe pops off like a soda cap. Wow, these things are sharp. Ed howls in pain as blood spurts from the wound.

Jax slaps Ed's face so that he stops focusing on the pain in his foot and looks at him, again. "You see how this is gonna work now?"

Ed nods his head.

"How long have you been watching me?"

"Only while you were here on honeymoon," he sniffs.

"But the photograph of me and Shannon? That was from way before that?"

"The photograph of you fucking my wife?" Ed says, as though suddenly he has a little fire in his belly.

"She wasn't your wife then," Jax snarls. "You two weren't even together."

"Because she was too busy screwing you every chance she got to notice me," he sniffs. "Not until Huxley..." he trails off as though he's said too much.

Jax narrows his eyes as though fishing for a memory. "Her dog, Huxley? Someone hurt him real bad and left him on her front porch," Jax hisses. "She was heartbroken. She even phoned me while I was in LA to tell me. You patched him up. You knew exactly how to treat his wounds so he wouldn't die, because you caused them, didn't you?" Jax snarls.

Ed nods his head. "I gave him a sedative while I did it, so he wouldn't feel anything."

"No, you gave him a sedative so he wouldn't know it was you who hurt him and bite your fucking face off when he woke up," Jax barks.

"It was the only way to get her to notice me," Ed sobs, full of self-pity and not a thought for the poor dog he abused.

"You are evil," I spit at him.

Jax puts an arm around me and presses a soft kiss on my head. "It's okay, baby. We'll make him pay for everything, I promise," he whispers before he turns back to Ed. "So you took that photograph and what? Just kept hold of it? How many others did you take?"

"None of the two of you. I swear."

"And Lucia and me? You filmed us at the barn?"

Ed stares at him, his mouth open and no sound coming out.

"You're up, Luce," Jax says and I step toward him with my shears.

"Yes. Yes I did it," Ed admits.

I feel like chopping all of his toes off for that, but I know I'm not allowed to yet.

"Why?"

"He's blackmailing me. He said he'd tell Shannon about what I covered up back in Virginia. He had that girl killed but the trail wouldn't lead back to him, it would lead straight back to me and Vince."

"Vincent Kane? The coroner?"

"Yeah. He told me that you knew about it. That you were the one who dug it all up again. That was why I had to leave my home town," Ed sniffs.

"And then I went and fucked the woman you wanted to marry?" Jax snarls.

Ed simply nods as he glares at him.

"Who told you all this? Who is blackmailing you?"

"Foster Carmichael, who else?"

"But you were happy to help him out just so you could get a little revenge too, right?"

"I was just supposed to take a few pictures of you that we could use to set you up..."

"The pictures with Toni Moretti?" I ask him. "You fabricated those?"

"Yep," he says with an air of pride. "You can do anything with photoshop these days. But you two went and gave me so much more, didn't you."

I swear there is an arrogant sneer on his face. Like even though he is tied up and about to die, he still can't help being a disgusting piece of shit. I feel the anger in Jax beside me, but I don't give him time to act. I raise the shears and smash them into Ed's face, busting his nose open like a ripe peach.

"You sick, twisted piece of shit!" I shout, ready to hit him again, but Jax catches my arm.

He pulls me to him, pressing his lips against my ear. "I

know, baby, but I need to know what he did with those videos first, okay?" he whispers so that Ed can't hear.

I drop my hands and nod my agreement. Ed is going to know pain like he could never have even imagined, and he's going to deserve every second of it.

CHAPTER 31

JAX

I press my nose against Lucia's hair and inhale her sweet scent until it grounds me. Tuning out the sound of Ed's sniveling in the background, I listen to her ragged breathing instead. I feel the anger in her and I wish that I could let her smash his face to pieces right now, but I need some more answers first. And there are things I need to say to him that I'd rather she didn't hear.

"Why don't you step outside for a few minutes, Luce?" I suggest. "Get some fresh air."

She looks up, her face pale as she blinks at me. "Okay," she whispers.

"Good girl," I kiss the top of her head and watch as she walks out of the door, leaving Ed and I alone.

I give him all of my attention now. "If you want this to be over, I'm gonna need answers and fast, Ed. No more fucking about. What did you do with the videos?"

"I sent them to Foster."

"How?"

"E-m-mail."

"And the originals?"

"On my cell phone. In an encrypted cloud folder."

I pick up his cell phone. "Password?"

"One – one — zero – three – nine – six."

I type the numbers in and unlock his phone. "And the encrypted folder?"

"It's the picture of the cat," he says. "It's supposed to look inconspicuous."

I tap on the screen and it asks for a thumbprint. "Gonna need that print, Ed."

He nods his head, no doubt expecting me to lift the phone to his thumb. Instead, I take my knife from the table, reach up and slice off his thumb before he even knows what's happening. A second later he's shrieking in agony again.

"You are the noisiest fucker I've ever had the pleasure of torturing. You know that?" I say as I press his thumb onto the phone and the folder opens. There are a number of videos in there.

"Who are in the rest of these?" I ask.

"Me and Shannon," he sobs.

"She know you took em?"

"No," he shakes his head.

"You really are a disgusting pile of dog-shit, Ed."

I put the phone and his bleeding thumb onto the workbench.

"Are there any other copies of those videos of my wife?"

"No. I swear," he whimpers, blinking as blood from his hand pours down onto his face.

Now that I have what I need, I can finally let some of this rage inside me out. I grab hold of his hair and pull hard, twisting his head so I can look into his eyes. "Did you enjoy watching me fuck my wife, Ed? Did you enjoy watching her come?"

"No," he wails.

I jerk his head back. "Why not? She's fucking beautiful. Don't you think she's beautiful?"

"No, y-yes," he snivels, unsure of the correct answer, because there isn't one.

"So you did enjoy watching her?" I punch him in balls and he vomits on himself.

"Did you like seeing her getting her pussy eaten out, Ed? Did you wish it was you?" I punch him in the stomach now and the force sends him flying so that he loses his footing and spins on the hook. "Did you jerk off while you watched her?" I spin him back around until he's facing me.

"N-no," he whispers, his eyes pleading with me now that he knows his crying has no affect.

"You saw my wife coming, Ed," I snarl. I grab hold of his head, pressing my thumbs into the corners of his eyes and pushing inside.

"Argh!" he screams again as the pressure pushes his eyeballs from their sockets. But I'm not done. I want his eyeballs rolling on the fucking floor.

I dig harder, pushing and pulling until his eyes are in my hands instead of in his head.

Ed's face drops forward. His body trembles and shudders as he goes into shock from having his eyes gouged out. My blood pounds in my ears and my heart still races but damn that felt good. Between Ed's busted nose and missing eyes, his face is a mess of blood and tissue. I could finish this right now, but I still need to let my girl have her chance to work out some of the shame and anger he's caused her.

I'm about to walk outside and get her when she walks back through the door. "I heard screaming. Did you get what you needed?"

"Yeah, baby," I say, letting Ed's eyeballs drop to the floor.

The soft thud makes her look down and she watches them roll a few feet before she looks back up at me.

"He looked at you," I offer in explanation for what I've done. But seems she didn't need any. She crosses the floor and wraps her arms around my neck. "I love you," she whispers.

"Love you too, angel."

We stay like that for a few seconds before the sound of Ed jerking his arms in his chains distracts us. He's making a last ditch attempt to free himself. Like he'd get anywhere with no eyes and Lucia and me right here. But it's human nature to rail against death, even when it's inevitable.

I reach down and pick up the shears. "You want to?"

She blinks at me. "He looks kind of pathetic hanging there like that."

"So end his suffering then, baby."

She nods her head and takes the shears, stepping close to him and swinging the shears like a baseball bat. "This is for helping your friend blackmail my father," she snarls as she hits him in the chest. "This is for filming us." He takes a blow to the dick with the metal blade that is so hard it splits him open. He screams and shakes as his dick hangs by a thick thread of sinew and skin.

I wince instinctively.

"This is for trying to come between Jax and me." She hits him on the kneecap, shattering the bone.

She sucks in a breath. Tears are running down her face, but she needed to let all of this out. "And this is for Bethany Cooper and that sweet little dog."

The final blow is to his head. It splits it wide open and cracks his skull. Ed falls silent. His body twitches and spasms a few times and then he's still. The chain creaking above his head is the only sound that can he heard.

Lucia drops the shears to the floor with a loud clatter. She lifts her hand to her face and then she stars to sob. Deep, soul cleansing sobs. I pick her up and carry her to my work bench, sitting her on top of it and wrapping her legs around my waist as I pull her close.

"It's okay, baby," I whisper.

She buries her face in my neck and I stroke her hair as her hot tears fall onto my skin.

CHAPTER 32
LUCIA

J ax and I showered at our barn after dealing with Ed. My incredible husband washed every single part of me with a soft cloth, making sure that every last trace of that sick fuck's blood was gone from me.

Now we're sitting around the huge table in the kitchen with my parents, all looking at each other as the reality of what we just discussed sinks in.

I look at my mom. This is going to be so hard for her. I mean she already knew her father was a piece of work, but now she knows that he raped and murdered a teenage girl, along with her unborn child too. I guess that's a lot to take in. Not to mention sitting here planning his demise.

"Are you sure about this, princess?" my father asks her. "You don't have to be a part of this."

She narrows her eyes at him. I know what's going through her head right now. She thinks him asking her that is because he perceives her as weak, but it's not. It's because he loves her so much, he can't bear to see her in pain. And no matter what he did, I can't imagining that being a part of her father's death is going to be easy for her. Especially not considering what my father and Jax do to their enemies.

"He used my own daughter to extort money from you, Alex. Yes I'm sure," she snaps, her eyes full of fire as she glares at him. But there is a tremor in her voice too. She is terrified of what she's about to do, and I can't say I blame her.

"So we're all clear on this?" my father asks.

"Yes," Jax and I reply while my mom sits in silence.

He sighs softly as he looks at her. I know how much he wants to deal with this for her. If he had his way, he'd send her back to LA with my little brothers and go to New York alone. But she knows her father better than any of us and if he's as smart as she says he is, then we'll need her by our sides too.

CHAPTER 33
ALANA

I pull Molly's huge cardigan around me as I walk through the garden in the darkness. It gets kind of chilly here at night. I take a seat on the old wooden bench and glance around me. My husband's men are scattered around this entire property, but I don't see any right now.

Taking my cell out of the pocket of the cardigan, I open it up. My fingers tremble as I dial the number. It isn't stored in my phone, but it is etched into my brain like one of those things from your childhood that almost becomes a part of you. I mean, I forget my computer password every other week, but I can easily remember the phone number of my parent's house in New York, a place where I haven't lived or called for years.

I take a deep breath as it rings. Suddenly, I hope he doesn't pick up.

"Hello?" his voice is the same as it always was. Deep and soothing. It hits me in the chest like someone just punched me right in the heart.

"D-daddy?" the word gets stuck on my tongue. I haven't used it in so long.

"Alana?" I hear the gasp as though he's as affected at the sound of my voice as I am by his.

"Yes, it's me," I whisper.

"What? Why?" He takes a deep breath. "How are you, sweetheart? It's been..." he pauses.

"Five years," I finish for him.

"Feels like longer," he adds softly.

My heart is racing and a whole raft of emotions wash over me. I feel like I'm going to pass out. But I need to do this while I still have the nerve. "I need to tell you something, Daddy."

"Anything, sweetheart."

"Alejandro knows about the five million dollars."

Silence.

"He knows that you blackmailed him, Daddy. He's going to kill you."

That certainly gets his attention. "How do you know about this?"

I close my eyes. The man's arrogance is astounding. Just because he shares nothing of his life with my mother, he assumes that all men treat their wives the same way.

"Because he told me all about it. He and Jackson are going to ask you to meet them at your lake house in Virginia. But it's a trap, Daddy. They're going to kill you."

"And why are you telling me this? You chose your side, Alana. You chose him over your mother and me."

"This isn't about choosing sides, Daddy. This is about saving your life," I snap. "No matter what you have done, you're still my father."

He's silent for a little longer. "Thank you for telling me, sweetheart. I always knew you'd be there for me if I needed you."

"I will always be your daughter."

"Yes you will. So, it's a trap, you say? They're onto me?"

"Yes. They'll both be waiting for you, and my daughter Lucia too."

"Right."

"You have to promise me you won't hurt them though, Daddy. They're my family and I love them too."

"Of course, sweetheart," he says softly in that deep, soothing politicians voice that reminds me of my teenage years.

"You promise? Because I would die if anything happened to them," I ask again. I need him to know what I'm potentially giving up for him here.

"Promise," he assures me.

"Okay. I have to go before Alejandro notices that I'm gone. Bye, Daddy."

"Bye, sweetheart."

I slip the phone back into my pocket. I know that was the right thing to do, but I still feel like I'm about to throw up.

I suck in a lungful of cool night air, push myself up and make my way back to the house.

CHAPTER 34
LUCIA

Foster Carmichael's lake house is actually kind of beautiful. At least the huge, open plan living area is anyway. My mom told me that her own mom decorated the place and I guess that's where she got her good taste from.

I've never met either of my grandparents, but I've often wondered what they were like. My mom never, ever talks about them, but I guess I'm about to meet dear old Grandpa.

Jax and my father said that they'd be waiting for him at eight p.m. and it's five to, so it shouldn't be too much longer. The clock on the mantelpiece ticks softly and it's the only sound that can be heard, apart from the soft breathing of the people sitting either side of me.

It's the whooshing sound that I hear first, followed by the shattering of whatever glass object the bullet hit. I wince instinctively, even though I'm not in that room. I'm nowhere near it.

I'm sitting in an office with my mom and our friends, Jessie and Shane Ryan, in New York. Together, the four of us watch via a camera as the whole room is torn apart by bullets.

Anyone in there would be incredibly lucky to have made it out alive.

I glance at my mom and see her wipe a tear from her cheek. She reaches for my hand and squeezes it tightly. I guess she thought maybe her father might have had a shred of decency left. He just proved that he doesn't.

When the shooting stops, there's the sound of boots stomping through the house.

"It's clear," a figure dressed in back shouts as he comes into view. Then at least half a dozen more come into view, holding automatic rifles as they move through the room.

The sound of feet running up stairs. "There's no-one here."

"It's a trap."

"It's time," Shane says and I press the designated key on the laptop. There's a deafening explosion and the splintering of wood before the camera cuts off.

"Are you both okay?" Jessie asks.

"Yup," I nod.

Although it feels kind of strange thinking about what happened in that room. All of those men believed that I was in there, along with my husband and father. If we had been my son would be an orphan. That kind of takes the breath from my lungs. But that was never the plan.

"I told him you would be in there. You and your father," my mom says with a shake of her head.

"I know, Mom."

"I mean, I was prepared to do this anyway after what he did to you and poor Bethany, but now..." she sucks in a breath and suddenly I feel sorry for Foster Carmichael. Alana Montoya doesn't get pissed very often, but when she does — well, even Satan himself would move out of her way.

"How about I get Mikey to make you both one of his famous soothing hot chocolates while you wait for Alejandro and Jax,"

Jessie says, pushing herself to her feet and taking her husband's hand.

Well, he's one of her husbands. She has four of them. The Ryan brothers have been friends of my father's and Jax's for years and they've kindly let us use their apartment and basement while we're here in New York. I only met them at mine and Jax's wedding less than two weeks ago, but I love all of them already. Especially Jessie, who's just a few years older than me. We needed somewhere we could keep Matthias and the twins safe while we dealt with Foster Carmichael, and the Ryan's basement also has the perfect place for the next stage of the plan.

"Sounds perfect, thank you," my mom replies.

"Not a problem. Full disclosure though, the soothing part is Irish whiskey, just so you know."

"Sounds even better," my mom says with a smile.

Jessie and Shane walk out of the office leaving my mom and me alone.

"I was about to say that I can't believe that he did that, but the really sad thing is that I can," she says softly.

I don't have a response for her. The truth is, it was my mom who told us all that her father was too smart to accept a request for a meeting without getting suspicious. This entire plan was her idea — well most of it. The double bluff.

A request for a meeting, no matter how it was done, would put Foster on high alert, given that he's just extorted five million dollars from my father, and the fact that neither of my parents have spoken to him for five years. There was no way to do that and not raise his suspicion.

So my mom made him believe that she was betraying my father, telling Foster he was onto him and that he was setting him up. It would not only confirm that he was behind the extortion, but also make him think he was in the clear. A man who thinks he has vanquished his enemies is a much easier target than a man on the defensive.

So, earlier today, some of my father's men drove to the lake house in Virginia, broke in, set up our camera and the explosives, closed the blinds and turned on the lights. Then they left two SUV's outside to make it appear like there was someone there.

Meanwhile, my mom and I came here with the boys, while my father and Jax have been following Foster all day. They have a link to the camera at the lake house too and will know exactly what he tried to do and that they need to act fast before his hired guns don't check in with him to tell him that the job is complete.

I sit back in my chair, confident in the knowledge, that right about now the man who tried to destroy our family will be in the capable hands of my husband and my father.

CHAPTER 35
JAX

"It's time to move, amigo," Alejandro says as the feed to Carmichael's lake house is cut off.

"We just gonna walk up to his house and expect him to let us in?"

"I'll break in if I have to," he says with a shrug. "But his housekeeper will open the door. He thinks he's untouchable. He thinks we're dead."

I nod my head in agreement. A man who thinks he has nothing to fear is a much easier target.

We climb out of the car and walk up the steps of the old Brownstone. Alejandro rings the buzzer and sure enough, the housekeeper opens the door a few moment's later.

"I have a meeting with Mr. Carmichael," Alejandro says with that disarming smile he has. He could have been a politician himself.

She blinks at us. "I'll just go check."

"No need. He knows about it," I say, pushing the door open and allowing us both to walk past her.

"You can't..." she shouts after us. "Mr. Carmichael," she yells louder and a few seconds later he walks out of the sitting room at the back of the house.

His face turns an unnatural shade of grey when he sees us.

"Meeting at eight, right?" Alejandro says.

He opens and closes his mouth.

"Sir, shall I call Fitz?" the housekeeper asks.

I turn to her and shake my head. "If Fitz is the big Irish guy who's supposed to be outside watching the house, you won't find him."

She swallows and blinks at me.

"It's okay. He's fine. His employers gave him the night off is all."

"How? I vetted him myself," Carmichael snaps.

I smile as I remember how pissed he was when he found out that a previous personal security detail turned out to be working for Alejandro all along.

"Well, he doesn't work for me. But some friends of ours know his boss. You know how it is," he says with a smile.

One of the many advantages of having the Ryan brothers as friends, is that they know every single person worth knowing in New York. A quick word in an associate's ear was all it took for Fitz to leave early. There was a time when Carmichael had a whole team of security, but since he lost the financial backing of Montoya Inc. his star has faded somewhat.

"Could you give us a moment?" I say to the housekeeper.

She looks at her boss, but he just stares at her.

"I'm pretty sure this piece of shit doesn't pay you enough for this, lady?" I say, pulling a wad of hundred dollar bills from my coat pocket.

Money makes the world go round. And Foster Carmichael is a self-centered, entitled, arrogant prick. I know without a doubt that he does not treat his staff well.

She looks at the cash and then at her scumbag boss. Then

229

she takes it from my hand, pulls her coat from the night stand and walks out of the house.

"Rosie," he shouts after her, but she doesn't even look back.

"Shall we?" Alejandro says as he gestures toward the front door.

Foster looks between his son-in-law and me, blinking in shock. "You seriously think I'd go anywhere with you?"

"I don't see that you have much choice," I say.

"You can't just walk in here and kidnap me. I'm Foster fucking Carmichael. People will notice I'm gone."

"Like who?" I frown at him. "Your housekeeper who just walked out of here for ten thousand bucks. Or your wife, who's so out of her head on pills that she doesn't even know what fucking day it is?"

He glares at me as he realizes that no-one gives a shit about him. Treat people like crap long enough and they will do the same to you.

"You come with me or I kill you right now and make it look like a suicide," Alejandro snarls. "But your daughter wants to look you in the eye. And believe it or not, she is your only hope of making it out of this alive. Because, despite how much I fucking despise your guts, you sick *hijo de puta,* I would spare your life if I thought it would ease her pain. Now move."

Carmichael remains frozen to the spot for a few moments before his feet finally stumble forward and he moves toward the direction of the front door.

Just five minutes later, he is in the back seat of the car with me for company as we drive to our friend's building where Lucia and Alana are waiting.

CHAPTER 36

JAX

I sent a text to Lucia to let her know we were on our way, so when we arrive at the apartment building, I'm not surprised to see our buddy, Conor Ryan waiting outside for us to let us in.

"What the hell? You're taking me to a nightclub?" Carmichael sneers.

"You wish you were going to a nightclub, you sick fuck," I snarl at him. Part of the building's basement and most of the ground floor is a nightclub, but there are also soundproof rooms down here too.

"The place you're going to is a whole lot quieter and with less people," Alejandro laughs as he drives through the huge steels doors and rolls the car to a stop. I climb out first, reaching in and pulling Carmichael out with me.

Conor locks the garage doors and walks over to us as Alejandro steps out of the car.

"The ladies are on their way down. The room you need is over there," he nods to an open steel door tucked away in the corner of the basement, "and I'm sure anything else you might need is in there too."

"Thanks, amigo," Alejandro says with a nod of his head.

"What the fuck is going on?" Carmichael wails, trying to wrench himself from my grasp. "Do you know who I am?" he directs this question to Conor.

"Yeah," is all Conor says, before winking at us and heading back through the basement to the elevator. The doors open a few seconds later and Lucia and Alana step out. Conor speaks to them briefly before he steps into the elevator. The doors close behind him and Lucia and Alana make their way over to us.

"Alana!" her father says as soon as she's close enough to hear him. "How could you? I'm your father."

The righteous indignation is practically seeping through his pores. I realize that he genuinely believes she is in the wrong here. A true narcissist.

She glares at him, her eyes narrowed in anger and disgust. "My father? You stopped being my father when you sold me for three million dollars. I would say that I'm your only child, but that wouldn't be true would it? Poor Bethany Cooper was carrying your baby when you had her murdered," she spits and his face blanches at her accusation.

"No father of mine would ask his sick, twisted friends to spy on my daughter and film some of her most intimate moments just so he could exploit her the way he has everyone else. And he most certainly wouldn't have a team of assassins trying to kill my family." She takes one step closer and then slaps him so hard across the face that his head snaps back with the force of it. "You are *nothing* to me," she hisses.

"You heard her, asshole," I push him toward the back of the huge basement.

"Alana, please?" he wails, "you can't let them do this to me."

She walks ahead of us, ignoring her father's sniveling and pleas for his life. He sounds pretty damn pitiful to be honest. I mean, I knew she was tough but it's gotta be hard hearing the man beg for his life like that.

"Think of your mother. She'll be lost without me," he wails, and it's that which makes her turn on her heel and glare at him again.

I stop walking, holding onto his arm still and wondering if he's about to get another slap, but instead she rears her hand back and punches him in the jaw. His knees give way from under him and he drops to the floor, taking my arm down until I let go and let him fall.

"My mother will be a damn sight better off without your cheating, murderous ass in her life. Maybe now she'll finally wake up from the goddamn haze she's been walking around in for the past fifteen years."

Carmichael rubs his jaw as his eyes roll in his head.

"Damn, princesa," Alejandro whistles, sidling up to her and wrapping an arm around her waist. "Remind me never to get on your bad side."

Lucia laughs softly and I wink at her. I can't wait for this to be over with so we can get back to our normal lives. Not that our normal lives are much less dramatic.

Grabbing Carmichael's collar, I drag him back up and over to the basement room. I push him inside after Alejandro walks in.

He sees the old dentist's chair in the center of the room. The wooden table. The array of torture devices that adorn the walls

"W-what? N-no," he starts to cry now. Huge, snot ridden sobs that vibrate through his body. "Alana," he drops to his knees in front of her, his hands clasped together as he pleads for his life.

She doesn't even look at him, instead she focuses on her husband. "I can't watch," she whispers.

"I know, princess," he says with a reassuring nod. "Wait outside. You won't hear anything once we close the door."

I look at Lucia and she rolls her eyes at me. I make a mental note to spank her for that later. "I'll keep mom company," she says with a sigh.

"Thank you, sweetheart," Alana replies.

Then the two of them walk out of the room, closing the door behind them.

Now there is just the three of us. Foster Carmichael looks up at me. His eyes pleading with me for mercy.

Alejandro laughs loudly. "You'd be better saving those puppy dog eyes for me, Carmichael, because Jax here is going to fillet you like a fish for what you did to my daughter."

Carmichael starts to dribble and piss himself with fear, as though he only just realized that it was my wife he was jacking off over.

I bring my face closer to his. "Did you like watching her, you sick fuck?"

"No, I swear, I never..." he shakes his head. "That was all Ed. He was into that, not me."

"Too old for you, is she? You prefer high school girls?" I snarl.

I hold out my hand to Alejandro who passes me the small electricians drill. "Who else saw those videos?"

"N-nobody," he shakes his head vigorously until I grab hold of his jaw, squeezing hard as I hold him in place.

I flick the switch on the handle. It roars to life like it's been waiting for this moment – I know I have. When his mouth opens on a scream, I press the drill head against the groove on one of his back molars and push until tooth and blood are swirling around his mouth. He sputters and chokes through his screams of agony.

"You got plenty more teeth I can do that to, you sick fuck. Now who saw those videos?"

"N-no," he sputters, shaking his head and causing blood and spittle to fly out of his mouth.

I grab his jaw again and repeat the process. By the time I've drilled through all of his back teeth, Carmichael is a gibbering, trembling wreck.

"We still need him to talk, amigo," Alejandro laughs darkly as he hoists his father-in-law up by his shoulders and sits him in the chair.

"He can nod and shake his head. That's all I need," I snarl as the adrenaline courses through my veins. I want to tear every fucking limb from his body with the rage that burns through me.

"The images are on your personal computer?" I ask and Carmichael's head lolls backward.

Alejandro grabs him by the hair and holds him upright. "My friend asked you a question."

"The videos and pictures? Are they on your computer?"

He nods as best he can.

"Where did you print the photographs?"

"Ofsh," he mumbles.

"Your office?"

Nodding.

"Your home office."

More nodding.

"Are there copies anywhere else?"

He shakes his head.

"You know what I do, Carmichael. You know I will find out if you're lying to me."

He nods.

I narrow my eyes at him. "I expect you know by now that you're not leaving this building alive."

Tears run down his face.

"But the one thing you do have is your legacy. You're the great Foster Carmichael, right?"

"Hmm," he whimpers.

"But if I find out you've lied to me, then the whole world will learn what you did to that little girl from Virginia. Everyone will find out what a snake you are. Are you lying to me?"

"Nuh," he snivels.

"So once I destroy the videos on your computer they'll be gone? You didn't print any extra for you or your buddies to jerk off over?"

"Noooo," he wails as Alejandro tugs his head back further.

"You think he's telling the truth?" Alejandro asks.

"I don't think he has the balls to withstand this level of pain. He's gotta be, right?"

"Hmm. Just checking," he says, letting Carmichael's head go until it drops forward onto his chest. "We're still gonna torture him though, right?"

I frown at him. "He watched my wife, amigo."

"I know. I'm just making sure we're on the same page."

"Aren't we always?"

He grins at me while Carmichael sobs in the chair. "Yeah."

HALF AN HOUR LATER, we walk out of the room, leaving Carmichael's mutilated body behind. I'll help Conor dispose of it properly tomorrow. They have an incinerator somewhere. I'll toss Carmichael's computer into it too.

"Alex! Jax," Alana gasps out loud and I look down at myself and then at my best buddy. We are covered, head to toe in blood and bits of body tissue.

"You knew we weren't going to tickle him, princess," Alejandro says.

"I know, but..." she swallows hard. "I know."

"The videos? Where are they?" Lucia asks.

"On his computer at home. I don't believe he sent them to anyone else. I'll deal with it tomorrow. Right now I need a shower."

Lucia wrinkles her nose at me. "Yeah. You kinda do."

A FEW HOURS LATER, after I've showered and we spent a few hours eating pizza with the Ryans, Lucia and I are lying in bed. I have my arms wrapped around her and she's nestled against my chest as I run my fingertips up and down her spine.

"You okay?" she whispers.

"Hmm," I kiss her hair. She smells so good. "You?"

"Yep." She snuggles closer.

We lie in silence for a few minutes. "You think everyone else is asleep?" she asks.

Her parents are in the room down the hall and Matthias and the twins are in the room next to us.

"The kids are. Everyone is probably fucking," I whisper and she giggles.

"Jax," she nudges me. "We can't do that here. We're guests."

"Pretty sure that's not an issue, angel," I slide my hands to her ass. "Unless you don't want to?"

She shifts her hips, rubbing her pussy against my hip, and my cock, which it seems is always at half-mast around her, springs to life. "I always want to."

"Yeah you do," I roll her onto her back, forcing her thighs apart with my knees so that I can lie between her legs. I grind my cock against her. "Why are you wearing panties anyway?"

"Because the rules are I don't wear panties in your bed. This isn't your bed. Pretty sure this is your buddy, Shane's."

"No," I shake my head and she bites on that juicy bottom lip of hers, driving me fucking feral. "What is the rule about beds?"

"Any bed I'm in is yours," she whispers.

"Damn right, baby, now get the panties off right now."

She stares into my eyes and they are full of wicked delight. "Make me," she purrs and the rush of blood to my cock damn near makes me pass out.

I am going to fuck her into a coma and I don't give a damn who hears her screaming my name.

CHAPTER 37

LUCIA

TWO WEEKS LATER

T take a deep breath and knock on the door to Toni's gym. Jax stands beside me, a comforting hand on my back. It's been three weeks since I last saw her because she's been on the road. We could have called her, but she's always super busy, and besides, I wanted to see her face to face when we tell her that we dealt with Foster Carmichael.

The day after what happened in the basement, my mom went back to that old Brownstone she swore she'd never set foot in again and told her mom that her father had packed up and moved to Havana with his long term lover, Ed Sawyer, and wouldn't be coming back.

Jax and Jessie Ryan set up a trail of emails and correspondence dating back months between Foster and Ed, declaring their love and planning their getaway. My mom said that her own mom actually smiled when she told her, and well, let's hope Foster Carmichael's departure from this earth ends up being a good thing for her too.

The same information was sent to Shannon back in Dallas, along with the videos that Ed recorded without her knowledge and an email telling her he had confessed to hurting her dog, Huxley too. I hope that she is able to move on. After all, she is definitely better off without that pig of a husband, and at least now she knows the kind of man he really was.

Jax took Foster's computers and destroyed them as well as the cloud files with the videos of the two of us.

It all worked out kind of perfectly, but the only person we still need to speak to is Toni. The longer we stand here waiting for the door to open, the lower Jax's hand slides until it's resting on my ass.

I look sideways at him. "Do you have to?"

He shrugs. "You're my wife and your ass is fucking beautiful. So sue me."

Even though I love that he always seems to have his hands on me, I roll my eyes at him.

"Oh, you're gonna pay for that, angel," he whispers just as the door opens and Toni is standing there grinning at us.

"You two are so darn cute," she says, crossing her arms over her chest and leaning against the door jamb.

"Were you watching us?" Jax asks feigning a scowl.

She shrugs. "I heard you two were into that now?"

"Too soon, Moretti," Jax says and she starts laughing before stepping aside and allowing us into her gym.

"That's what we wanted to talk to you about, actually," I say as she closes the heavy metal door behind us.

"Oh, you find something out?" she asks as she walks to the back room and we follow her.

"You could say that," Jax says as he looks around the gym. "Where's Benji?"

I only just noticed that he's not here either. He trains Toni and looks after her gym. I've never known him not be here when she is.

"He's packing," she says with a shrug.

"Packing?" I say.

"Yeah. I got a new sponsorship deal, but they want me to move my training to Chicago."

"You're going back to Chicago?" Jax asks with a frown.

"I guess so. Bye bye sunshine. But, I got to go where the sponsors want me, so..." she shrugs. "I figure a few more years and then I'll retire and go live in Bali or somewhere."

"So you'll be back in the loving bosom of the Moretti family?" Jax laughs softly and I feel like I'm missing a joke.

"Ha," she snorts. "Fat chance." Then she looks at me. "Looks like you'll need to find a new trainer, princess. Sorry about that."

"I'll take over Lucia's training," Jax says and Toni arches an eyebrow at him.

"What?" he says with a frown.

"Like you two could do anything involving that kind of close contact without fucking?"

"She kind of has a point," I mutter and Toni winks at me. I feel a pang of sadness as I realize how much I'm going to miss her.

"So, you wanted to tell me something?" she looks between Jax and me.

I swallow hard. I still feel so guilty about dragging her into the whole video mess. "Only that we found out who took those videos and we made sure that every copy was destroyed."

"Along with the people responsible," Jax adds.

"You didn't keep a copy just for yourselves?" she asks with a wicked grin. "I mean, 'cause if you did, I wouldn't mind taking a look myself."

"No we didn't," I say, rolling my eyes.

"Shame," she says with a soft sigh.

"We just wanted you to know it was dealt with."

"I appreciate that," she says, her tone more serious now. "That must be a relief, right?"

"God, yes," I agree.

"Then I'm glad you sorted it. And maybe I'll see you both at another fight some time?"

"Maybe," Jax agrees, but I have a feeling this might be the last time I ever see Toni. It makes me feel a little sad, but she doesn't seem the type of person to ever settle in one place.

"I'll miss you guys," she says. There is none of her usual snark or wicked humor present, just a genuine, friendly affection and respect.

"I'll miss you too," I tell her.

"You're one of a kind, Moretti," Jax says as he pulls her in for a hug. She pretends to fight him off but then she wraps one arm around while pulling me in with the other.

"Don't you two dare make me cry," she whispers.

Matthias is helping Jax prepare a sauce for dinner while I chop vegetables. Our son talks non-stop about everything he did in school today and Jax listens intently. The two of them together still make me smile.

I'm still smiling when a sudden wave of nausea washes over me. I hold my hand to my mouth because I think I might just vomit right here onto the kitchen counter, but then the feeling passes almost as quickly as it came.

I glance at Jax and Matthias again, who are still deep in conversation. I've experienced that strange kind of sudden nausea before.

"Just going to use the bathroom," I say as calmly as I can.

"Okay," they say in unison, smiling at me.

As soon as I'm out of the kitchen, I run to the bathroom.

Opening the small wooden cabinet, I pull out the paper bag from inside. I stocked up on a few pregnancy tests when I was at the pharmacy the other day. Jax seems to be on a mission to impregnate me as soon as possible, so it seemed like a good idea to have some in the house.

A FEW MINUTES LATER, I sit on the edge of the bath, staring at the white stick. I don't dare turn it over yet. My stomach is in knots and waves of nausea wash over me, and I'm not sure if it's from nerves now or something else.

There is a soft knock at the door. "You okay, baby?" Jax asks.

I draw in a deep breath. He should be here for this, right? I'll just have to deal with his disappointed face if there is only one line on that test.

"Come in," I croak out the words.

A second later, he steps inside, his face etched with concern. "What's wrong?"

I nod to the lid of the toilet.

His eyes grow wide as he sees the test sitting there. "Are you late? What does it say?"

"I don't know if I'm late. I only stopped my pill three weeks ago. I have no idea when to expect my period, but I felt really sick just before in the kitchen. And also I don't know what it says," I say all of that so fast it makes my head spin.

He walks over and sits beside me. "Fuck, Luce," he whispers.

"It's probably nothing," I whisper back as he takes my hand in his and squeezes tight. "Will you be disappointed if it isn't?"

He stares at me, a soft frown on his handsome face. "No, baby."

I narrow my eyes in suspicion.

"I will be over the fucking moon if you are pregnant, but we

243

only just started trying. I'll be fine if you're not. There's no pressure here. Okay?"

"Okay," I whisper.

"Is it time to look?"

"Yeah. You want to do it?"

"Ew, no. It's your pee," he says with a wicked grin, diffusing the tension and making me giggle in the way that only he can.

"What? You would drink my pee if I asked you to."

"Nope," he shakes his head. "I'll give you pretty much anything you want, angel, but golden showers are a hard limit for me."

I snort-laugh so hard that I almost pee again. Damn I love this man and his ability to put me at ease. He is just so freaking perfect. Reaching over, I pick up the test and turn it over in my hands. My stomach does a full one eighty flip.

"Oh," I gasp for breath.

"What?" Jax asks, his eyes full of concern now as he stares at my face instead of just looking at the damn stick.

I hold it up for him. "We're having a baby."

He blinks at the stick and for the longest time he says nothing and I'm wondering if he's changed his mind about the whole baby thing. But then he stands up, scoops me into his arms and starts smothering my face with kisses as he walks into our bedroom.

"You." Kiss. "Are." Kiss. "Fucking." Kiss. "Incredible."

"Jax," I giggle, kicking my legs as I squirm in his huge arms. "Stop. Matthias will hear."

"So?"

"We can't tell him yet," I whisper. "It's too early to tell people."

He lays me down on the bed. "Okay," he agrees as he lies next to me. "But everything will be okay, you know that, right?"

I smile at him in response because I can't lie. Nobody ever knows that.

He slides a hand onto my stomach. "Fuck, Luce," he breathes.

"I know," I whisper.

"I love you so fucking much, angel."

"Love you too, cowboy."

EPILOGUE
JAX

My cell vibrates in my inside jacket pocket as Alejandro and the mayor discuss his upcoming campaign for re-election. Half a dozen other men in suits sit around the table with us while we talk business. Mostly, I listen rather than talk.

My cell vibrates against my ribs and I take it out of my pocket. I have two cell phones these days. This is my personal one. Only Lucia, and my family have the number and that includes my dad now too. Lucia, Matthias and I try to get to our barn at the ranch for at least a weekend a month. Seeing the two of them with my father and aunt has reminded me how much I have shut my family out over the years. I guess that old saying is right - time really does heals all wounds.

It's been nice getting to know my father again, and seeing him with Matthias in particular, helps me to remember what a good man he is. He is anxiously awaiting the birth of his next grandchild and has restored a beautiful old crib just like the one I talked about. It's waiting for us at the barn back at the ranch for when we visit next month.

My incredible wife is currently eight and a half months

246

pregnant with our daughter and I am on emergency standby. I slide my cell out of my pocket and read the text from her.

Hey, cowboy. When are you coming home? I really need you. Like now!

I type out a quick reply.

Is everything okay?

A few seconds later another message comes through. It's a photograph of her hand sliding into her panties.

Fuck! My dick is instantly hard. She has become the horniest woman on the entire fucking planet since she fell pregnant just after our honeymoon. Not that I'm complaining, but sitting here with my cock busting the zipper of my pants isn't exactly ideal.

Alejandro glances across the table at me. He arches an eyebrow. He's also anxiously awaiting the birth of his next grandchild too. I shake my head to let him know that no, it's not about the baby, and then I send her a reply.

You do know I'm in a meeting with your father, right?

Yes (laughing emoji)

And you remember who he is and what he does to people who upset him?

Sure do

This is followed by a second image of her fingertips glistening with her cum. Fuck! Me!

You are making it very difficult to concentrate. All of the blood in my body is rushing straight to my groin.

I just wanted to remind you what is waiting for you at home, cowboy xxx

I look up to see Alejandro glaring at me now and realize I have a stupid fucking grin on my face.

"Everything okay there, amigo?" he asks, his tone clipped.

"Yeah." Then I look to the other men around the table. "It's just my wife. She's pregnant and it could be any day now."

They all nod and offer words of congratulations and understanding before going back to the meeting.

When a third photograph comes through, I can't resist opening it, even though I know I'm going to regret it. When a picture of her pink cotton panties stained with her cum fills the screen I swear I almost shoot my load right here.

I put the phone back into my pocket and look at her father instead, sure that will cure my raging boner. He frowns at me, letting me know he's pissed. But all I can think about it getting the fuck out of this meeting and home to my wife.

LUCIA

I giggle when I hear the front door slamming shut. I knew it wouldn't be long before Jax was home after I sent him those photographs. It's become a whole new thing with us. You'd think that after what happened, I'd shy away from any sort of pictures like that, but I never show my face or anything else identifying, and I only send them to Jax's cell phone and that man has taken online security to a whole new level. I swear the CIA couldn't get into his phone even if they had it in their hands.

I lie back against the fluffy pillows with the sheet pulled over me. He runs into the room a few seconds later and I can't help but laugh at the look on his face. He's trying his best to pretend he's mad at me, but he's staring at my naked form beneath the thin cotton sheet like he's about to nail me into oblivion.

"You have any idea how much trouble you almost got me in?" he says as he starts pulling off all of his clothes and tossing them onto the floor.

"Me?" I feign my ignorance. "I was simply sharing my afternoon activities with you and asking when you were coming home. It's no fun being here on my own."

"You looked like you were having a whole lot of fun to me. I think I have at least eight speeding tickets and traffic fines, angel. I jumped every red light to get home as fast as possible."

"I'm sure you can work something out with the mayor," I giggle, aware that Jax has been helping him with his campaign.

He takes off the last of his clothes and crawls onto the bed. "I was in a meeting with the mayor when you were sending me pictures of your hand in your panties, angel," he growls before he presses soft kisses on my stomach through the sheet. "What the fuck am I gonna do with you? You can't keep dragging me home to fuck you every few hours," he says as he fists the soft cotton sheet and pulls it off me.

"But I get so horny," I whimper as he slides a hand between my thighs.

"So, play with your toys I bought you."

"They're not the same as you, Jax," I hiss as he slides a finger inside me. "Nothing feels as good as you."

"Well, I can't be mad about that now, can I?" He smiles at me before he starts to kiss my breasts.

They're so sensitive now, but he knows the exact amount of pressure and teasing to have me on the edge. He sucks a nipple softly into his mouth as he works his finger in and out of me, making me purr like a contended cat.

"Dammit, Jax, stop teasing me. I need all of you," I whimper as the ache in my pussy grows even stronger.

His lazy finger fucking just isn't going to cut it right now. He's so much more gentle with me these days, since my bump became so huge, and we have to be more creative finding comfortable positions, but he still manages to take care of me multiple times a day.

"You mean you need my cock, baby?" he chuckles against my skin.

"Yes, your huge, magic cock," I hiss, clawing at his neck as I become more frantic with need.

"Fuck, Mrs. Decker, you're turning feral, you know that?" He slides his finger out of me and pushes himself up. "Roll onto your side, baby."

I do as he tells me and he lies behind me, lifting my leg slightly before he slides his thick cock deep inside my pussy. The sudden rush of pleasure and heat makes me moan — loudly.

"This what you really need, Luce?" he whispers, pressing his lips against my ear.

"Yes," I whimper now as he presses deeper, hardly moving at all while he rubs the tips of his shaft against the delicious spot inside me that has my legs trembling.

"You feel so fucking good, baby. So wet for me," he groans too as he slides slowly in and out.

I bring my knee up, resting my foot on my calf and allowing him to glide his hand over my rounded belly until he finds my swollen clit. His fingers brush it softly first, making me tremble with need, until he adds a little more pressure.

"Yes, Jax," I hiss.

"So fucking needy."

"Yeah," I rock my hips against him.

"You gonna come all over my cock like a good girl?"

Damn! My orgasm detonates in my pussy so hard that my entire body shudders, and as my inner muscles squeeze and release him, he gives a few final thrusts, cursing in my ear as his own climax hits.

We lie on the bed face to face and I can't help smiling at this man who is always so willing to give me exactly what I need. I have loved him for such a long time, and sometimes I can still hardly believe that he is mine.

He narrows his eyes, searching my face and making me wonder what's going on inside his head.

"Were you this horny when you were pregnant with Matthias?"

"No," I shake my head. "Although I kind of had a lot of other stuff going on. But, still. Nothing like this," I blush. "I crave you every second, Jax. Like if your hands aren't on me," I shudder. "I hope it wears off once the baby's born."

"Hmm. If it does, I'll just knock you up again," he laughs softly.

"It's not funny. I'm a slave to my hormones. You walked out of here in that new suit this morning and I swear I was seconds away from following you outside and mounting you in the driveway."

"Well our driveway is completely secure and gated, so..." he winks at me.

"Don't give me any ideas, cowboy," I whisper as I curl my fingers in his hair. "Damn you are so freaking handsome."

My cheeks flush with heat and he laughs loudly. "You could go again right now, couldn't you?"

"I can always go. It's not funny," I push against his chest. "I've become some kind of sex addict."

"Well, I think you were always one of those, baby."

"Well, if I am, it's because you made me this way, Jackson Decker. You insisting on me asking for what I want and giving me mind blowing orgasms. Is it any wonder I've become a teenage boy trapped in a woman's body?"

"I'm an evil genius and I've created a monster."

"You are and you have." I cup his face in my hands and pull him to me for a kiss.

He rubs a hand over my swollen belly and our baby girl kicks him.

"Those endorphins she keeps getting a hit of must be wearing off," I giggle at him.

"If I give you any more endorphins, angel, you won't be able to walk down the stairs when our son comes home from school in an hour."

"This is true," I say with a sigh.

He leans down, kissing my belly. "Your momma is a nymphomaniac, baby girl. If you don't come out soon, she's gonna kill me."

"You can't say that to our daughter," I admonish him.

"Okay," he laughs softly and then he rests his lips against my bump again. "Your momma is the most incredible person you will ever meet, baby girl. She is smart, and kind and beautiful, and she is going to be your favorite person in the entire world, because she's the best momma you could wish for."

A few tears run down my cheek and I swat them away but not quickly enough and he sees.

"Why are you crying, angel?" he asks pulling me into his arms.

"You're so sweet," I sniff. God, I am just a walking bag of hormones. "I love you so much."

"I love you too"

I press my face against him and feel his next words rumble through his chest. They are the words that make me quite literally melt for him. "Who do you belong to, Luce?"

"You, Jax. Only you."

ALANA

I watch my two sons running around the garden, squirting each other with super soakers and can't help but smile. They're four years old now and such a handful, but they bring a joy to our lives that is indescribable.

As I'm thinking about the news I got today, I feel a pair of warm, strong hands sliding over my hips and onto my stomach. He pulls me toward him, pressing my ass into his groin.

"*Buenas noches, princesa,*" he whispers in my ear.

I lean back against him, my body sagging against his hard chest. "*Buenas noches,*" I reply as he presses soft kisses on my neck. "The boys have been waiting for you to get home."

"I'll go see them soon," he growls. "I want you all to myself for a few minutes."

I turn in his arms and wrap my hands around his neck.

"You look tired," he says with a frown.

"I am," I stifle a yawn.

He arches an eyebrow at me. "How about an early night?"

"Your early nights are never about sleeping, Alex," I laugh softly.

"No," he trails soft kisses along my collarbone. "But after I fuck you, we can watch TV and I'll rub your back while you fall asleep."

"That sounds good," I admit. And I need to talk to him about my visit to the doctors today. I feel a knot in my stomach as I wonder at the best way to tell him. Maybe I should just do it now? Like ripping off the band aid?

"Papi!" Dario and Tomás shriek as they come running through the French doors and see their father is home, holding their super soakers in the air.

"Ah and the peace is broken," he grins at me, giving me a soft kiss before he chases after our twin sons.

I smile as I watch the three of them. Our boys laugh and shriek with delight as he catches each of them and scoops them into his arms. Our perfect little family. And I'm about to throw a mini grenade right into the middle of it.

I lie on the bed while Alex deals with bedtime. I feel exhausted. The doctor told me it's perfectly normal given the circumstances.

I look up when Alex walks into the room. He's wearing his dress pants and a white shirt which is open at the collar and damn he is still the most handsome man on this planet. How is it possible that he still gives me butterflies every time I see him? Even after all this time.

"Did they go down okay?" I ask.

"They always do, princess. I think they wear themselves out so much all day with their constant energy," he laughs softly.

"I could do with a shot of their energy right now," I sigh.

He looks at me with concern as he starts unbuttoning his

shirt. "So Jax went home early again today," he says with a roll of his eyes.

"Did Lucia need him? Is she okay?"

He tosses his shirt into the laundry hamper and then lies on the bed beside me. "We both know she's fine and that there is only one reason why he has to drag his ass home at least twice a day. It's getting ridiculous. You're going to have to have a word with her?"

"Why me?" I laugh. "You're the one with the problem."

"Alana," he scowls at me. "What am I supposed to say? Stop booty calling your husband during working hours?"

That makes me laugh harder. "You can hardly talk. If I remember correctly, you were home more than you were working when I was pregnant with the twins."

"Ah yes," he smiles at me. "You were even more insatiable than you are now."

"I am not insatiable," I whisper.

"No?" he smiles as he starts to kiss my neck.

"I'm always satisfied."

"Fuck, yes you are," he growls as his hand slides beneath my tank top.

"Alex," I whisper, placing my hand over his.

He stares at me, his eyes narrowed. "What's wrong, princess? Are you sick?" he places a hand on my forehead.

"You know I've been really tired lately?"

"Yes. I told you you're working too hard. You need to get someone in to help you."

"Well, I agree. I think I will. I'm going to write up a job description tomorrow."

The frown on his handsome face deepens as he regards me suspiciously. "While I'm very happy about you getting some help, you're freaking me out, princess. You've always been so resistant to the idea."

"I know, but I went to see the doctor today, you know because of the tiredness."

He scowls now. "And you didn't tell me this?"

"I just called by on my way home and she could squeeze me in."

He blinks at me. "What did she say?"

"I'm pregnant," I whisper.

"What? But you can't..." He sits up, running a hand through his hair as he blinks at me in shock.

"They said it was very unlikely I would conceive naturally, but not impossible. I'm pregnant, Alex. Two months."

"Two?" he shakes his head in disbelief.

"Yeah, two," I bite on my lip and now I'm not just talking about months. "We're having another set of twins."

"Fuck!" he hisses, and I wonder if he's as happy about this as I am. But then he rolls on top of me, smothering my face with kisses.

"I would have called you to come to the scan she did, but she was about to close and go home and..."

"Stop, Alana. It's okay," he says, lacing his fingers through mine as he pins my hands beside my head. "Just when I think I couldn't possibly love you any more, you go and surprise the hell out of me."

"I was kind of surprised myself."

"You're happy though?" he asks as he stares into my eyes.

"Yes. Ecstatic. You?"

"Fuck yes," he says before he seals his lips over mine, sliding his tongue into my mouth before he kisses me. It is full of fire and passion and leaves both of us panting and wanting so much more. I buck my hips, rubbing myself against his hard length.

"Did the doctor say we were okay for this...?" he groans as he rocks his hips against me.

"Yes. It's a normal pregnancy. We're fine to have sex."

"Thank fuck." Then he seals his mouth over mine again and as his hand slides down my body and into my pajama pants. "Because I would lose my mind if I didn't get to fuck you every day, princess."

ALEJANDRO
NINE MONTHS LATER

"Dario, stop standing on your brother's face," I shout at my son as he wrestles with his twin brother while my grandson, Matthias plays at being referee. The three of them are a giant ball of energy, but I wouldn't have it any other way.

"These kids wear me out, amigo," Jax says with a laugh as he walks up behind me, carrying my eight month old grand-daughter, Alyssa, in his arms.

She reaches out a chubby hand and grabs at my beard.

"You love it," I remind him as we watch our boys playing together.

"I sure do, and it's a damn good job I do too," he says with a grin and a twinkle in his eye that makes me suspicious.

"Have you knocked my daughter up again, amigo?" I scowl at him.

"I couldn't possibly tell you that until after the twelve week scan," he says with a shrug, "which is in two weeks by the way."

"You..." I'm stopped by the sight of my daughter coming out of the house holding one of the newest additions to our family.

Alana gave birth to two more beautiful boys six weeks ago, Javier and Diego.

"So many babies," I say as she reaches us instead.

She glares at Jax. "You told him?"

He holds up his free hand in surrender while Alyssa giggles at her mama. "I-I," he stammers. He can't lie to her and I like that.

"Relax, *mija,* I forced it out of him." I can lie to her though, I'm her father. "And congratulations." I wrap my arm around her and kiss her cheek.

"Thank you, Papi."

"Where's your mama?"

"She's just dressing Javier, she'll be right out."

"Good. I'm starving and I want to barbecue."

She rolls her eyes and stands beside Jax, who slides his free arm around her waist and kisses the top of her head. He whispers something in her ear that I don't hear, but that I'm sure I don't want to know because it makes her blush.

It was hard to accept the two of them for a long time. But I should have known that of all the men in the world, the man I trust more than anyone, would be the right man for my daughter. Her eyes shine with happiness whenever she's around him. And Jax, well I've known him since I was fourteen years old, and I have never seen him so happy either.

I look around the garden and can hardly believe that just six years ago, I lived here alone, thinking that I had it made and that nobody could touch me. It's only now that I realize I had nothing. Nothing until she came along and filled my life with family and children and love. She is where all this began. She is where I begin and where I end.

I paid her father three million dollars for her hand, and it wasn't anywhere near enough. But I would sell my soul to make her happy.

As though even the thought of her brings her to me, she walks out of the house cradling a sleeping Javier in her arms.

Her eyes meet mine and she smiles. And fuck me if she isn't still the most beautiful thing I have ever seen in my life.

I walk over to her, leaving Jax and Lucia holding Alyssa and Diego, and pull my wife into my arms, careful not to crush our son as I seal my lips over hers and kiss her so hard that it makes her moan softly. And that makes my cock twitch so I have to pull back, leaving us both wanting. And that, right there, is the only drawback of having all these kids running around.

"What was that for?" she whispers.

"Just because I can, princesa. Have I ever told you how much I love you?"

"Maybe once or twice," she says with a soft laugh that I feel in my bones.

I slide my hand to her ass and squeeze and the skin on her neck turns that subtle shade of pink that drives me crazy. So sweet, but so wickedly sinful at the same time. She is perfect in every fucking way.

"I love you too," she whispers.

I stare into her deep brown eyes, wondering what the hell I ever did to deserve her. I might not be worthy of her, but I would burn the entire world to ash before I ever let her go. And then I tell her the words that I have spoken so often, I hope I have carved them into her heart. *Mi reina. Eres todo para mí.*

My Queen. You are everything to me.

If you haven't yet read Alejandro and Alana's story. You can read find them on Amazon and Kindle Unlimited.

Fierce King
Fierce Queen

ALSO BY SADIE KINCAID

Want to know more about Jax and Alejandro's buddies, the Ryan brothers and their wife, Jessie? Find out all about them in Sadie's internationally bestselling New York Ruthless series. Available on Amazon and FREE in Kindle Unlimited.

Ryan Rule

Ryan Redemption

Ryan Retribution

Ryan Reign

Ryan Renewed

As well as the super spicy New York Ruthless short stories/ novellas

A Ryan Reckoning

A Ryan Rewind

A Ryan Halloween

If you'd like to read about London's hottest couple. Gabriel and Samantha, then check out Sadie's London Ruthless series on Amazon. FREE in Kindle Unlimited.

Dark Angel

Fallen Angel

If you enjoy super spicy short stories, Sadie also writes the Bound series feat Mack and Jenna, Books 1, 2, 3 and 4 are available now and FREE in Kindle Unlimited.

Bound and Tamed

Bound and Shared

Bound and Dominated

Bound and Deceived

About the Author

Sadie Kincaid is a dark romance author who loves to read and write about hot alpha males and strong, feisty females.

Sadie loves to connect with readers so why not get in touch via social media? Or follow her on TikTok

Join Sadie's reader group for the latest news, book recommendations and plenty of fun. Sadie's ladies and Sizzling Alphas

ACKNOWLEDGMENTS

As always I would love to thank my incredible readers, and the members of Sadie's Ladies and Sizzling Alphas. My beloved belt whores! You all rock.

And to all of the readers who have bought any of my books, everything I write is for you and you all make my dreams come true.

To my beta readers Kate and Michelle, for turning this around at lightning speed. And also my fantastic ARC readers for their enthusiasm and support.

A huge thank you to two of my dearest friends, Mandy and Mary for your constant support. And to my fellow romance authors, but especially Vicki H Nicolson, Nicci Harris, Elle Nicoll and BJ Alpha - you all make this journey so much more enjoyable.

As always, a super special mention to my lovely PA, Kate, who puts up with my impulsiveness and tendency to go off grid when I'm busy, like a champ.

To my incredible boys who inspire me to be better every single day. My amazing family, who support me even though they are not allowed to read any of my books! And last, but no means least, a huge thank you to my husband, who is my rock, my biggest supporter and continues to support every crazy idea I have.

I couldn't do this without you!

(And a final note of thanks to Alejandro and Alana Montoya for giving me the courage to follow my dreams)

Printed in Great Britain
by Amazon

29581710R00162